In Bloom on Jekyll

Gem of the Golden Isles Series
Book Two

BEACH HOUSE
PUBLISHING

In Bloom on Jekyll

GEM OF THE GOLDEN ISLES SERIES BOOK TWO

SANDY MALONE

BEACH HOUSE
PUBLISHING

BEACH HOUSE PUBLISHING

Beach House Publishing

544 Old Plantation Road

Jekyll Island, GA 31527

ISBN: 979-8-9901756-3-1 (paperback)

ISBN:979-8-9901756-2-4 (ebook)

Library of Congress Control Number:2024906145

Cover design by: Patricia Tait, Gravitait Design

Printed in the United States of America

Disclaimer

This is a work of fiction. Unless indicated below, all the names, characters, brides, grooms, businesses, places, events, venues, and incidents in this book are either the product of the author's imagination or used in a fictitious manner. Any resemblance to actual persons, living or dead, or actual events is purely coincidental.

Patti Tait, Rita Rich, Andy Pagan, and Jamie Sanders are all real, as are their business names. However, their roles in the book are fictional. Their names have been used with their permission. The author endorses and recommends Gravitait Design, Rita Rich Media, Potomac Floral Wholesale, Jekyll Market, and At Your Service Jekyll Errand Girl.

Dedication

To my mom, Robin Corridon, for letting me study journalism in college despite your worst fears I'd end up spending the rest of my life writing obits on the overnight shift somewhere in the midwest.

Thank you for loving me, teaching me to be a good human, and showing me how to properly plan a party. All have come in handy on a regular basis.

I hope this series is the first of many "beach reads" I write for you to critique from a chair beside me on the sand. I love you very much.

Sandy

JEKYLL
ISLAND

← St. Simons Island

← Driftwood
Beach

← Tally's
House

Intercoastal
Waterway
↓

Jekyll River

Jekyll Causeway

Brunswick

The Wharf
→
● Jekyll Island Club Hotel

↑
Historic
District

← Beach Village

← Jekll Ocean Club

← Glory Beach

St. Andrews →
Beach

ATLANTIC OCEAN

Cumberland Island
↓

Chapter 1

November 2018

The ceremony was almost over, but Tally wasn't sure they were going to get through the wedding vows before the sky opened. The clouds had been getting blacker by the second for the last 20 minutes and the photographers were giving the wedding planning team worried looks. The weather was rolling in from behind the ceremony, which meant that when the rain started, everybody would be running into it to get to their cars. Half of the guests were driving open golf carts. It wouldn't be pretty.

Tally had tried several times to get the bride and groom to agree to move their wedding to an indoor location. She'd had a backup plan – she always had a backup plan for inclement weather – and when she saw the forecast on the Wednesday before Josh and Rachel's wedding, she didn't play games. She immediately put Plan B into motion and joked with her new assistant, Kayla, that she was going to get her first crash course in wedding damage control.

But that wasn't what happened.

When the bride and groom arrived on Jekyll, Tally and Kayla sat down with them at the beach house they'd rented and reviewed their wedding weekend schedule. Then Tally also gave them an alternate schedule to pre-approve for inclement weather. Just in case it was needed.

Josh and Rachel weren't having any of it and refused to even discuss the possibility their wedding wouldn't be held on the famous Driftwood Beach, where so many scenes from "The Walking Dead" had been filmed. Seriously. Tally was just glad the ceremony didn't have a zombie theme because the undead had been alluded to in several of the items in the couple's welcome bags.

The wedding itself was an unusual one for the wedding planner because it was the first time Tally had encountered the Noahide religion. The groom, who was heading up the wedding planning because his bride was busy studying to take the bar exam a few weeks after their big day, had explained Noahide to Tally as "Jewish Lite." It focused more on the Noah part of the Old Testament and there were a number of rainbows featured in their décor. The prep list had given Kayla the worst case of the giggles, but they were completely justified. It was the weird stuff like this that Tally loved. It kept her job interesting. It was the first time in her career that she'd actually gotten to use those crazy-looking rainbow roses in a wedding decor. And the clients weren't even gay.

Tally tried to get the bride and groom to see reason because the forecast was calling for a 90 percent chance of rain every day their wedding week. She pointed out to her clients that even if their wedding guests didn't melt, they had chosen a rather unusual décor for their chuppah that involved handmade paper flowers in rainbow chains that Rachel and her bridesmaids had created at her bridal shower. Also, the ketubah – a traditional Hebrew marriage license - was a hand-painted watercolor that had been a very expensive wedding gift from the groom's grandmother. If it got wet, it would be ruined.

Josh and Rachel sat politely and listened to all of Tally's concerns, and they agreed to discuss it again on the morning of the wedding. But by and large, the couple weren't worried about the weather and didn't care what it did.

"If it rains, God sent us that rain. And he will send us a rainbow, too," Rachel told her wedding planners.

Kayla looked over at Tally to see what she would do with that one, and Tally had to look away so that she didn't crack up.

"Okay, so instead of putting together Plan B, you'd rather I figure out how to make Plan A work no matter what. I don't suppose you'll let us set up a tent?" Tally asked.

Josh laughed at her. "Haven't we been over this?"

"We have. But you hired me to give you good advice and plan a perfect wedding, and no matter what God has planned for your life, Mother Nature isn't cooperating this weekend. I don't want you to regret your decision when all of your guests are soaking wet and cold at your reception," Tally warned. "Are you sure you don't want me to find ponchos that we can hand out to guests?"

"It's okay, Tally. God will provide," Rachel said, and reached over to pat her wedding planner's hand in what felt to Tally like a rather patronizing way. Her tone of voice had bugged Tally from the beginning of their client relationship. Even through the phone, she felt like Rachel was always looking down her nose at Tally. It wasn't any better in person.

Tally and Kayla didn't stay to argue with the couple after the decision was made. They left a few minutes later, after making sure that the bride and groom didn't need anything. The welcome bags had been delivered to all of their guests' accommodations and the activities didn't start until the next evening. The couple appeared to be pretty self-sufficient and would have been considered easy if they'd been willing to at least talk through the inclement weather plan that would inevitably have to be used.

Tally kept her mouth shut until they were out of the driveway and then she couldn't hold back her rant.

"God will provide? What will God provide? Does he have 75 ponchos and something to protect that freaking priceless ketubah?" she asked Kayla in a shrill voice, not expecting an answer. "Will God provide hair dryers when all the women look like shit in the pictures? The reception is at a restaurant. It's not like they're staying at the venue and can freshen up in their rooms. At this point, they're all going to look like drowned rats and most of them will be freezing their asses off in the air conditioning."

Kayla looked at her boss, surprised. Tally was usually the one to point out a bright spot in every problem.

"Where's all this doom and gloom coming from?" she asked. "I thought you said an optimistic, well-rested wedding planner can handle anything."

"She can," Tally allowed. "But unless this guy really does have a direct line to God, we are so screwed. Ugh!" she yelled in frustration. "I know this was their call, and ultimately, their decision. But Kayla, I'm afraid you're about to get your first taste of getting screamed at for something that we warned the clients not to do. It happens, but it's not fun."

That happened too often, unfortunately. One of Tally's first weddings on Vieques was a bride and groom who insisted their cake be displayed outside for their entire wedding ceremony and reception. In August. In Puerto Rico. She'd told them it was a bad idea and that the cake wouldn't hold up or look good for pictures if it sat out in the heat, but they poo-pooed her guidance. Tally also warned against using cream cheese frosting in the Caribbean heat. It would be in the high 90s with a million percent humidity. The couple also ignored this advice and ordered a three-tier cake with cream cheese frosting.

To add insult to injury, they'd brought a godawful cake topper with them. It had been made to look like the wedding couple, sort of, and it weighed a ton. So much that Tally suggested putting it on the table beside the cake instead of on top of it, but the bride wouldn't hear of it because her sister had made it. Before the ceremony had even ended, the topper started sinking into the cake. Slowly at first, then faster, inspiring lots of quicksand jokes when the guests finally saw it.

Then the weight of the topper split the back side of the cake's top layer in half. Tally and her staff had jumped in to save it, removing the topper and taking the cake into the kitchen for the caterers to triage. Afterward, the father-of-the-bride had torn Tally a new one for letting the cake collapse. Even though she'd advised against doing exactly what caused the fiasco. She had a sick feeling that the Noahide wedding was going to end the same way.

Unfortunately for the wedding guests, Tally had been right on target about the weather. The big day dawned gray and gloomy, and when the wind picked up as Tally was doing a site check on the beach in the late morning, she got sprayed in the face with sand. It was not pleasant. The crappy weather had stirred up the Atlantic Ocean and even at low tide the night before, the waves had been twice as far up on the beach as usual. Driftwood Beach didn't have much beach to speak of when it came to space for chairs. It also didn't have any driftwood.

The beach located on the far northern end of Jekyll Island had taken a beating and over the years, the coastline had crept back to the point that there were trees growing below the waterline. Those trees died but mostly stayed put, pretending to be driftwood when they were really just dead trees. But that little factoid didn't bother any of Tally's clients who wanted to get married there. And normally she didn't mind. It was really, really pretty and ranked as one of the best beaches in the United States. Also, she got to use their wedding pictures on her marketing pages.

But Josh and Rachel's wedding was going to be the exception to the rule. The walk from the street-adjacent parking to the exact spot that the couple had "felt the right energy" for their ceremony was close to 100 yards. Tally and Kayla got dressed earlier than usual, in outfits that wouldn't turn into wet t-shirt contests or blow up over their heads when they were trying to help little old ladies get back to their golf carts in a monsoon. They dressed for the weather when they headed out to the beach to see how bad things were going to be. Both women wore slickers – little kid-style raincoats with hoods. Tally told Kayla to just leave her shoes in the car before they walked down the sandy path to the beach. It was going to be that kind of nasty day.

On the plus side, there was nobody to get in the way of the wedding pictures on Driftwood Beach because of the awful weather. Usually, they had to set up staff to stop random fat people in bathing suits from walking through the background of the wedding pictures. Driftwood Beach was always packed with tourists playing photographer. An empty beach would be great if not for the reason it was empty today. The tide was up way too high for the time of day, but it had been almost up to the roadway a day earlier, and that meant it wasn't going to go much lower. They would be lucky to have enough room for all the chairs that needed to be set up, and the wet sand would make a questionable foundation for the guests. Tally could almost guarantee that somebody's chair would sink at an unfortunate angle and dump its guest into the wet sand.

"Let's see if we can get a couple of sheets of plywood to put underneath the first few rows on each side of the aisle," Tally told Kayla. "Call Mike at the hardware store and see if he's got anything here on Jekyll that would work. And if they do, see if you can bribe him to drop it off here. Otherwise, one of us needs to head to Home Depot on the mainland five minutes ago."

Propping up the first two rows wouldn't keep everybody dry, but at least the mothers and grandmothers of the bride and groom were unlikely to end up on their butts in the wet sand. There were no guarantees of course, but it was always a good idea to try to take care of the people who had been signing the checks.

Mike delivered the plywood to the beach in less than 30 minutes and helped the wedding planners hide it with sand – bless him for thinking to bring a shovel, Tally thought. Then the three of them made quick work of setting up the chairs the bride and groom had rented for the ceremony. Thankfully, they were wood and didn't have fabric seats to protect. The plywood wasn't as visible as Tally worried after they'd trekked back and forth across it setting up chairs with sandy feet. She mentally crossed her fingers that it would work. She had never tried to do a ceremony on a beach that was this wet. This is such a bad idea, she repeated in her head. But she tried to be optimistic for her staff.

Black clouds had gathered at the same time the wedding guests started arriving at the beach ceremony, and the violinist insisted on being draped in plastic to protect her instrument. Half of the guests were wearing rain gear, half were not. Those who were not looked positively miserable. It wouldn't have been uncomfortably cold if the sun was out, but instead it was wet and windy and those sundresses all the little 20-somethings were wearing just weren't cutting it. Kayla and Tally joked that you could tell the relationship status of the guest couple based on whether he was trying to keep her warm and dry and had given her his jacket.

Thunder started at the same time the Noahide rabbi imported from Ohio began the vows, and it was raining bucket-style before they were finished. Kayla had executed the ketubah protection plan – holding it safely inside a trash bag until the very last minute when they were about to sign it. The bride tried to stop Kayla from bagging it but her mother intervened, proving at least somebody in the family had some common sense.

There was literally nothing Tally could do for damage control when a wind gust - later estimated at about 60 mph - whipped through and took the bamboo chuppah with it before the ceremony ended. They probably looked like a cartoon trying to stop it. Nobody was hurt, but it was total chaos. Literally a wedding planner's worst nightmare.

It was raining as Tally and Kayla helped guests back up the sandy path to the road where they'd parked. The photographer had already told Tally that she was only going to take about five minutes of pictures if the rain didn't stop. Even with all her protective equipment, it was too risky for her expensive cameras. Tally understood but groaned inwardly because the bride and groom wouldn't want to get out of the rain. She needed to be off the beach before they started arguing with their photographer so she didn't have to get involved.

***

As predicted, everybody froze to death at the wedding reception held at The Wharf at the Jekyll Island Club Hotel. Cocktails were supposed to have been held outside on the deck during sunset, but there was no sun to see set. Instead, guests watched crazy lightning over the Sidney Lanier Bridge through the windows instead. A quick-thinking Tally had called up to the front desk of the hotel and asked for lots and lots of big plush bath towels, explaining what had happened at Driftwood Beach. Most of the wedding guests were staying at the hotel anyway, but it was a bit of a hike from the hotel to the reception venue. The club hotel did not disappoint, and the restaurant turned off the AC and the ceiling fans at Tally's request.

By the time the guests had a few cocktails in them, most had quit bitching and started to forget that they were so miserable at the wedding.

"It's still coming down," Kayla told Tally as she came in through the back door of the restaurant's bar, carrying a sealed tub of wedding favors they were going to hand out as the guests left. Because the wedding had already been the absolute max number of people The Wharf could hold, losing the space on the deck they'd planned to use had complicated a few things. Nothing that couldn't be overcome, however. And Tally smiled to herself as Kayla began spreading out the cleverly-wrapped, handmade rainbow candles she'd specially ordered for the bride and groom from Wicks & More in Mississippi.

"I think everybody is happy now," Tally said, helping with the display.

"I'm not. My underwear is still wet," Kayla grumbled quietly.

"Mine too. Yuck. But the clients seem happy."

"I don't know why. They've gotta have wet skivvies too," Kayla joked. "Guess they can celebrate not having gotten concussions when the chuppah took flight."

Tally giggled. "Little Miss Negativity today, aren't you? I'm not used to this Kayla."

"This is wet Kayla. If you want my sunny optimistic side, you have to keep me dry. Isn't there something about that under OSHA?"

Tally gave her a gentle shove and laughed. "Complain to God. According to the bride, this was all planned."

"Then God has a terrible sense of humor."

Chapter 2

Tally woke up when her phone wouldn't stop buzzing on the bedside table. She'd turned the ringer off when she went to bed after Josh and Rachel's wedding because there were no more wedding events scheduled. There was no farewell brunch that she had any responsibility for – the guests were just planning to eat at the hotel and then check out. The bride and groom had been thrilled with everything and thanked their wedding planners. The bride handed Tally a big tip to share with her staff at the end of the night and thanked her for being a good sport about the weather.

"It was one of the more unusual requests we've had, but certainly not the most unpleasant or difficult," Tally told her, smiling. "If you want to get married in the rain, who am I to stop you?"

Both women laughed and hugged and then Tally had made a run for it. Saying goodbye to clients at the end of a wedding weekend could be a long process because there were so many people she'd chatted with who wanted to thank her and say nice things about Jekyll Island.

In less than a year, Tally had raised Jekyll Island's profile as a wedding destination immeasurably. BRIDES magazine had featured it in two different stories and Conde Nast's Traveler had written a neat story about the Caribbean wedding planner who was saving brides' dreams on another tiny island after Hurricane Maria. They'd made the covers of a few wedding magazines, too.

Tally had become a bit of a local Cinderella story after a crazy florist had tried to ruin her first big wedding on Jekyll 10 months earlier by stealing the flowers for the bouquets. She'd gotten a lot of press around that – most of it pretty flattering, considering what had happened. Then Tally started marketing to brides who'd had their destination weddings cancelled. The tiny historic Georgia barrier island had become the first choice for brides who'd had to scrap wedding plans in the Caribbean because of the total devastation wrought by Hurricane Maria.

Jekyll Weddings' social media had blown up immediately. The pictures from beautiful weddings Tally had planned on Vieques were getting thousands of likes from random strangers on Instagram and she'd been invited to host a number of wedding planning chats on Twitter and Facebook. Kayla was in charge of posting the really good wedding video clips on TikTok and they'd picked up a lot of followers there, too. Tally wasn't a huge fan of social media except for keeping up with news and wedding trends, but she'd embraced it fully as the free marketing tool it really was. Her blog was getting thousands of clicks. The interesting thing was that the older posts still got as much traffic as the new ones. She worried she'd be screwed if she ever ran out of new topics.

Tally's phone started buzzing again on the bedside table and she rolled over and picked it up, annoyed. She saw it was Kayla and answered. Kayla shouldn't be awake, either.

"What?" she asked in a snippy tone her assistant did not deserve.

"I'm sorry. I'm sorry. I knew I was waking you up but I think you should see this," Kayla said.

"See what?"

"Look at your text messages. I sent you multiple links."

Tally's stomach sunk because Kayla wouldn't be calling if it wasn't something bad. She sat up in her bed and wiped the crunchy sleepers from the corners of her eyes. She could see in the mirror on her closet door that her blonde curls were doing their impression of a Troll doll so she looked the other way. Tally put the phone on speaker and went to texts and clicked on Kayla's name. Then she clicked on a link to a Tweet and groaned. Somebody had posted a video of the Noahide wedding when the rain was at its most torrential. The wind was whipping the chuppah and those wet paper flowers were being destroyed and Kayla was on the sidelines holding a black trash bag. Tally could see herself off to the side in her pink slicker, and even at a distance in a video, she looked annoyed.

The clip was only 30 seconds long but it sure looked like a miserable wedding. The bride and groom were smiling but the guests all looked like they were in hell. Then, all of a sudden, out of nowhere, a gust caught the chuppah and the bamboo structure flew up into the air, the table holding the ceremony stuff went flying, the groom caught the bride before she fell over in her dress, but nobody caught the rabbi, who landed with a splash on the foamy beach. The clip was actually hilarious, if you had no connection to the wedding. But Tally couldn't laugh. She wanted to cry.

"Ugh," Tally said. "I don't think this was filmed by a wedding guest. Do you? The angle is wrong."

"Tally, you've gotta click some of the other links that I sent you. Some of the comments and captions are brutal."

"Oh boy." Tally did as she was told and cringed when she started reading. Most of it was benign, but some of it was mean. And some of it questioned the fact the wedding was held in the rain and some asked whether it was God telling the couple not to say "I do."

"WTF? Why didn't their wedding planner move them inside?" one of the posts asked.

She was still scrolling when Kayla broke more bad news.

"Tally, we're trending," her assistant said.

"Oh no. Under what hashtag?" Tally couldn't imagine what would be funny under those circumstances.

"#Bridesbcray."

Well, at least it was accurate. Most brides were crazy, she thought.

"It's going to be an awful day, isn't it?" Kayla asked.

Tally flopped back onto her pillow and sighed before answering.

"This is something we can't do anything about. We did what the clients wanted and they were thrilled. That's all that matters. I'll send it to Rachel and Josh so neither of them gets blindsided, but I'm not sure they're going to be mad about it. I think there's a chance they're going to think it's absolutely hilarious."

And they did.

Chapter 3

Tally's boyfriend, Mitch Durham, had Monday off, so he asked her to block off her calendar, too. Mitch was a state trooper assigned to a nearby barracks - not the one on Jekyll Island, but the next closest one to the little barrier island they both lived on. He was a Georgia State Patrol legacy – both his father and grandfather had been troopers, and so were two of his older brothers. A third brother was a sergeant with the Glynn County Police Department.

Mitch had served out most of the prior year assigned to the little barracks on Jekyll Island after he was on the scene of a controversial officer-involved shooting at Georgia Tech during his rookie year. The brass had parked him on the sleepy island that was a state park with its own trooper post to keep him out of trouble while the Georgia Bureau of Investigation, better known as GBI, conducted its investigation. Mitch hadn't actually fired his weapon during the incident, but all of the law enforcement officers who were on the scene were under investigation. His superiors had sent him to Jekyll Island, where nothing bad ever happened, to work until he was formally cleared.

All of Jekyll Island was a state park. It was seven miles long and about a mile wide, including the marshes. It had once been the winter playground of the very, very wealthy. The Rockefellers, Pulitzers, Goodyears, and many other well-known families built their own "cottages" beside the original club building, in the early 1800s, creating Millionaires Row. Their families arrived by yacht and train right after the holidays to spend the season hunting, boating, fishing, and socializing together.

After World War II, the state bought the entire island from the millionaires and changed it into a state park. They eventually built a causeway and turned Jekyll into a year-round beach resort. It had a rich and interesting history, and many of the original buildings have since been restored.

The Jekyll Island Authority was chartered by the state to run the island and act as a de facto homeowners' association for the less-than 1,000 full time residents. The island became financially self-sufficient from the revenue from facilities, gate fees, and taxes paid by the homeowners. The island has no crime on it, unless you count the unfortunate bathing suit choices some tourists made. But bad taste wasn't actually illegal, even though it should be.

It was considered a busy week for the 10 Georgia State Patrol troopers assigned to Jekyll when they caught a drunk driver on the causeway, so most people considered the Post 35 assignment a joke. Everybody sent to Jekyll Island was either about to retire or was an overenthusiastic rookie who needed to be put on ice until they cooled off a bit. Mitch had fallen into the second category after the shooting at Georgia Tech. He'd been out of the academy for less than a year and was in the process of setting up a recruiting table on the Atlanta college campus when the radio call went out about an armed man at one of the dormitories.

A student active in the PRIDE movement had written three suicides notes and then called 911 to report a man with a knife and "maybe a gun" walking around outside a dormitory. Four officers responded to the scene, and Mitch was one of them because he happened to be there when the call went out.

Scout Schultz was waiting for law enforcement outside the dorm, dressed in an outfit that matched the suspect's description that was given to law enforcement. Schultz had something in their hand and the officers told them to drop it, multiple times. But the student ignored them and started walking toward the officers telling them to shoot. When the student ignored orders to stop, one of the Georgia Tech police officers opened fire and fatally shot them. It turned out that the student was carrying a multi-tool that contained a knife, but was not otherwise armed.

Mitch hadn't done anything wrong, nor was he accused of breaking any state police policies. But the protests over the controversial shooting were top of the headlines and it was explained to the rookie that if he wanted to get back on the street immediately, he needed to keep his head low and stay out of trouble until the investigation of the fatal officer-involved shooting had been finished. So, without further ado, Trooper Durham was transferred someplace there was no crime. It wasn't punishment, but it sure felt like it to him.

He'd moved into his grandmother's house on Jekyll Island when he was transferred from Atlanta, much to the amusement of his older brothers. His grandmother, Bonnie, lived in a house on Beachview Drive, just around the corner from Tally's Aunt Etah. Etah had raised Tally from the age of 12, after her parents were killed in a small plane crash off the coast of Amelia Island, not too far south of Jekyll. Etah was his grandmother's best friend. And Tally was named after the street they lived on, Tallu Fish Lane. The street was named for a famous Jekyll historian named Tallulah Fish.

Tally and Mitch had been born the same year and spent most of their childhood summers together playing in the sand or exploring the mysteries of the marshes on the magical little Georgia barrier island. Tally's parents left their daughter with Aunt Etah on Jekyll Island several times each summer when they were flying their plane to work on political campaigns in Florida, Georgia, and both of the Carolinas. Aunt Etah was her father's aunt, and when her parents were killed in a plane crash on their way to pick up Tally the summer before 7th grade, Etah became Tally's guardian.

After that, Tally had made Jekyll Island home when she wasn't away at St. Margaret's, an all-girls' boarding school in Virginia that her mother had attended. She and Etah had celebrated most of the big holidays with the Durham family across the street. Until Mitch made the stupid mistake of choosing his girlfriend over Tally the summer they graduated from high school. His girlfriend, Tara, had been terribly jealous of his friendship with Tally and did everything possible to discourage him from spending time with her. As a result, Tally and Mitch grew apart before they left for college and didn't reconnect until they'd both found themselves back on Jekyll a year earlier, after both of them had had their lives turned upside down.

Tally had evacuated from Vieques Island, Puerto Rico, a year earlier after Hurricane Maria wiped out the tiny island where she'd been living and working for a Caribbean destination wedding planner. Getting off the island after the storm had been a challenge and Tally had left behind the guy she'd been living with for almost two years, because he didn't want to leave with her. The island still didn't have power 14 months after the storm and Mitch had never heard her say that she wished she hadn't left. Tally launched her own wedding planning business on Jekyll Island and it took off like wildfire in its first year.

It was kismet that Tally and Mitch had both landed back on Jekyll Island at the same time after 11 years apart. They hadn't come together romantically right away – if anything, they'd dragged out taking things to the next level for as long as they could. It had been terrifying to both of them to realize the person they were meant to be with had been under their nose the whole time, or practically next door. It wasn't until after the same girl who drove them apart years ago reappeared to try to destroy Tally's new business that everything came together and made sense.

That was around the same time that the GBI finished its investigation into the shooting at Georgia Tech and declared that it was justified. No criminal charges were brought against the Georgia Tech officer who'd shot Scout Schulz, and all of the other officers involved in the scene were completely cleared and restored to duty. After months of praying to be able to get back to real police work, Mitch found himself wishing he could stay assigned to the Jekyll Island barracks. He wanted to be able to see Tally every day.

Fortunately for both of them, Mitch got assigned to Post 23 in Brunswick. It was literally the closest assignment he could have gotten without actually being on Jekyll Island. His barracks covered Glynn County, where Jekyll Island was located, as well as nearby Ware and Camden counties. It was close enough that Mitch had decided to keep staying with his grandmother for the time being. If he'd moved, it would have been to live with his parents or one of his brothers because it just didn't make sense for him to waste money on rent with so many available bedrooms in the same area. But only his grandmother's house held the attraction of Tally across the street. And Mitch had high hopes that it wouldn't be long before they moved in together.

Chapter 4

Mitch and Tally had promised each other an uninterrupted beach day. When Mitch was interrupted, it was usually family. Tally got constant calls and texts from her clients and potential clients who wanted instant responses to their wedding planning requests and worries. In order for her to truly take the day off, she'd asked Kayla to babysit her phone for the day. She didn't have to deal with any crises on her own, but she could shoot off quick "Tally is out of the office today" reply texts and answer the phone and take messages. It was the personal touch and feeling like somebody had actually heard them that made clients feel good about their wedding planning experience.

"You ready to go?" Mitch asked. He'd arrived a few minutes earlier and was standing in Tally's kitchen chatting with Kayla when his girlfriend came out of her bedroom carrying her beach bag.

The sun was bright, coming in through the floor-to-ceiling windows on the oceanfront house, and Tally's blond curls glowed around her tanned face. She had her bathing suit on underneath a beach coverup with turtles on it – turtles were a thing on Jekyll – and carried a ginormous floppy hat in one hand.

Tally dramatically placed a big pair of Tory Burch sunglasses on her face, hefted her beach bag up onto her shoulder, and struck a pose.

"Do I look like I'm on vacation?" she asked.

"Oh absolutely," Kayla assured her. "I like the new sunglasses!"

"Thank you. So do I!" She did a bit of a twirl but stopped, realizing she looked silly.

"I'm so excited to have a real beach day. Are you sure I shouldn't grab snacks?" she asked Mitch.

"I've got it covered," he assured her. But then he laughed at the look on her face. "You don't trust me, do you?"

"I can't help it," Tally confessed. "It's the planner in me. I like to know all the details. Who, what, where, when, how and why. When you handicap me with not enough information, it makes me anxious."

"Too bad," Mitch told her with zero sympathy in his voice. "I have everything handled today. And you, Little Miss Control Freak, are just going to have to suck it up for a little bit longer and then everything shall be revealed to you."

Tally groaned out loud and Kayla laughed at her. It was nearly impossible to surprise Tally with anything and her assistant was super impressed by the efforts Mitch had been making. In fact, Kayla knew where her boss was headed for the day and had helped with ordering some of the goodies Mitch wanted to take with them on their picnic.

Tally and Kayla worked out of Aunt Etah's oceanfront beach house. Kayla's office was one end of the dining room table and Tally's office took up the other end. The wireless printer sat on the cabinet under the television on the opposite wall in the living room. When they needed it clean and clear to meet with a client or vendor, or because Etah was coming home for a few days, they could stack everything up, unplug laptops, and hide it all within minutes.

Etah was a wire reporter and she traveled the world covering big international new stories and doing speaking engagements. She was rarely home and didn't mind the wedding chaos when she was there for it. She was just very relieved her great-niece had chosen to leave Vieques Island and come home after Hurricane Maria, and she was willing to provide whatever support she could for Tally's new wedding planning venture.

"Everything is in my truck if you're ready to go," Mitch told Tally, looking at his watch. She got the message and gave Kayla a hug.

"Call me on Mitch's phone if you absolutely have to," Tally told her assistant. "But try really hard not to have to. We don't have any weddings this coming weekend. That means nothing is an emergency unless the groom is actually on fire. If nobody is on fire, I will call them back. If somebody is on fire, call the fire department and then think twice about whether you really need to call me."

Kayla laughed and gave her a thumbs up. "I got it. I can handle the crazy brides for a day. And if I need you, God forbid, I will call Mitch's phone."

"Absolutely," Mitch nodded. He walked to the front door – which was actually the back door because the front of the beach house was the side that faced the ocean – and opened it. He stood holding it open for Tally but his girlfriend didn't move.

He watched her think and realized she was reconsidering whether she could walk away from her electronic leash, as he referred to her iPhone. Mitch felt guilty when he saw Tally hesitate.

"Babe, you can bring it if you want. You're the one who laid down the law on yourself about not bringing your phone today."

"No, I'm okay," Tally snapped out of whatever headspace she'd been in. "I'm ready. Call me if you need me. But please don't need me," she told Kayla with a laugh and then strode out the front door ahead of Mitch as if to prove she wasn't bothered about leaving her phone at home.

Mitch and Kayla made eye contact and cracked up. He winked and waved a conspiratorial goodbye at her and followed Tally to his truck.

Chapter 5

When they pulled up at the public boat launch on the south end of the river side of the island, Tally recognized Mitch's brother, Pete, standing next to a boat trailer that was hooked to his truck.

"Surprise!" Mitch said with a grin. "I borrowed Pete's boat. Don't leave any of your stuff in my truck because he's going to take it and we'll just bring his truck and boat back with us when we're done."

Tally followed instructions and carried her stuffed beach bag out of the truck with her. The boys made short work of backing the boat down the ramp and floating it. Tally helped by staying out of the way.

While she was standing on the boat ramp watching, Tally reached for her phone about 10 times. Ugh, she thought. She could have gotten so much done while they were getting the boat ready. But she dared not voice her thinking to Mitch. He already thought she was too available to her clients and worked way too much. Fortunately, he'd been assigned an evening shift – 3 p.m. to 11 p.m. – so Tally had plenty of free time in the evenings while he was working to write blogs or get caught up on paperwork. She always had emails to respond to and it never felt like she ever got ahead on things.

She was a list maker and nothing gave her greater professional pleasure than crossing off finished items.

Tally saw Mitch boost himself into his brother's boat, so she walked down to the edge of the water and stepped out of her flip flops. Pete handed her bag to Mitch to stow on the boat and then he picked Tally up as if she weighed nothing and boosted her up onto the side of the 24-foot fishing boat he'd named "Robin's Nest" after his wife.

"You guys have fun. Weather looks clear but you know how it can be around here, so keep an eye on the sky and the radar," Pete cautioned his little brother.

Georgia's barrier islands were known for unpredictable weather patterns. Tally loved the sudden thunderstorms that popped up on an almost daily basis, and Etah's oceanfront house gave her the best view on the island for storm watching. But she didn't want to do it from a boat.

"We'll be careful," Tally promised. She blew a kiss to Pete as Mitch eased the little power boat away from shore and headed south toward the St. Andrews Sound.

Tally sat down on the bench in the back of the boat while Mitch stood at the wheel. They weren't in the boat for that long because Mitch piloted the boat straight across the St. Andrews Sound to the privately-owned Little Cumberland Island and dropped anchor by a pretty sand beach in front of a mansion. Tally gave him a questioning look.

"We have permission to be here," Mitch told her. They both laughed.

Tally had visited Little Cumberland many times as a teen with friends, when they did not have permission to be there. The entire island was part of the Cumberland Island National Seashore, but Little Cumberland was private and only accessible to the wealthy folks who owned homes there. It was located just four miles south of Jekyll Island, and Tally had boated over to Little Cumberland Island by moonlight with friends many times and had bonfires on the beaches. It wasn't a terribly safe or smart thing for them to have done, but nobody ever got killed or caught. She'd never been there with Mitch before because he'd refused to participate in obviously illegal shenanigans.

Mitch jumped out of the boat first, and Tally handed him her beach bag and a cooler that he'd brought with him. He carried the supplies to shore and came back for her. She took off her coverup and left it in on the boat. Then she handed her sunglasses to Mitch and jumped off the side of the boat. He gave her back her glasses and followed her to shore. Once there, Tally pulled a big beach towel out of her bag and spread it on the sand. They sat down next to each other and enjoyed the late fall sun on their faces.

"You know that's my favorite bathing suit, right?" Mitch asked her.

Tally laughed. "That's why I wore it."

"That bikini made me fall in love with you," he told her, remembering when he saw her wearing the yellow polka dot bathing suit on the beach shortly after she returned to Jekyll.

"Well, that's just sad. I bought it on sale at Target for $12."

"The day you came back to Jekyll was the happiest day of my life," he told her sincerely, not letting her derail the conversation that he wanted to have.

"I thought being assigned to Jekyll was the worst thing in the world," Mitch continued. "It felt like I'd been sent to state police purgatory and I couldn't even complain too much because my mom and grandmother were so freaking happy that I was home."

Tally laughed at him.

"I'm glad you were sent back here, too. Or we may have never reconnected," she told him. "And I am so glad that we found each other again."

"Me too," Mitch agreed. He leaned over and kissed her on the lips.

Tally looked at her boyfriend sitting beside her. He was tall and tan and handsome, with dark, thick hair cut military short and an amazing body, but he was also a really good person. Being with him felt entirely different than her relationship with her last boyfriend, Eduardo, on Vieques Island. Eduardo never wanted to leave Vieques, and would be content to give biobay tours to visitors for the rest of his life. Not that there was anything wrong with that, but Tally wanted more.

Mitch had goals and plans and he wanted to be a success on every level. They'd talked about having children one day and, unlike her Puerto Rican boyfriend who expected her to give up her career when the time came for a family, Mitch had talked about how they could have it all and manage it together. It was very different from the way Eduardo had made her feel about the future. And Tally loved it.

Spending time together was easy. They enjoyed talking about things that interested each of them, and their careers were so dramatically different that they each proved to be a good sounding board for the other. A part of Tally wished she could spend every afternoon on the beach with Mitch for the rest of her life.

Bonnie had packed an amazing picnic, and they finished it up by gobbling down a selection of treats from the Smallcakes bakery on St. Simons Island. Tally suspected Kayla had been in on the planning when she saw the mini cupcakes, but she didn't call Mitch out on it. She loved that he wanted to make her happy and went to such lengths to get her favorite treats.

"I got some good news at work," Mitch told her. "We could probably celebrate."

"What's up?"

"I'm being assigned to work with a federal drug interdiction task force for a few months," he told her.

"What does that mean?"

"It means I get to do more than just run radar and direct traffic around car wrecks on Interstate 95," he explained. "The task force is made up of guys from like six different federal and local agencies, and me, for the state police. This is the kind of stuff that looks good on your resume when you try for a promotion later on."

"That's great," Tally said enthusiastically, but she didn't really mean it. What she wanted to say was "that sounds dangerous," but Mitch was so excited about the new assignment that she didn't want to burst his bubble with her own insecurities. She was still learning how to mentally cope with dating a member of law enforcement.

"Best part is my schedule is going to change around so I'll be home some evenings and we'll be able to spend more time together," he said. "I may even end up working four-day weeks while I'm on the task force."

"That'll be great. I'm jealous. I'd like a four-day work week. What will your hours be?" she asked.

"Well, it'll change on the regular from what I understand because part of the job is investigative and then we move and shut down the operations. I'm not entirely clear on what they'll have me working at first – I'm the lowest guy on the totem pole, I'm sure – but I know the hours will probably change on a daily basis based on what they have me doing."

"Ew," Tally said and made a face.

"What?"

"That sounds like a nuisance. Like it's going to be super-hard to make plans," she explained. "We already struggle to have date nights and a 'normal' relationship. This is going to make it a lot harder."

Mitch was quiet for a moment and then reached for her hand.

"We wouldn't have a shortage of time if we lived together," he said.

Tally didn't reply. He tried to look her in the eye to see what she was thinking but she was looking away from him, across the water.

She wasn't sure if Mitch was making an observation or a suggestion. Was it a question? Was she supposed to reply? He already spent the night at her house a few times a week, but only if she was still up when he got home from work or they'd done some preplanning. He still lived around the corner with his grandmother, and Tally never intended to do the "walk of shame" from Bonnie's house to home in the morning. Etah had raised her better than that. Her aunt knew what was going on and that Mitch spent a lot of time at her house, but he didn't sleep over when Etah was home, just out of respect for her aunt. Etah had let her know that she wouldn't be upset if she ran into Mitch in their kitchen making coffee in the morning, as long as he didn't break the Nespresso machine that she loved more than Tally. But Tally felt weird about it and hadn't suggested it to her boyfriend. Mitch had been her best friend when she was little and now, he was her best friend and lover as an adult. But their lives and families were so intertwined that it was a little overwhelming to think about at times.

She realized she still hadn't said anything about the idea of moving in together when she caught Mitch staring at her with a slight frown.

"Well, what do you think?" he asked.

"I think I'd love to live together but the practical side of me says neither one of us has a home. We both live with other people, basically. I don't think we can make plans to move in together until we're moving someplace different. And right now, I can't move off of Jekyll Island because my whole marketing schtick is that using a local wedding planner who lives on the island is better than bringing in an event coordinator from somewhere else," Tally explained.

"But that's not forever is it?" he asked.

"I guess not. But at least for a few more years until the company is better established. But Mitch, think about how much more exponentially difficult my job would be if I didn't live here," Tally said. "When I have to do weddings events on St. Simons, it screws up my whole week. I get home so late. I spent half my work hours driving to and from the venues. And remember, my job isn't like yours. When you get off work, you take a shower and turn off work. When I get home from a rehearsal dinner at midnight, I have to work for a couple of hours to fix the reception seat assignments if we had no shows at the wedding rehearsal and make sure the prep tubs are ready. Plus responding to a million texts from nervous brides-to-be and their mothers. And sometimes, we're up late making bouquets because the florists around here still hate me.

"It's not that I have to live on Jekyll," Tally conceded. "But it makes my job and my life a whole lot easier. I'm happy here. I don't want to move. I'm still figuring the business out. And I do think knowing I'm actually a resident here makes a big difference to some of the bigger-budget potential clients."

"So, if I wanna live with you, I need to save up to buy a house on Jekyll?" his question was asked in a joking tone, but Tally knew Mitch was dead serious.

"Something like that," she replied. "But I'd think it's more like 'we' need to save up to buy a house here together. And I think that with our incomes combined and a down payment from my trust fund, we could probably afford something that isn't on the water and needs to be renovated."

"So our biggest challenge is going to be waiting for somebody with an original house to die?" Mitch asked.

"Basically." Tally said, and she wasn't joking. Only a small part of Jekyll Island was developed because it was a state park. It was a great way to preserve the beautiful nature and history on the island, but it made home ownership completely impossible for most first-time homebuyers. There were some condos and townhouses to be had that were under a half a million dollars, but Mitch and Tally had agreed they didn't want to be that close to their neighbors.

It was as standing joke on Jekyll that people started house-hunting when they heard an ambulance on the island. Sirens were so unusual on the quiet state park that when somebody was transported to a hospital, everybody knew about it within minutes. There were so few homes on Jekyll and no more space allocated for building – only 35 percent of the island could be developed by law – that it wasn't far-fetched to say that realtors kept an eye on local obituaries.

Most houses never even made it onto the open market. Bonnie and Etah were forever gossiping about deals that had been made behind closed doors for when so-and-so passed away. Houses that weren't passed down in the family were usually quietly purchased in deals that had been made as part of the estate planning. Only a handful of houses, at most, went on the market each year and those usually received multiple offers.

Fortunately, for Mitch and Tally, if they let their families know they were house hunting, their chances of finding something they could buy on Jekyll Island skyrocketed exponentially. But they weren't there yet. Keeping the status of their relationship private had been important to both of them. Asking for home-buying help would kick up pressure on them to make other moves they weren't ready for yet.

The weather started to look a little funky after they'd been on the beach for a couple of hours, so the couple waded back to the boat, which was considerably farther out with the incoming tide. Mitch boosted Tally back over the side before climbing back into the boat himself.

The water was rougher on the trip back because the wind was whipping up, but the rain didn't start until after they had gotten safely back to the boat launch and finished hauling the boat out of the water with Pete's trailer.

Mitch had been quieter than usual on the ride back and Tally thought she'd hurt his feelings by not showing equal enthusiasm for moving in together. She was being practical and he was being romantic.

Tally didn't want Mitch to think she didn't want to make a future with him because she did – just not yet. She'd gone through so many changes in the past year and overcome so many challenges. Tally absolutely saw Mitch in her future, she just wasn't willing to give up her independence yet.

They were almost home when Tally screwed up the nerve to talk about it.

"Hey Mitch, I want to explain something," she began, reaching across the center console to take his hand. "I do want to live with you. Just not yet. I'm not ready to make a move right now. But it has nothing to do with the way that I feel about you. I love you very, very much. You are my best friend and the most amazing man I have ever loved. I just want to take things slow because I'm juggling so much."

She squeezed his hand, and he squeezed back.

"I love you, too, Tally, and I just want to spend more alone time with you," he told her honestly.

"Etah is gone for another few months. You can stay over anytime you want to. You can even let yourself in after I'm asleep if you want to," she offered.

"Careful what you wish for," he teased. "I might wake you up."

"That's the nicest kind of wake-up a girl could ask for," she told him. "Having a hot state trooper climb in bed with her. How did I get this lucky?" she asked as they arrived home.

Mitch parked his brother's truck, with the boat trailer, in front of Bonnie's house on Beachview Drive. Tallu Fish Lane had a tight corner and he was pretty sure he'd get himself stuck getting back out if he tried it.

"I'm not as good at maneuvering it as Pete is," he told Tally. "I'm not going to take any chances. I can just pull it straight out from here and take the long way around the island."

"All the way around the island?" Tally asked, grinning. It was an age-old joke about mile-wide island. It was a phrase that dated back to hot August afternoons when they'd tried to get the adults to give them a ride somewhere instead of biking in the heat.

Mitch laughed with her.

"All the way around the island," he replied.

He walked her back to her house, all the way up to the front door, and stopped there. He bent over and planted a deep kiss on Tally. The intensity of it took her balance, but Mitch had his arms around her for support.

"What was that?" she asked him with a slow smile when they finally came up for air.

"That was me showing you why you should want to go to sleep with me every night and wake up with me every day," he said.

"I already do."

Chapter 6

The rest of the week went by in a blur. Tally had two weddings – an elopement on Driftwood Beach on Thursday and a 200-guest, black tie affair on the lawn of Crane Cottage at the Jekyll Island Club Hotel on Saturday. The elopement was easy. After a year, Tally had executed so many tiny weddings on Driftwood that she couldn't remember the details of each anymore. It had become a weekly wedding ceremony spot for her, thank God. The fact that anything was already "weekly" after she'd been in business for just a year was a tremendous accomplishment.

Tally offered elopement packages for couples who wanted to do a small beach ceremony with 10 guests or fewer, followed by a dinner party at a local restaurant. The package included a welcome basket at their accommodations upon arrival, a bouquet for the bride, a boutonniere for the groom, a minister, help planning the ceremony, a professional wedding photographer for one hour, and the marriage license paperwork. It also included two tickets for a sunset dolphin cruise with Captain Phillip that departed from the historic wharf at the hotel. Those tickets were good for a year if the couple didn't have time to use them on their wedding trip.

Tally had booked a ton of her elopement packages in the first year because none of the other wedding planners along the Golden Isles coastline catered to small-budget couples. Tally had lots of big budget clients, too. But when you added up the time it took to plan a big wedding and the manpower required to pull off a whole weekend of events for a large group, she was probably earning more by the hour at the end of the day for the little elopement packages.

The big wedding on Saturday was one that Tally had been dreading ever since the bride and groom had rebooked their Vieques wedding on Jekyll Island. The couple were in their 40s, and when they'd come to Vieques on a planning trip, she'd gotten a definite gay vibe from the groom. So had Isabelle. But they kept their ideas to themselves because wedding planners knew that it took all kinds to make the world go round. Their job was to make the wedding happen, not wonder if it should.

Tonya was an attorney and Ronald was a "philanthropist." By the time the wedding rolled around, Tally had figured out that meant he lived off his trust fund and spent his parents' money going to charity events like it was his job. She'd gotten to know him rather well because, unlike most couples, Ronald was the one who called her all the time to whine, not the bride.

"I just don't know what to do with her," Ronald had told Tally one day early in the planning when she finally called him back after he'd sent a couple of 911 texts. "I gave her the real engagement ring and she won't accept it."

"The real ring?" Tally was confused. Tonya had been wearing a huge rock when they'd come to visit and choose a wedding venue.

"When I proposed in Dubai, I gave her a gorgeous ring, but it wasn't the REAL ring because I wasn't able to get that one insured for travel in time for our trip. The real ring was my great grandmother's and it's

100-plus-year-old Tiffany ring with a five-carat sapphire in the center," Ronald explained.

"And you waited until just now to give her the real ring? And she doesn't like it?" Tally asked. She was still confused. Tonya was getting two engagement rings? Didn't sound like something to be upset about.

"It was in a vault at my parents' home and they were in Europe for The Season, and so I presented it to her last night at a big family dinner we catered at our place. We had a photographer there and everything for the big reveal," he said and paused like she was supposed to be impressed.

"Go on," Tally told him, looking at her watch. She had a call with a potential client scheduled in the near future and Ronald was a talker.

"I gave her the ring with a champagne toast after dinner and she loved it," he said, further confusing the wedding planner. "Everything was fantastic all evening until my father asked her to sign a legal document associated with the engagement ring."

"A what?"

"The ring is a priceless family heirloom," Ronald explained. "It's actually owned by the family trust. So, if Tonya and I were ever to get divorced, the ring would have to be returned to the Babcock Family Trust."

"And that's a problem because?"

"Because Tonya completely flipped when she found that out," he yelled through the phone. "She hit the goddamned ceiling. She cancelled the wedding and broke up with me. She threw her first engagement ring off our balcony and it took the doormen a couple of hours to find it in the bushes."

Tally struggled to contain a snort of laughter. "But they found it? That's good." The couple lived in a fancy-schmancy condo co-op on the Upper West Side of Manhattan. The property was also owned by the Babcock

Family Trust. Tally knew that because of something snarky Tonya had said to Ronald during an earlier conference call.

"Thank God. I gave them each $100 for looking and sent an email to the management singing their praises," he bragged.

Tally was not terribly impressed. She'd be willing to bet the ring they'd recovered for their badly-behaved tenants was worth at least $20,000.

"So, Tonya doesn't want the family ring?" she tried to get the whiny groom back on track.

"Not unless she can keep it if we ever get divorced. She gets to keep the first ring if we get divorced – just not both of them."

"That sounds fair."

"Not according to her. She's refusing to budge on that. And you know, she's a lawyer. So now she's got her back all up and wants us to figure out the prenups as soon as possible in case we run into a conflict there, too," Ronald explained.

"That's not a bad idea," Tally told him. "If you guys are cancelling weddings over jewelry, figuring out a prenup is gonna be rough. I'd advise y'all to get that ironed out now. That way if you're pissy about it afterwards, you have some time to get over it before your wedding week."

The ring blowup had ultimately been resolved when Ronald took Tonya to Tiffany & Co. and dropped $50,000 on the engagement ring of the bride's choice, one that she could keep forever even if the marriage didn't last. She'd texted pics of the new ring to her wedding planners and Tally and her friends had a really good laugh over it. Tonya was outrageous. But so were the wedding plans.

Ronald's parents had a family compound in Martha's Vineyard and their family traditions included competing in sailing regattas quite successfully over the years. The groom had decided to carry a nautical theme across their entire wedding, complete with shipping Tally all the silver cups from the sailing races to use as part of the reception table centerpieces. He'd used nautical maps that included Jekyll Island, St. Simons, and Cumberland Island as the background for the placecards, the menus, and the table numbers. The dinner napkins were embroidered with the happy couple's monogram in pink and green. But the weirdest thing about it all was the fact that Tonya had nothing to do with it. Ronald made all the wedding decisions. But he wasn't a Groomzilla. He was just way too interested in the details of flowers and décor to be considered an average groom. He was more of a bride.

After 18 months of planning Ronald and Tonya's wedding twice – once in Vieques and once on Jekyll – Tally just wanted it all to be finished. Nothing about this group was going to be easy. But it did all start making more sense when, a week before the wedding, she learned that Ronald's sister was married to a woman and had been disowned by their parents years earlier. That meant Ronald was left as the only child for this massive money dynasty. He wasn't allowed to be gay. And, in order to get the keys to the kingdom, under the terms of the family trust, he also had to be married. Enter Tonya.

Tonya was a strange bird. She'd come across as warm and friendly when they'd visited before they hired Vieques Weddings, but once the planning started, she'd been a lot less fun. She never dialed in for conference calls on time, she acted put out when she needed to send information to her planners, and she was constantly irritated with Ronald. She'd opined to Tally that Ronald's dancing had gotten worse after they took lessons to learn a special first dance. Tally had suggested they try having cocktails before the lesson, but Tonya hadn't been amused. She didn't have a sense of humor.

Prep for Ronald and Tonya's wedding had been a nightmare with so many little details and family heirlooms like the sailing cups. Tally knew good and well from experience that they were going to be even more difficult when they arrived on Jekyll, so it was important to have everything finished that could be done ahead of time. There wouldn't be any downtime while these clients were on the island.

***

The unhappy couple arrived on Jekyll Island the Tuesday before their wedding and within an hour of checking into their suite at the historic Jekyll Island Club Hotel, Tonya texted Tally that the wedding was cancelled.

"Here we go," Tally muttered to herself.

With any other clients, Tally would have freaked out. But this was par for the course for the Stoner/Babcock wedding. Yes, Tonya's last name was Stoner and she was planning to keep it. She hadn't even giggled when Tally suggested a Stoner conference call at 4:20 one day, and that was when Tally decided she probably didn't like this client.

Tally texted Tonya back and told her it was too late to cancel the wedding, and volunteered to come talk to them about whatever was going on. Tonya told her to hurry, and Tally rolled her eyes as she showed the message to Kayla.

"This is going to be a fun one," Kayla remarked, not meaning it at all. She wore shorts and a t-shirt and had her long hair up in a pony tail as she sorted goodies into welcome bags for the last of the guests.

"You wanna come with me?" Tally had the Jeep keys in her hand and was headed for the front door. She was carrying her overstuffed purse with the Stoner/Babcock file in it over her shoulder.

"Oh gosh, I wish I could," Kayla said unconvincingly. "Got to get these bags delivered."

"Oh, c'mon. You have time," Tally joked. "You should totally come with me to see them now."

"I'd rather get a bikini wax from a blind beauty shop trainee," Kayla said with a straight face. Then they both cracked up.

Tally was feeling the same way as Kayla about 15 minutes later as she watched a Mexican standoff unfold between her clients. She'd left her SUV with the valet at the hotel and gone straight up to the bride and groom's suite, but the conflict had already escalated to what Tally would have called the point of no return for any other clients. But Tonya and Ronald were different.

It turned out the couple hadn't dealt with their prenup six months ago when Tally advised them to get it done. Instead, Ronald had waited til they arrived on Jekyll Island to present Tonya with a draft prenup created by the family trust's attorneys. They got into a screaming fight, Tonya announced she was cancelling the wedding just as Tally arrived.

"Is this something you guys can work out today? Because it needs to be resolved before your guests start arriving. You don't want them seeing you at each other's throats," Tally warned.

There was no doubt in her mind that the wedding was happening and all this drama was just a massive waste of her time.

"I need more time than what he's giving me," Tonya announced. "I need to send it to my attorney. I don't even know if he's available."

"But Tonya, you're an attorney," Tally pointed out. "Can't you two work this out between the two of you?" Before your guests arrive and you embarrass the hell out of yourselves, she wanted to add. But she didn't.

"Oh no, we can't," Tonya said dramatically. "Because this wimp won't sign anything that his mommy and daddy's attorneys haven't pre-approved. He just wants me to sign this piece of crap," she said, hurling papers to the floor that Tally assumed were the offensive legal agreement.

When Tally left the hotel about 45 minutes later, nothing had been accomplished. Neither half of the couple was willing to budge and Tonya was still declaring their wedding cancelled. That was fine with Tally, if it were actually being cancelled. But common sense and experience with the crazy couple told her that everything would be fine by the next morning when guests started arriving. Until the next blowup.

Chapter 7

The wedding guests turned out to be the easiest part of the Stoner/Babcock wedding weekend. They were all wealthy and polite to the help, including the wedding planning staff. Isabelle had taught Tally early in her career that no matter how much a couple liked their planners, wedding planners were "the help" as much as anybody else at an event. And even the nicest of brides could turn on a dime and treat Tally like a servant if she got too stressed out and popped her cork. She'd experienced it more than once.

The first two days of events, after the prenup blow-up, ran smoothly for Jekyll Weddings. Ronald and Tonya hosted their welcome party on the deck at The Wharf across from the historic hotel where most of their guests were staying. The groom's sister and her wife were staying at the Jekyll Ocean Club, on the opposite side of the island, with their children, as were a few other guests who were on Ronald's parents' shit list. Tally and Kayla noticed that Ronald's parents and his sister's family had managed to stay at opposite sides of the venue for the entire evening.

It was all very civilized. The sister's family was very nice and their toddlers were adorable. But the kids didn't even seem to know that the

Babcocks, standing 25 feet away from them, were their grandparents. The vibe was weird if you knew what was going on. And Tally assumed that most of the guests knew more than she did.

"At least they don't get drunk and beat the crap out of each other," Tally told Kayla. "We've had that happen more than once and it wasn't fun to break it up. Although, people usually chilled out pretty fast on Vieques when we told them getting arrested meant going to the big island on the ferry wearing handcuffs and leg chains."

"This is a higher-quality crowd than your average wedding down there, though. Right?" Kayla asked.

"I wouldn't necessarily say that. We did all kinds of weddings for all kinds of people. One of the worst groups we ever managed was a groom who worked for World Bank. Every girl working the events got manhandled by wedding guests at some point that weekend."

"Ew," Kayla made a face. She'd heard a lot of destination wedding horror stories from her boss.

"Exactly. Big ew. We didn't expect that to happen with that group and Isabelle made some new security rules after that. Up until that point, she'd based security needs on the size of the group. After that, we did a safety assessment with the bride and groom ahead of the wedding to figure out what we were facing."

"Huh. I wonder if this group would have been worse down on Vieques," Kayla said.

"Everybody was worse in Puerto Rico. That whole lack of accountability thing." It was a simple fact – wedding guests were much better behaved when their behavior could have consequences. Something about the Caribbean made them think they could do anything they wanted and get away with it. Most of the time they could.

***

The day after their welcome party, the Babcocks hosted a mini sailing regatta for their guests, followed by the rehearsal dinner, at a yacht club on St. Simons Island. Tally hadn't had to do much for that, other than to make an appearance to make sure everybody was having fun. Using top-tier venues with their own reputations to protect made Tally's job so much easier. Kayla had dropped off the placecards and décor a few days earlier and the yacht club would have it all boxed up again afterward and help load it into Tally's Jeep. Centerpieces had been delivered directly to the club that morning by a florist from Savannah and Tally gave them to VIP guests to take after the party, as she'd been instructed by the groom.

Tally went home after the rehearsal dinner with plans to get to bed before midnight. She'd sent Kayla home to get some rest before the dinner even ended. This group was wearing them out both physically and mentally. Her assistant needed sleep. She wasn't used to going for days on end without snapping like her boss.

Tally had already put on her pajamas and was in the process of filling up her water bottle when the phone rang. It was Ronald. Ugh, she thought.

"Hi there. What's up?" Tally asked with a smile in her voice, picking up after the second ring. She was afraid to hear the answer.

"Tonya has sunburn," Ronald announced dramatically, as though he was telling Tally that his bride-to-be was dying of cancer. "I don't know what we're going to do."

"Where is she burned?" Tally asked. She didn't laugh but she wanted to. It couldn't have happened to a more deserving bride. But she stopped herself, not wanting to bring bad karma down on herself.

"The back of her neck. She was wearing a halter-style top with this cool patterned strap in the back, and she's managed to burn the pattern onto her back," Ronald sounded like he was going to cry.

Tally struggled to remember what the bride had been wearing during the regatta that afternoon and was able to picture the web that was probably burned onto her back. She'd changed into a dress with a high neck for the rehearsal dinner so Tally hadn't noticed the burn.

"Ronald, isn't she wearing her hair down for the wedding?"

"She totally is. I bought the best extensions," he bragged, totally distracted. "I went to the store without her and was able to choose the exact right color. I'm good at that stuff. They weren't cheap but they're gorgeous."

Definitely gay, Tally thought and not for the first time.

"So won't her hair cover the burn on her back so you can't see it above the back of her dress?" Tally asked. "It's not the perfect solution, but we'll be able to hide it for the pictures. Also, if she's burned tonight, it might not show as badly tomorrow if you coat her in aloe or put tea bags on the worst part to draw it out."

"Can you come over here and help her?" Ronald asked, whining.

"Me?" Tally squeaked. "It's after midnight, Ronald. I need to get some sleep so that you have a beautiful wedding tomorrow." The last thing in the entire world that Tally wanted to do at that moment was get dressed and go over to the hotel to stroke a narcissist's ego.

"She really needs help putting the aloe on it. And she won't let me in the room to help her because it's bad luck to see each other the night before the wedding," he explained.

"What about her friends?" Tally asked. "This is what she has brides-maids for." She used a light, joking tone but she hoped he was picking up the message that this was asking a bit too much.

"Nobody's here. She's not that close to those women. Can you just come do it?" he whined again.

"Yeah, sure. I'm on my way," Tally said and hit end on the call. Then she let out a brief muffled scream, conscious of not wanting to frighten everyone on the street, and released some frustration. She got dressed in jeans and one of the new uniform t-shirts that had just arrived, thinking to herself that at least if she ran into anybody, she looked like a dedicated wedding planner.

When she got to the historic hotel, Tonya answered the door to her suite stark naked. Tally wasn't sure where to look – it was awkward – but it didn't seem to bother the bride. She flopped on her tummy on the bed and ordered Tally to put aloe on her back in an imperious tone Tally imagined she used on most people who were trying to do something nice for her.

While they waited for the aloe to dry so Tally could apply a second coat, Tonya bitched and moaned about Ronald and his family. It took everything Tally had not to ask the bride why she was going to marry this obviously gay man that she clearly didn't think that much of. But she worried that would set off a series of events that would lead to catastrophe, and Tally wasn't taking any chances with this loopy couple. Her job was to plan and execute the wedding, not get involved in her clients' lives. Some of her clients from Vieques were good friends on a personal level now. Tally did not want to stay friends with Tonya and Ronald. She almost hoped she'd never see them again.

Tally finally scooted out of the bridal suite almost an hour after she arrived, feeling mentally drained. She also felt a little sad for Tonya. She couldn't remember another bride who was alone on the night before her wedding when she didn't want to be. She figured it was indicative of the life Tonya and Ronald led back home in New York City and shook it off.

Tally was exhausted and she was headed straight home and into bed, as she was about to do when Ronald called and screwed up her plans.

***

Her childhood stuffed animal, Plops, was keeping the bed warm and she'd left her water bottle and book on her bedside table. The only thing missing in her room was Tally and she intended to get there as quickly as possible. She sent Mitch a voice text letting him know what was up in case he saw her car coming and going so late and worried. She was a little bit relieved when he didn't reply because that probably meant he was asleep and had turned his phone off. She didn't have the energy for a cuddle session tonight.

Her phone rang as she was getting into bed 15 minutes later and she swore aloud. She told herself that if it was Ronald or Tonya, she was letting it go to voicemail. But it was Mitch.

"Hey babe," she answered. "Did I wake you up with my text?"

"No, I'm on duty," he told her. "I'm pulling my first shift with the task force tonight."

"Oh wow. Okay, I didn't realize that would start so fast," she said.

"Me either," Mitch admitted. "But they told me to report to task force headquarters today and I did. And the DEA agent in charge of the group dumped a file box full of background materials on a desk and told me to sit and read til I was familiar with all of it."

"It's almost 2 a.m."

"Yup, and I'm halfway through the box," he told her, sounding proud. She couldn't help laughing.

"When did you start?"

"3 p.m. But it's okay, I can see a light at the end of the tunnel now. And it's all overtime anyway. I can earn as much overtime as I want without prior approval while I'm assigned to the task force. How sweet is that? If this gig lasts long enough, we might be able to afford a home on Jekyll before we die," he joked.

Tally groaned. "Maybe."

"How was your night?" Mitch asked her.

Tally told him about the emergency call for aloe application and he was horrified.

"What do you mean she was naked?"

"Without clothing. The usual definition," Tally said lightly.

"But why? Was the burn that bad?"

"Nope. In fact, she barely has any sunburn at all. She's just nucking futz and wanted somebody to come hang out with her, I think. I don't know where the bridesmaids were – I'm going to find the maid of honor in the morning and explain her responsibilities for the next two days. I will not have time to stroke Tonya's ego all day if she actually wants to have a wedding. That's what her bridesmaids are for," she said in a grumpy voice.

They chatted for another minute and made plans to get together on Sunday evening, unless Mitch had to work. He wished her luck on the Stoner/Babcock wedding and they both laughed at Tonya's name again. Mitch agreed with Tally that Tonya would be easier to deal with if she was actually a stoner instead of a high-maintenance, type-A diva.

"Text me after the wedding tomorrow and let me know you survived," he told her.

"I will. You stay safe, Mitch." Tally said that every time she said goodbye to him when he was working now. She'd heard his grandmother, Bonnie, use the same phrase with Mitch's dad, Tom Durham, and all of his older brothers. Tally understood it to be a police thing, and now that she was in love with Mitch, she was part of that "blue family."

Chapter 8

Tally broke every rule in the book and turned off the ringer on her phone after she said goodbye to Mitch. She had to be up at 7 a.m. and she couldn't afford to deal with stupid calls all night. It was a risk – something she never would have done on Vieques, where a middle-of-the-night phone call could mean Isabelle was needed to help translate so an ambulance could find the villa where the bride's grandmother was staying. But on Jekyll Island, if somebody called her with a medical emergency instead of 911, they were just stupid.

When her alarm went off at 7 a.m., Tally sat up and grabbed her phone. Her heart skipped a beat when she saw five missed calls and 17 text messages waiting.

Tonya and Ronald had gotten into a big fight at about 3:30 in the morning on their wedding day, apparently. She listened to a screechy voicemail from Tonya, a weepy message from Ronald, and a message from the manager-on-duty at the Jekyll Island Club Hotel asking her to call immediately about some drama with her clients.

Text messages revealed the fight had been about the prenup, again. And it appeared the argument had gone on for several hours, based on the messages. Some of the texts were ugly, and she couldn't imagine Tonya actually marrying the man she was writing those things about just hours before she was supposed to say 'I do.' But Tally kept reading.

It appeared the happy couple had made up about 6 a.m. because the last text came in 6:30ish informing her that since she'd "been unavailable" to them all night, they'd worked things out themselves. So, Tally could go ahead and disregard all the voicemails and text messages.

Tally had been awake for less than five minutes, but she didn't feel rested at all. She felt like she'd been hit by a two-ton truck that was getting ready to back over her again and again for the next 18 hours.

Isabelle had taught her on Vieques that there were some crazy clients that couldn't be tamed. They would act like idiots to their own detriment and ruin their weddings themselves no matter how hard she tried to fix things. Tonya was definitely one of those brides. So was Ronald.

She felt the outside shower calling to her, and she grabbed her bathrobe off the back of her bedroom door and headed down the hallway. Aunt Etah had built an amazing outside shower right off her bedroom on the back deck – which was actually the front deck of the oceanfront house. She'd used incredible tile that looked like sea glass and put in a wooden bench for leg shaving, but the "peekaboo" window was the very best part of the outside shower. There was a door in the front wall of the shower that, when opened, gave the person inside a view of the Atlantic Ocean less than 50 yards away. Tally loved to watch pelicans fishing for breakfast and schools of dolphins making their way along the coastline while she washed her hair.

She couldn't use the outside shower when she was in a hurry because she daydreamed too much and wasted time. It was a luxury. But this morning was the exception to the rule because Tally needed to do anything she could to delay the conversation she had to have with hotel management about whatever had gone down in the bridal suite overnight.

She finished showering and went back to her room to dress. She was towel-drying her long, curly blonde hair when Kayla called out from the front door.

"I'm here," her assistant yelled. She did that every time she let herself in after she'd scared the crap out of Tally one morning.

"Good morning!" Tally called back, padding out to the kitchen on bare feet. "Did you get a lot of rest I hope?"

Kayla looked fantastic. Her long, straight blonde hair was in a tight French braid, and she wore a khaki skort with her new Jekyll Weddings uniform shirt. The shirts were white with her snazzy company logo on the chest and the slogan "Get Married on Jekyll" in swirly hot pink writing across the back. Tally was wearing khaki capris and the same top. Both women wore crisp-looking white tennis shoes on their feet. The footwear had not been planned.

"I love it. You look great," Tally told Kayla.

"So do you. And I sorta love that we don't have to think about what to wear to setup," Kayla admitted.

"Me too. I always wore a uniform in school, and when Isabelle handed me uniform shirts in Vieques, I was like 'sweet, no more fashion dilemmas,'" Tally joked. "But really, they look super professional and make us easily identifiable to arriving vendors when we have a massive setup like the one at Crane Cottage. Don't forget your clipboard. Uniform shirts and clipboards and people will do whatever we tell them to do."

"That's so true," Kayla agreed. "The clipboard has magical powers. I didn't believe it until I saw the way you used it at the first wedding rehearsal."

"Oh my God, would you stop reminding me of that? It was not my finest moment," Tally turned her back to Kayla and started the Nespresso machine. She needed coffee badly.

"Tally, it was freaking hilarious. There we were, surrounded by a wedding party made up of absolutely-wasted 40 year olds who wouldn't shut up and listen to you. You did what you had to do. It was my first wedding rehearsal after you hired me and I was impressed."

"Really?"

Tally had held her clipboard up in the air and yelled to get everyone's attention. When they ignored her and kept up the shenanigans, Tally had blown the lifeguard whistle on her keychain to get their attention. That had worked.

"Okay guys. We have to get through rehearsal so you can be at the rehearsal dinner on time. We don't want people getting confused to-morrow since it's a beach ceremony and the guests can see everything," Tally began. But the groomsmen had already turned their backs to her and were pouring shots into plastic shot glasses that somebody had pulled out of a seersucker pocket.

"Alright," Tally yelled really loud. "I need your attention. We're going to play a game. Like summer camp."

She held her clipboard up in the air over her head.

"When my hand is up, your mouths are shut," Tally waved her clipboard in the air the way her camp counselor had done when giving the same speech to first-time campers at Camp Arrowhead on the Rehoboth Bay when she was seven.

Seventeen executives – most of them important Wall Street honchos if they worked with the bride and groom – shut their mouths and listened like little kids while Tally told first the men, then the women, where to walk and where to stand, before she had the bride and groom practice walking down the aisle. When the drunk wedding party got giggly again, Tally gave a short blast of the whistle and held her clipboard up in the air until they got quiet. Then she continued the wedding rehearsal. It was funny, but it was a bad memory.

"I was lucky they were so wasted that they thought it was funny, Kayla. Some people would have gotten really pissed at me for talking to their friends like little kids."

"They were acting like little kids. It was ridiculous."

"But they're paying us to run their wedding. If that's the kind of people they are, that's probably how everything they do goes. They're always late, they're always drunk, and everything they plan is a clusterfuck. That's good, actually. That means the bar for success is so much lower for us. We know how to keep them on time and on schedule and make the wedding seamless even if the entire wedding party skips rehearsal, because that's what we do. My handling of that situation was less than professional and I'm not proud of it."

"It was funny as hell. And you'll never change my mind on that. And the bride and groom gave us fantastic reviews on Wedding Wire, so the rehearsal couldn't have been that bad," her 25-year-old assistant argued.

"They were so drunk they didn't remember the rehearsal," Tally said and rolled her eyes.

"Probably," Kayla agreed. "That's why they hire us."

"You're catching on, grasshopper."

Chapter 9

Tally decided to face the music at the Jekyll Island Club Hotel in person, so she and Kayla loaded up what they needed for setup and headed across the island 30 minutes before they needed to meet the lighting people at the tent.

"Okay, drop me under the portico at the hotel and then head over to the venue," Tally told her assistant. "It's the first left after the Georgia Sea Turtle Center. Follow the road around and follow the signs that say 'Crane Cottage Guests Only,' or something like that. Get as close as you can to unload. Text me if you have any problems. I'll be getting my ass handed to me by hotel management. This is not going to be fun."

"Maybe it's not a big deal, maybe they just heard some yelling," Kayla suggested optimistically.

"Maybe. But nothing that has happened with Tonya and Ronald has been no big deal so far," she sighed. "I'll be over at Crane Cottage soon, but call me if you need something before I get there."

Kayla saluted and pulled away as Tally started up the staircase. She thought about trying to sneak across the hotel and get more coffee before she faced the dragon, but the hotel's latest general manager was standing in the lobby and she saw Tally before Tally saw her.

"Shit," she muttered under her breath and then put a smile on her face. "Good morning, Mayra! It's a beautiful day for a wedding, isn't it?"

When she got close, Mayra leaned in conspiratorially. "Yes, it's a beautiful day for a wedding. But tomorrow will be an even more beautiful day after these hideous clients of your check out of this hotel."

Mayra was smiling as she said this and nobody else in the area could have heard her, but her tone of voice conveyed that she was furious. Tally respected that. Mayra Hernandez was a professional. Who knew if anybody wandering through the lobby or halls of the hotel was a wedding guest. The Stoner/Babcock wedding was humungous and not everybody had attended the welcome event. Several of the guests were arriving that afternoon by private planes at the Jekyll Island airport. It certainly wouldn't do for somebody associated with the wedding to overhear the hotel manager and the couple's wedding planner talking smack about the bride and groom.

Tally followed Mayra back to her office and shut the door behind her. Both women sat down, but only one of them was smiling.

"If this wedding hadn't booked out almost every room in this hotel, I would be telling you to find the bride and groom somewhere else to stay," Mayra told Tally in a serious voice.

Uh oh, Tally thought. "What happened?"

"What didn't happen? I got called in here at 5 o'clock this morning after the bride screamed and yelled and made the overnight desk clerk cry because she wanted room service and we don't offer that until 6 a.m."

It could be worse, Tally thought to herself. "I'm so sorry. She had a bad sunburn and felt miserable."

"She was wasted, Tally. So was the groom. They had a screaming fight in the hallway. The bride wouldn't let the groom in the room and so they screamed through the door at each other. For more than an hour," Mayra gestured dramatically. "And when security went up to ask them to pipe down, the bride opened the door and lobbed an empty bottle of champagne at him."

"Oh my God." Even for Tonya, that was bad. "Was he hurt?" Tally asked.

"Fortunately, it missed him. It took out a light fixture on the wall behind him, though. If that bottle had hit him, we'd be talking about why your client was sitting in the Glynn County jail on her wedding morning," Mayra told her.

"I believe you."

"And she was naked."

"I believe that, too."

"Look, Tally, they're moving over to Crane Cottage this morning. This can't happen over there. The bride was throwing things and really tore up the room. Crane Cottage is a historic landmark and some crazy New York lawyer isn't going to destroy it having a bridal tizzy."

"I understand," Tally said. "I won't let that happen."

Tally texted Ronald to let her know when he was awake while she was sitting with Mayra, and he replied just as she was leaving the GM's office.

"I'm up. Tonya isn't," the groom wrote.

"Sounded like you guys had a really bad night. Are you okay?" Tally asked.

"We're okay," he texted back immediately. "Just wedding stress."

That was not normal wedding stress, Tally thought. But that's not what she typed. Instead, she briefly explained that their bruhaha in the hallway had management concerned about a repeat performance in the beautiful villa built by Chicago plumbing magnate Richard Teller Crane, Jr. in 1917 as part of the historic district's "Millionaires Row."

"If Tonya's gonna go all WWE again tonight, you guys should stay someplace else. Seriously," Tally typed. She was trying to make light of a serious situation but she had a feeling that Ronald, the trust fund baby, would get her point.

"We'll be fine," he texted back. Tally doubted that. But she didn't have any more time to bullshit with him.

"Okay, it's on your credit card," she texted back. "Please tell Tonya to let me know when she and the girls are all set up over at Crane Cottage. The hair and makeup team is supposed to be there by noon."

Ronald replied with the ubiquitous thumbs up, but Tally read his true meaning. She didn't reply, and instead, pocketed her phone and hoisted her overstuffed purse onto her shoulder for the short hike over to the wedding venue.

Chapter 10

"Oh my God," Tally's friend, Cheryl, gasped, when Tally called to post-mortem the Stoner/Babcock wedding late that night. "You cannot make that stuff up."

But Tally had only gotten to the point in the story where she got yelled at by the hotel manager.

Cheryl had been the in-house wedding planner at the Jekyll Island Club Hotel for several years before a rumble between two drunk groups of groomsmen on the croquet court had caused her to quit.

"No kidding," Tally said. "But hang on, it gets worse. The bride went down the aisle like 40 minutes late because nobody could get her dress zipped."

"What?" Cheryl practically shrieked. "Had she gained weight?"

"No, she had those chicken cutlet boob boosters on upside down under her tatas, and that's why it wouldn't zip. But I didn't figure that out until I made her take off the dress – and the fake boobs – to start over. It zipped when she put it back on. I've seen way too much of this chick naked," Tally complained.

"For sure," Cheryl agreed.

"She had weird boobs."

"A lot of them do." The girls chuckled.

"They missed their entire cocktail hour having pictures taken because things started so late. Dinner went fine, but then everything fell apart during the first dance," Tally continued.

"Why?"

"Well, they'd taken dance lessons and had some routine worked out to their favorite song – one of those cringeworthy Jack Johnson ones that everybody uses – and about 10 steps into the song, the groom stepped on the bride's foot.

"Of course, nobody but the bride knew it happened because nobody can see their feet with all the wedding gown," Tally continued. "But Tonya freaked the fuck out. Ronald tried to recover and keep dancing, but Tonya hiked up her dress and stomped off the dance floor in the middle of the song. Everybody was just standing there watching and trying to figure out if it was real or some kind of prank."

"She did not!" Cheryl was horrified.

"Oh yes, she did. So I followed her to the bridal suite and tried to talk her off the ledge. Total waste of time. That bitch is bonkers. She missed like 45 minutes of her own wedding reception during that tantrum, and then when we had to shut things down at Crane Cottage at 11 p.m. as per the contract, she told Ronald that he wasn't allowed to go to the after-hours that they'd booked at The Wharf for their guests."

The Wharf was a restaurant located at the end of the historic pier across from the hotel, and walking distance from Crane Cottage. Nothing on the island was open after 9 p.m. so Tally frequently booked private, late-night after-parties for wedding groups in different venues that were part of the resort. If they were staying at the historic hotel, it was perfect because nobody had to drive to get back to their rooms. And it was far better than having the guests create their own spontaneous after-party somewhere on the property that would bother other guests.

Tonya and Ronald had booked a 90-minute after-party at The Wharf and prepaid for a massive top-shelf, open bar during that time period. Tally had dropped off the décor with the restaurant's manager that afternoon and it would be a fun party with an amazing view of the moon over the water and a totally clear sky. Tally had no plans to attend the after-party – she had to deal with teardown and cleanup at the wedding venue – but it would get the guests out of the Crane Cottage area quickly because everybody loved an unlimited open bar. When Tally announced that the wedding reception bar was closing and the party was moving, she didn't have to tell the guests twice.

"Tonya decided that neither of them was going to the after-party," Tally told Cheryl. "It was so bizarre. She told Ronald that he'd had enough to drink and that if he went to the party, he didn't need to come back to their room afterwards."

"What happened?" Cheryl asked, aghast.

"I honestly don't know. Last I saw, Ronald was headed to The Wharf with his friends and Tonya had sworn not to leave their room. I'm so done with that crazy woman."

"I hear you on that one. I'm not sure how much longer I can do this for a living and not end up in prison for beating somebody to death with a flower arch," Cheryl joked. She had taken over wedding planning at The Cloister on Sea Island after she left Jekyll. It was the fanciest venue in the area and she dealt with really snooty clients. Plus, Sea Island had a million of its own crazy rules.

"I'm just hoping that the shit doesn't hit the fan overnight. Mayra told me she'd kill me if I turned off my ringer again. And I'm freaking exhausted," Tally complained.

"Mayra gets it. She's cool," Cheryl said. "She called me after she took over for the asshole at the hotel, and we did lunch. She asked what it would take to bring me back to Jekyll Island Club Hotel and I told her there wasn't enough money in the world."

"Aw," Tally felt sorry for Mayra but knew Cheryl was dead serious.

"I think she respected my honesty. I didn't waste her time trying to bribe me back. And now we're friends and we can refer events between properties when we're already booked solid. It's all copacetic," Cheryl explained. "Go to bed now. You don't know what's going to happen in an hour."

"Don't even joke like that," Tally growled.

"It wasn't a joke."

"I really, really hate this couple," Tally admitted to her friend. "And if I have to see them in the middle of the night again, I might actually tell them that. Unfortunately, their wedding was gorgeous, and I want to use the pictures on my website. So, I can't burn any bridges before they leave Jekyll Island."

"Oh, the sacrifices we make," Cheryl joked.

The girls made plans to meet for lunch the following week and then said goodbye. Tally went to bed a few minutes later and she was out before her head hit the pillow.

Chapter 11

Thanksgiving was upon them before Tally could blink, and she was grateful for the standing holiday invitation at Bonnie's house because, if she'd been left to her own devices, she would have probably just eaten a peanut butter sandwich. Etah was in Russia covering something – Tally didn't even try to keep up with her famous wire reporter aunt, she moved too fast – and wouldn't be back on Jekyll Island until Christmas.

Because he was assigned to a task force at the moment, Mitch actually got to eat Thanksgiving dinner with them. He'd told Tally he would have to go into work later that night for a few hours, but his father, a 30-year veteran of the Georgia State Patrol, endlessly mocked his millennial son for getting to enjoy a holiday meal in real time while he was still basically a rookie. Tom Durham swore he worked through every holiday meal for the first 10 years of his career.

"Sounds like you didn't know how to work the system, Dad," Mitch teased as he filled up his plate at the buffet.

His father threw one of Bonnie's famous rolls at his son and it bounced off Mitch's head and came down in the gravy boat, causing quite a splash.

"Enough," Mitch's mother, Roberta, yelled at both men. "If you want to act like kids, you should go outside and eat at the kids' table in the yard."

"I didn't do anything!" Mitch protested. "It was all him."

"You antagonized me," his father claimed, trying to look innocent. "Okay, okay, sorry. We promise to be good. Right, Mitch?"

Tally realized how much Mitch looked like his father, when they faced Bonnie with matching expressions.

"I wasn't the one misbehaving. I'm always good," Mitch quipped and then scooted to a chair at the opposite end of the table before his father could cuff him.

Mitch held Tally's hand while the family said grace, and then he didn't let go right away afterwards. Everybody knew that Mitch and Tally were dating but they hadn't done any public displays of affection and Tally still felt like everybody was watching them whenever they were together. Sort of like an ant farm.

***

After dinner, including three kinds of pie, Mitch walked Tally back around to her house. They went out on the front deck and watched the waves together while the sky got dark and talked about holiday plans. Mitch had signed himself and Tally up to work the Toys for Tots collection booth at a nearby shopping center and she added it to their shared calendar app. It was the only way either one of them could reliably make plans because Tally was booked so far ahead with weddings and parties. After one year in business on Jekyll Island, she was booked 18 months ahead with at least three big weddings a month, and sometimes a bunch of elopements on top of that. Things were going very well in her work life, but that made having a social life difficult.

"I really like doing the task force stuff," Mitch said. He told her about the deputies from Glynn, Camden, Charlton, and Brantley County sheriff's departments who were assigned to the task force with him. There were also a couple of DEA and FBI agents assigned to run the task force, and another guy from ATF.

"Sounds like you're meeting every cop in southeast Georgia," Tally observed.

"Nah, just a few from every department. The cool thing is that I'm also getting to work with the task force team from Florida and I'm learning all about the problems at the border between Florida and Georgia. Apparently, the same problem exists where the panhandle touches other states. But those spots aren't my problem.

"Florida has medical marijuana but Georgia and South Carolina do not. So that's a problem because people just go south to get what they want and bring it back," Mitch explained. "Florida is also a major drug entry point for narcotics coming in from Latin America. That's what we're primarily focused on, thank God. Because trying to catch 100 kids coming back from Jacksonville with an ounce of weed isn't the best use of task force time."

"Could be entertaining," Tally suggested.

"It's always entertaining. Anyway, there's a huge push to stop the flow of drugs from Florida across the border into other states and show numbers proving progress before the end of the year," he explained.

"Oh great. A whole month! No pressure," Tally joked.

"Seriously," he nodded. "If we meet our goals, it's entirely possible the task force will get federal funding for another full year. And if I'm part of what makes it a success, it ups my chances of staying on it."

"You really love it that much more than patrol?" Mitch looked like a little kid the way his eyes lit up when he talked about working on the task force.

"Tally, this is the coolest stuff. I'm getting access to investigative technology that I've only read about. I'm getting to put the crime scene certifications that I got while I was cooling my heels on Jekyll last year to use finally. It's so much fun that it doesn't even feel like work," Mitch declared. "I only lucked into this position and I want to keep it as long as I can."

"That's amazing, babe. I'm so proud of you," Tally leaned over on their favorite bench and planted a quick kiss on her boyfriend's lips.

"And speaking of work, I need to get out of here in a minute. I promised Agent Bond – yes that's her name, Melanie Bond – that I'd get there a little early to help with the analysis on today's intel. All of the targets were home for Thanksgiving, and Florida and Georgia need to have summaries exchanged so we can coordinate tonight's operation," he told her enthusiastically.

It was all Greek to Tally, and she hated to admit it, but she'd sort of started tuning out his police babble. She loved that he talked to her about work, but she found it hard to stay focused when he talked for literally an hour about the different ammo brands the other agencies used and what was considered the best for "LEO off-duty carry."

LEO stood for law enforcement officer. She'd learned that after she asked Mitch who "that Leo guy" was that he was always talking about. Police slang wasn't unlike Puerto Rican slang. She had to listen closely to figure out what the hell they were talking about. Some people said L.E.O. and some just said "Leo." It was like Puerto Ricans dropping the "s" off of words.

Tally's schedule wasn't as bad during Christmas as it might have been. She'd decided to focus on booking some local holiday parties and hadn't accepted any wedding clients from December 15 to January 15. That didn't mean she wouldn't be working on weddings. It just meant that she could do more of what she wanted over the holidays and spend time with Aunt Etah while she was home.

Her former boss and current mentor, Isabelle, had warned Tally from the launch of Jekyll Weddings that she shouldn't give up her life to serve her clients. She told Tally to avoid overhead expenses like renting an office space until she had to, and to keep her costs low so she could pick and choose her clients. Isabelle told Tally she was confident that Tally could knock the whole thing out of the water and do 100 weddings a year, but she wasn't sure that was a fun or healthy way to live life. Once you got into the bad habit, she'd warned, it was really hard to get out of it.

Isabelle was loving life at her mountain chalet near the town of Londonderry in Vermont. She and Tally talked on the phone almost every day and she'd helped Tally unfuck something she couldn't figure out more than once. She'd come to town twice to help with weddings when Tally first got started, but after that, she'd begged off and told Tally she'd rather visit when she didn't have a wedding going on.

"I've done enough of them, my love. I would always run down here to help you in a pinch, but let's not do it intentionally," Isabelle had told her.

Tally understood, and her friend was scheduled to come down for a few days in early January when she could finally meet Aunt Etah and spend time with Tally without brides. Tally was really looking forward to her visit.

Mitch looked at his watch again and Tally caught the cue. She walked her boyfriend to the front door and they embraced for a minute. She rested her head on his chest.

"Oh Tally," Mitch groaned. "You are not helping me make a good impression on the new bosses. I'm starting to feel really sick. Maybe I should call off work."

"Yeah right," Tally laughed and stepped back. "You wouldn't play hooky even if you had tickets to the Savannah Bananas." The Bananas were a local team that was baseball's equivalent of the Harlem Globetrotters. Their tickets were sold out two years in advance.

"Where are the seats?" Mitch asked with a twinkle in his eye.

"Would it matter?"

"Not a bit," Mitch laughed. He planted a kiss on her nose and stomped out the door with purpose.

"Stay safe," she called after him.

Chapter 12

Christmas was fantastic.

"I haven't had that much fun during the holidays since I was a little girl," she told her Aunt Etah and Isabelle as the three women sat on the roof deck of 1509, a relatively-new restaurant atop a boutique hotel in historic downtown Brunswick.

Isabelle and her aunt had hit it off as expected, and it appeared they were in cahoots when they ambushed her at dinner.

"Tally, you must make a point to do the same thing with your schedule next year," Isabelle told her. "Block that month and say 'no weddings, no matter what.' Don't listen to sob stories, don't do any favors for the hotel, and don't take on more holiday events on Jekyll than you can handle."

"I thought you were very wise to say no when they tried to book you to handle all of the Jekyll Island Authority Christmas parties," Etah agreed. "All but one of those is pretty low budget and wouldn't have been worth all the time you'd have spent running around setting them up. But it was smart of the JIA event planner to try to farm them out," she chuckled.

"You're hitting the point where you have to set limits, or you have to hire more staff," Isabelle said. "Kayla's fantastic and you'll be able to promote her to a full-time wedding position soon. But that's more money because you still need an assistant. So you have to figure out how many weddings or parties you have to do in order to make payroll every month.

"I'm telling you, Tally. My first five years running Vieques Weddings, there were a lot of nights that I didn't sleep worrying that I wasn't going to be able to pay myself. I always paid my staff and my vendors, but there were too many months I didn't pay myself in the beginning and that was a rough hole to get out of. You want to avoid it and you do that by not growing faster than you can afford," the veteran planner said definitively.

Tally had been trying to avoid hiring anybody else right away because things were already getting kinda crowded in Aunt Etah's house. Yes, they could hide everything, but the company was getting to a point where it deserved an office space where things could be pinned to the walls and left out overnight. Etah had told her numerous times that she could do anything she wanted to the house to make it more functional, but she'd interpreted that to mean within the context of not screwing up the walls in the process.

"I feel like if I'm going to hire more people, I'm going to need office space," Tally told Isabelle and Etah, cringing.

"Why?" Etah asked.

"Aunt Etah, you have no idea how bad your house looks sometimes when you're not here. Sort of like a wedding storage locker exploded. With schedules and prep tubs and stuffed welcome bags everywhere for a week before the clients arrive. And when we have to do flowers – that's not often, but it does happen – we make a huge mess. We actually made a rule that we have to do flowers outside on the deck unless it's too hot or cold out for the flowers," Tally confessed.

"Well, that's a bit extreme. You always managed to keep it together at my house," Isabelle pointed out.

Tally had worked for Isabelle in Vieques for two years. Isabelle had also owned Vieques Flowers and had done all the flowers on the island for weddings, hotels, and funerals.

"I didn't keep squat together," Tally argued. "Yaya was always the one in charge of flowers, not me. I just did what she told me to do. And you had tile floors everywhere that were easy to clean.

"Yaya kept your house from looking like somebody had just weed-whacked inside it. She used to make me and the interns sweep in between bouquets if we'd made a mess," Tally laughed. "She was strict!"

"Yaya was smart to stay on top of it," Isabelle agreed.

"I miss her," Tally sighed. The stylist-cum-florist had been her best friend on the island besides Isabelle. She'd grown up there but had gone to New York for school, so she knew everybody and knew how to get anything done. Yaya taught Tally about surviving and thriving on Vieques. Other than Isabelle, Yaya was the only person Tally really missed on Vieques.

"How is she?" Isabelle asked. "Do you hear from her often?"

"We talk about once a week on the phone, and we send snarky messages back and forth on a regular basis," Tally said.

"What's she doing now? I heard that only half of Vieques has real power back. It's only been what, 15 months since Hurricane Maria? Sounds like they're right on schedule," Isabelle said sarcastically.

"Yeah, town has power now most of the time," Tally said. Yaya's little shop was in Isabel Segunda, the town on the north side of the island that was the island's capital.

"But now she's getting screwed with on her permits. Insurance companies are dropping coverage on the island and even though Yaya didn't make any claims, she lost her liability coverage. So, the health inspector shut her down until she finds new coverage and that's creating a mess. I feel so bad for her. She moved into that sweet little space only a year before the storm, and she put a fortune into making it feel like a spa.

"It's messed up because all the nail girls who are doing nails out of their houses and not paying taxes are still in business – hell, some of them have little shops on front porches now since there's no power – and nothing is being done to shut them down. It's like she's being punished for trying to do things properly," Tally ranted.

"She should get out of there," Isabelle said.

Tally had noticed that with every month Isabelle was gone from Vieques Island, she sounded a little more bitter when talking about it. She didn't blame her friend – her villa had been destroyed by the storm and what was left had been looted, right down to the copper wiring. In one night, she had lost a company she spent years building, and because of the nature of Puerto Rico and her age, it was pointless and foolhardy to try again.

Isabelle would be in insurance limbo for a long time with the size of her claim. And once that was settled, she had every intention of putting her property on the market to sell immediately. Let somebody else tear it down and start over, Isabelle had decided that she was too old to do that herself.

"You know, Tally, if you were to open a flower shop here on Jekyll Island, you could have Yaya run it," Isabelle suggested, not for the first time.

"Yaya lives on Vieques, not Jekyll," Tally pointed out.

"I bet she would move if you gave her a business to run," Isabelle suggested. "Also, you'd have to get space for a flower shop but you could use it for office space for your wedding staff, too. *If* you set it up right. And owning a flower shop in an area without one, and where wholesale flowers are available, could be a goldmine. I still can't believe that with the number of hotels on this island that there isn't a florist," she added.

"There have been in the past. And that's not a good sign. The fact that they went out of business," Tally pointed out. "But I don't know why."

"There are a couple of spaces coming open in the Beach Village," Etah volunteered, ignoring her niece's comment. "I saw something about it in the JIA monthly meeting notes on the residents' page. No idea which spaces they are or how much they'd cost, but you could get that info super easily. Heck, I could call and get it for you in the morning before you even wake up."

"Whoa! Slow your roll, ladies," Tally felt panicked. "I haven't decided to open a flower shop."

"But you also haven't decided not to open a flower shop, my dear," her aunt pointed out. "You said you need more space. The island needs a flower shop. And Yaya might want a job that would solve all your problems and bring a good girlfriend of yours to Georgia. Sounds win-win to me." Etah made the statement like it was all a done deal.

"I agree," Isabelle nodded. "You should do the research now and just find out what the spaces rent for. You should also check out the bigger hotels and see if any of them have an interest in having a flower shop somewhere on their property. You never know what's available until you start asking. You might be able to have a space that doubles as a gift shop."

The server brought the check at that moment and Tally snatched it, handing him her American Express card before he could get away. "My treat," she announced. "You two are always so supportive of all my crazy. Let me thank you."

She excused herself to powder her nose and then stopped by the bar and signed the tab. When she returned to the table, she didn't sit down. Instead, she grabbed her purse, signaling to her guests that she was ready to go.

"You can't run away from this conversation," Isabelle told her when they were in the elevator back to the street level.

The elevator doors opened and Tally dashed out.

"Watch me," she called over her shoulder as she ran down the block to the Jeep.

***

Aunt Etah went straight to bed when they got home. Tally had noticed that her aunt did that more and more often these days. When she was younger, the two of them ended most evenings on the front porch looking at the moonlight reflecting on the water.

Etah would be 80 next year and had been talking about retirement since she got home from her latest trip. She complained that just because she didn't look 80 didn't mean that she wasn't feeling her age. Tally understood that her aunt was doing less actual writing and spending more of her trips visiting with old friends and resting up between important interviews. She was also making a pretty penny giving speeches to various international journalism groups. But she'd been sounding like she was tired of all the travel.

It made Tally sad to think about her only family member getting older. Etah was the most important and influential person in her life. Thinking about losing her someday made tears well up in Tally's eyes.

She shook her head to get the depressing thoughts out of it and sat down at her computer to knock out a blog before bed. People were reading her blogs, and she thought they were helping to attract a lot of potential clients to Jekyll Island. Tally loved it when she talked to Isabelle because her mentor reminded Tally of all the crazy they'd endured from clients on Vieques Island. Those conversations gave Tally endless material to blog about.

Tonight, at dinner, they'd laughed until their stomachs hurt telling Etah about the bride who turned her hair green the night before her wedding. It was one of those stories that didn't sound real until you heard all the details, but even then, Tally had to pull out her phone to show Etah the pictures and prove the unnatural disaster had actually occurred.

Katrina was an absolutely exquisite bride and she and her groom were getting married in a waterfront home in Monte Santo Playa. The couple, the brides' parents, and the wedding party were all staying in the nine bedrooms at the wedding venue. There was a pool in the yard and the property had steps that went down to a private-feeling beach where the couple planned to get married. Tally was not fond of that location because she had done a faceplant going up that staircase more than once – with an audience - when she was in a hurry after rehearsal.

The bride had long, platinum blonde hair that fell to the middle of her back. It was super pretty and she intended to wear it down on her wedding day. She'd been growing it for two years and talking about it since the planning started. But on the morning of the wedding, Katrina called Isabelle hysterical. She'd woken up with green hair!

After the rehearsal dinner the night before, the wedding couple and their friends took a dip in the pool. And Katrina left her hair down without thinking about it. Unfortunately, she'd just had her hair bleached platinum a couple days earlier so it would be perfect for the wedding and she hadn't even washed it yet. She left it down when she went in the pool, and she never actually dunked her head under the water so she didn't think about her hair getting wet. Until she woke up the next morning. In the light of day, there was a clear line across her hair at shoulder height. Everything below the line – the hair that had gotten wet - had turned green. A really bright green. It was awful.

Fortunately, for everyone, Katrina found the situation sort of funny. She sounded panicked when she called, but she trusted that if the problem could be fixed, her wedding planners would handle it. Tally put in an emergency call to Yaya and the hair wizard was on her way to the bride's villa in short order.

Tally didn't know what chemicals Yaya used in the bride's hair to fix it, and she probably didn't want to. Yaya had Katrina lie on a lounge chair and hang her head over the end. She coated the 12 or so inches of hair that were green in something thick and submerged it in a bucket and had the bride lie there. Tally had to look away when she passed by them during setup because it really wasn't funny and she was going to crack up if Yaya looked at her. That was the bad part about working with best friends. It made keeping a straight face when something went wrong even more challenging.

Tally checked on Katrina's hair progress through the day, and more than once tried to convince her to just wear it up. The green was only from her shoulders down. Yaya could roll it up underneath and camouflage it. But that wasn't what the bride wanted.

Two hours before Katrina was supposed to go down the aisle, Tally went to check on their progress. The bride was being giggly with her girlfriends and seemed not the least bit concerned about looking like a mermaid when she walked down the aisle. But Tally knew Katrina really did care. A lot. She stepped out into the hall to talk to Yaya.

"It's still green," Tally said.

"No shit, Sherlock," Yaya replied.

"We're out of time."

"I realize that."

"So, what's Plan B?" Tally asked. She figured Yaya would get the bride to let her put it in an updo that hid the green.

"Look, I'm going to try one more chemical on her before I signal defeat. But will you be mad if all her hair breaks off at the green line tomorrow?" Yaya asked.

"Did you ask Katrina that?"

"She said she didn't care."

"Then neither do I," Tally said honestly. "But I'm going to have her sign something saying that, if you don't mind."

"Excellent idea."

The bride was almost blonde when she walked down the aisle and, from what Tally heard afterwards, her hair didn't fall out the next day. But the whole catastrophe made for an excellent blog topic for brides – "How Not To Turn Your Hair Green" before your wedding.

Tally uploaded the blog as soon as she finished writing it. She added some pictures from the wedding with before and after shots of her hair, but not the bride's face. Katrina probably wouldn't care, but Tally wanted her permission before identifying the star of such a blooper story. Really, the pictures of her hair were enough to make the point, and Tally had a feeling this one might go a little viral.

Chapter 13

Mitch got home from work really late, but he resisted the urge to go straight to bed.

He'd spent the entire evening sitting in a bar waiting for a suspect to show up and meet with members of a drug smuggling ring that authorities suspected had been bringing a ton of marijuana flower and edibles across the Florida line into Georgia. But after five hours of pretending to drink and watching sports on the TVs suspended over the bar, nobody ever arrived. He got a text telling him to break it off a little after midnight. Mitch went back to task force HQ and wrote a report that said nothing before heading home.

Like many hole-in-the-wall bars in rural Georgia, nobody had seemed too concerned about no smoking laws. Mitch thought he might have been the only guy at the bar who wasn't sucking on a cigarette, and he smelled like he'd been sitting in an ash tray all night. He'd noticed the odor in his truck on the way home and he didn't want to take it into his grandmother's house. He stripped down and showered in the outdoor shower they used after the beach, then left his smelly clothes in a pile on the outside deck. His grandmother did his laundry. She said she was already doing her own.

Anyway, he didn't have that much because his trooper uniforms went to the dry cleaner. Bonnie would know how to get the stink out of his favorite shirt.

Before he got into bed, Mitch looked out the window to see if there was a light on inside Tally and Etah's house. He didn't see anything. That was good. Too many nights, Tally stayed up ridiculously late working. He worried about her burning out or getting sick. He really didn't want anything to happen to her.

Mitch was head-over-heels in love with Tally, and he had every intention of marrying her. Heck, he would have proposed by now, but he could tell she just had too much happening in her life to add her own wedding to the list. The uncomfortable conversation they'd had about moving in together on the beach had been his way of testing the waters about their timeline. Mitch had promised himself that he would wait until after she got through the spring wedding season before he brought up marriage with her in a serious manner. But he was going to start ring shopping soon so he'd have it when he needed it. There was no doubt in his mind that he wanted to propose.

Tally was perfect, he thought to himself, as he stretched out on the queen-sized bed that had replaced the bunk beds in his grandmother's house. She was the entire package. She was smart and beautiful and motivated. And she loved him back almost as much as he loved her. It would be a fairytale ending when they finally got married. He just didn't want to push her. Losing her career in Puerto Rico and coming back to start a company was a lot in a year. He'd been lucky she'd had enough time to fall for him. But Mitch wasn't going to push his luck.

He understood how she felt because when he was trying to get into the police academy, and while he was in training there, he hadn't had time for anything else in his life. He didn't date – except for the regrettable nights spent with his ex-girlfriend, Tara, when she found out he was home – because he didn't have time for a relationship. Finding Tally again had changed how he felt about that. He was in a different place in his life and he was excited about everything in front of him. Besides, he wanted a life outside of work and he wanted to start a family with Tally.

Mitch set his alarm for earlier than he wanted to get up, and then he got up quickly when it woke him up the next morning. He pulled on a t-shirt and shorts and bounded down the stairs, almost running over his grandmother, who was in her bathrobe on the way into the kitchen.

"Slow down before you kill somebody," Bonnie told him in her grumpy, pre-coffee voice.

"I'm sorry," Mitch said, and planted a kiss on Bonnie's cheek. "I'm trying to get to the bakery before Tally wakes up so I can surprise her with breakfast and a Starbucks."

"Oh, fancy!" his grandmother was impressed. "Then you're forgiven for putting my life in jeopardy before 8 a.m. But you better get moving if you're serious about delivering her first coffee of the day. I think she starts early."

He told his grandmother about his stinky laundry on the porch and left for the pseudo-Starbucks in the Westin lobby. It wasn't a real Starbucks and it was only open for a few hours in the morning, but the coffee was pretty good. The Marriott Courtyard down the street had a Starbucks coffee cart in its lobby, too, but Mitch stopped at the Westin because it was closer.

***

He got back with the treats before Tally was up.

"You are ridiculous, and the sweetest man in the entire world," Tally sighed after she took the first sip of her coffee while sitting in bed.

Mitch bent over to kiss her and she pulled away. "Morning breath," she warned.

"I don't care," he replied and then kissed her anyway. "It's okay. You taste like a white chocolate mocha."

Tally crossed her legs and patted the bed and Mitch took a seat beside her.

"To what do I owe the pleasure of such a wonderful early morning surprise?" she asked.

"I missed you," he said. "I got spoiled spending so much time with you over the past few weeks and I miss you when I don't get to kiss you goodnight."

"I miss you, too."

"Good. You're supposed to."

After Tally pushed back on his suggestion to move in together, the couple had struck a compromise that suited both of them. On nights when Mitch had to work super late, he'd let himself into Tally's house after he got home and softly kiss her goodnight. Sometimes she woke up, but usually she didn't move beyond a sweet smile that would spread across her lips. He never stayed without an invitation. They reserved that kind of intimacy for when they were both actually awake.

Now that Tally's Aunt Etah was back home for a few weeks, he'd stopped the romantic nighttime ritual. Tally had been concerned that he would scare the crap out of Etah by coming in at 3 a.m. and give her a heart attack. He was having fun on the task force but its schedule was wreaking havoc on his love life.

"How's work? Still love it?" she asked.

"It's awesome." Mitch told her about the prior night's assignment.

"You were undercover?"

"Sort of. Not really. I guess you could call it that. I was in plain clothes," Mitch allowed. "I was watching for a suspect to come into a bar and I was wearing jeans and had my badge in my pocket. But my purpose was to spot the suspects' meeting, give a signal, and then watch them make the arrests. The suspects never showed up and I basically just had a really bad burger, watched a hockey game, and went home."

"Aw, what a bummer," Tally said.

"We can't get them all on the first try," Mitch told her. "We only catch the stupid criminals, you know. The smart ones go on to become White House staffers and Enron executives," he joked.

Tally laughed. She'd heard his father, Tom, say that more than once.

They went out to kitchen to eat breakfast together. Mitch would have liked to have had Tally for breakfast, but with Etah just down the hall for another few days, he was iced out. Food would have to suffice.

Chapter 14

By the end of January, with a lot of unsolicited advice from Isabelle and Aunt Etah, Tally had all the information she needed to launch a flower shop on Jekyll Island. She'd been bullied into it by her mentors, but they'd been right. She could clearly see it when she ran the numbers, but she wouldn't be able to do it by herself. Not only because she really hated doing flowers, but because she didn't have time between wedding planning and juggling brides on the island to also deal with the myriad of other people and businesses that would become flower shop clients.

It was time to call Yaya and make her an offer.

"Hola Chiquita!" she greeted her bestie when Yaya answered on the third ring.

"Hey Tally. How's the real world?" While some Viequenses were offended that gringos referred to the mainland as "civilization," Yaya had actually lived stateside and she knew what Vieques was missing.

"Everything is awesome."

"Are you still in love?" Yaya asked in a teasing voice. "Thanks for sending those pictures of you and Mitch. He's a hottie. You guys look so cute together."

"I'm totally in love," Tally giggled. "But that's not why I'm calling. I'm calling because I need a really big favor. And I have an offer for you."

"*Digame.*" Puerto Rican for "talk to me."

"I need you to move up here and run the new flower shop I'm opening on Jekyll Island," Tally said in one breath.

Yaya was silent on the other end of the phone.

"Are you there?" Tally asked.

"I'm here."

"What do you think?"

"I think you've lost your mind. You hate flowers."

"True dat."

"Then why are you opening a flower shop?"

"Because I need one. And I also need somebody to run it and you're the only person I trust. Will you come? Please please please," she whined.

Tally told Yaya how much she could pay her and told her she would pay for her flight up.

"You can stay with me at Etah's for the first few months until you're sure you like it here and want to stay. We have the Jeep and the golf cart to use, so you won't even need to get a car right away. Please say you'll do it."

"I need to think about it and talk to my mom," Yaya said. Her parents lived two doors down from her on Vieques, and the main reason she'd returned to the little island was to be closer to them as they aged. But now that the storm had wreaked havoc on all the basic utilities, her parents had moved to her older sister's house in San Juan so they would be closer to medical care and more likely to have power and water. Her older sister was a nurse at Centro Medico, the biggest hospital in Puerto Rico, and Yaya didn't know if their move was going to be permanent.

"That's fine. Take a couple of days if you need to. It's a big decision. But I'll make you a deal," Tally proposed. "If you hate it up here after six months, we'll find a replacement and I'll buy you a plane ticket home. I just don't think that's going to happen."

"I'll think about it," Yaya promised.

Chapter 15

Yaya did think about it and called Tally to accept the offer the next day. They agreed she would come north in six weeks because Tally would need at least that much time to get a lease and permits and everything else they needed in place. Yaya needed time to shut down her shop in town and ship north whatever she was going to need. The rest of her stuff was going to her sister's house on the big island until she decided where she would ultimately stay.

Some of the paperwork that Tally needed for the flower shop was just an extension of her wedding planning business license, but she wanted to make sure she did it all properly and got everything off the ground the right way from the start before they opened their doors. Etah had offered to front the deposit for the flower shop space, and Tally had taken her up on it. She'd wanted to make her aunt a partner in the business but Etah wouldn't let her.

"Some day, everything that's mine will be yours anyway. If you make scads of money and want to pay me back while I'm alive, that's fine. I'll just give it back to you when I'm dead. But repayment's not necessary. Consider it a gift," Aunt Etah had said.

"Oh wow. Will the house be mine, too?" Tally asked. It wasn't a greedy question, but rather a practical one. And her aunt recognized it as such.

"If I still have the house. It's a lot for me to manage on my own once you move out and get married. I'd always have a place here on Jekyll, but I might consider looking at those fancy new condos over by the marina. We don't have a lot of steps here, but at The Moorings, they have elevators and a sunset view," she said with a grin.

Tally wanted to talk more about the house because it was her favorite place in the world, but it felt awkward to talk about Etah dying when it was the last thing in the world she wanted to have happen. So, she turned the conversation back to how she was planning to set up the new flower shop space she and Etah had visited together a few days earlier.

Tally had ended up leasing a small storefront from the Jekyll Island Authority, located a few doors down from the Jekyll Market. She named it Jekyll Flowers. She would take possession of the space about a week before Yaya arrived, but she planned to wait for her friend before she started setting everything up. She already had an appointment to go back in and take measurements. Ordering signage, blinds, display refrigerators for the flowers, and an entire of supply of flower scissors, rose strippers, preservatives, tubes, ribbon, tape, vases, and a hundred other things they needed to fulfill flower orders from locals, brides, and local businesses would take some time. Tally was ready to get out the graph paper and figure out the space.

Yaya would get the one real office in the back. Tally would continue to work from home most of the time and there was space she could use in the back of the flower shop when she needed it. She planned to give Kayla office space at the flower shop so she could finally have a real desk, but Tally knew they'd still do the bulk of their collaborative work on Etah's dining room table.

Tally told her girlfriend, Rita Rich, a public relations maven she'd gone to boarding school with, about the new flower shop venture. Rita congratulated her and offered to send out a press release about the grand opening. The same girlfriend had juggled reporters for her a year earlier when the near-fiasco at the Bland/McLemore wedding made the news.

"Do you think anybody will care about a flower shop?" Tally asked. She had a list of local publications where she'd planned to look into advertising prices, but it hadn't occurred to her that her flower shop was newsworthy.

"You're the girl who saved the McLemore wedding last year after that crazy florist from Savannah tried to ruin it. I think the story will be easy to pitch," Rita laughed. "And we can peg it around your grand opening. Have you even started planning that?"

Tally groaned. "No. And speaking of Savannah, I bet this new venture of mine is going to go over like a lead balloon up there. You know Savannah florists handle 90 percent of the flower business on the island. They're going to want to kill me."

"Don't joke about that," Rita told her. "The last time was too close a call for my comfort."

Tally wasn't sure it was entirely fair to blame all of the florists of Savannah for what was ultimately a grudge held against her for 11 years by Mitch's ex-girlfriend, Tara. But Tara had been working for the illustrious Southern Blooms in Savannah when she stole the hydrangeas for the Bland/McLemore wedding bouquets last year. Tara had been determined to ruin Tally's first big wedding on Jekyll. So it was hard for Tally to separate her feelings. Southern Blooms was on her "never use" list. But so were several other wedding florists in a 75-mile radius of the Golden Isles who had been nasty to her. It was her turn to hold the grudge.

She gave Rita more details about the new business and a rough idea of the timeline they were working on – Tally had wanted to launch the storefront by Valentine's Day. Really, by February 1st so they could be taking pre-orders for the biggest flower holiday of the year. But it just wasn't possible, given that Yaya couldn't be there for six weeks and she had weddings to execute in the meantime. Making the launch of the flower shop financially feasible meant she needed to keep booking new wedding clients. She'd set a new soft launch date of the week before Easter.

Rita suggested she plan her launch party for Mother's Day so she had a month's cushion if things ran behind, adding that she could mention deals on prom and graduation flowers during any interviews they booked. Tally promised to keep her updated on the progress.

"From a pitch standpoint," Rita said, "this is going to be cake. We'll just go back to everybody who loved you last year and set up another round of interviews. Let me know when you're ready. What are you naming it?"

"Jekyll Flowers."

"Of course you are."

The rest of January and all of February felt like pure chaos to Tally and Kayla. Tally was temporarily working out of Yaya's new office so she could be on hand to take deliveries, deal with permit stuff, and generally troubleshoot until the real boss arrived. There was a big "Coming Soon" sign on the door of the small storefront, but that didn't stop people from stopping by and knocking if they thought someone was inside.

Tally could never be rude, no matter how annoyed she was by the interruptions. Most of the time it was a neighbor wishing her well – a few had even brought goodies – but some of the random knocks had led to wedding planning contracts. Tally began reimagining the signage she was in the process of creating. She had initially planned to feature Jekyll Flowers on the window, with Jekyll Weddings in much smaller print. But if the first weeks had proven anything, it was that many of the potential wedding clients – and their mothers – who visited Jekyll Island on vacation fell in love with the magical state park, known as the Gem of the Golden Isles. If they saw something that said weddings, they wanted more information. And Tally was happy to provide it.

Patti Tait, her lifelong friend and a professional graphic designer, had created the logos for both companies. They were similar in design and if someone saw one of Tally's businesses, they'd recognize the second logo. She called Patti and told her they needed to change up their plans for the storefront.

"People keep stopping in to ask questions. We finally just left the door unlocked because running to open it before people walked away was annoying. But we've picked up a few wedding clients, who will also be floral clients, just on walk-ins in the first 10 days we've been here. I don't know how long that pace will keep up, but I want to take advantage of it while I can. We need to make the 'Weddings' part of the sign just as big, or bigger, than the flower shop part of it."

Patti, who ran her own business, Gravitait Design, in the DC suburbs understood completely.

"Okay, let me rethink it. I still think you need to keep 80 percent of your glass clear for people to see in," Patti said.

"I'd rather they can't see us," Tally whined. She was already rethinking how to screen a back area for wedding planning so they didn't feel like a tourist attraction in the high season when the sidewalks were full of visitors.

"Yeah, well that's not how you sell flowers. It's good for them to see you guys creating beautiful arrangements and bouquets. And you've decided you're going to keep a limited selection in the coolers all the time for locals and tourists to buy? Right?"

"Absolutely. Once we get rolling with weddings, it's the best way to not lose money on the overage. Hydrangea wedding on Saturday, leftover

Hydrangeas for sale on Sunday. In big buckets out front if it's not too hot," Tally could imagine how pretty it would look and she couldn't wait for her ideas to come to fruition. "Sometimes, they don't want the centerpieces after the wedding and we can put those stems in a big discount bucket, too."

"Sounds awesome. I agree with you – you guys need a split sign of some kind. Let me play with idea in the context of your actual logos and measurements and we'll take it from there. I think we need to create a combo logo for you to use everywhere for your advertising. Why pay for twice as much space?"

"That's a really good point. Thank you for thinking of it."

"That's why you keep working with me," Patti joked.

They caught up on what each of them was up to – Patti's life was significantly more exciting than Tally's. She went to clubs and concerts and had a fun group of partying friends to hang out with whenever she didn't want to work. But from what she told Tally, she had so much work that she never ran out of things to do for clients.

The signage was scheduled to go up the first week of April. Easter fell late – on April 21st – and the marketing plan Tally and Yaya had come up with had included gifting massive amounts of Easter lilies to all of the nearby churches, along with their introduction materials and a discount coupon for future work. They'd notify the churches of the gift on April 1st so they wouldn't need to spend so much on their holiday flower orders.

The women were still working on their marketing plan for the hotels, but that was bigger and much more complicated than the churches. Tally wanted to wait until after Yaya arrived to put it all together in a timeline.

At the rate Tally and Kayla were booking new wedding clients, Jekyll Weddings was going to be very busy its first spring in business. They had added several last-minute elopements in early May and, with Mother's Day on May 12th, that would be the real test.

Tally had made a note to figure out if she needed extra drivers that weekend, and she mentioned it to Mitch as they sat on a bench along the bike path to watch sunset over the water.

"I can help with the Easter and Mother's Day deliveries," he offered. "If you're crazy-overloaded, my dad would probably help too. We could ask my brothers but you'd have to pay for their gas at least."

Tally was overwhelmed. "Well, of course I'd pay for everybody's gas. But I'd pay for their time, too. I don't want them to hate me," she joked.

"You're about to be family, Tally. This is what family does for each other," Mitch explained.

Tally was quiet as she digested what Mitch said. She would be a member of the big, nutty Durham family.

She had grown up as an only child. Her parents had been popular and successful political consultants who were killed when she was a child. But even before they died, growing up as an only child Capitol Hill had been unlike the experiences of children who grew up in suburban neighborhoods. Kids got snatched and shot even in the best DC neighborhoods and her parents kept her under close watch. But when she visited Aunt Etah, she ran wild with Mitch and his siblings. Aunt Etah's house had become home after her parents' plane crashed off the coast of the barrier island, and Mitch's family had been her family ever since.

Mitch noticed Tally's silence but misinterpreted its meaning. He thought maybe his comment about how she was about to become a member of his family had been a step too far. He hurried to reassure her.

"Tally, you know what I mean. You are family to everybody already, and I hope that someday soon, that status will be upgraded. But I wasn't pushing you," he said.

"Oh Mitch," Tally gasped when she realized he was confused. "I wasn't thinking about that. I was actually thinking about how I've never really had brothers and sisters before. Robin and Pete make me feel like I'm one of you when I'm there. They have since the very beginning, the same way you guys all did when we were kids. I was just thinking that I was lucky."

"I'm the lucky one."

"No, I am," she laughed, thinking they were starting the "no, you are" game. But Mitch didn't crack a smile.

"I'm serious, Tally. I love you. I think I have been in love with you all of my life. This isn't an official proposal because it's way too badly planned and I don't have a ring in my pocket, but I'm not kidding when I say that I want to marry you and spend the rest of my life with you as soon as you will let me," his face was so earnest that Tally fell a little deeper in love.

She scooched closer to him on the bench they were sharing to watch the sun set over the water, behind the Sidney Lanier bridge. Mitch turned to face her and they shared a kiss.

"Give me a little more time to get my life together, and I promise to say yes when you officially pop the question." It was more than she'd given him when they discussed it before. Mitch was elated.

"Permission to start ring shopping?"

"Granted."

"What style of ring do you love?" he asked. She was a wedding planner and he figured she had something very specific in mind. After all, she had to look at it all day, every day, for the rest of her life.

"Surprise me," Tally told him.

Chapter 16

It was the first big event that Kayla had run on her own and things were off to a less-than-stellar start. Tally felt terrible for the young wedding planner – she'd promoted Kayla just before Yaya arrived on the island – but she was also slightly amused. Everything was going just fine with the vendors for the events. It was the mother-of-the-bride who was the fly in the ointment. And it was important for Kayla to learn how to handle these sorts of problems because they were more common than most people realized.

Yaya and Tally had been busy with wedding flowers for a few days. There was another wedding on the island the same weekend, and they'd opted not to use Jekyll Weddings for their planning. They had gotten their flowers from Jekyll Flowers, though. And because they weren't wedding planning clients, they hadn't gotten the 15 percent discount on their flowers that Tally's bridal clients did, so the little flower shop was making a fat profit.

"I think I'm starting to like flower clients more than I used to," Tally told Yaya as she sat murdering roses on the floor of the new shop. So many brides loved to walk down a runway of rose petals and it was a million times cheaper to depetal them all themselves. Almost every wedding required somebody to spend about an hour removing the stems and the seeds from roses and loosening the buds so the petals would fall individually. Not difficult work. Kinda therapeutic, in Tally's opinion.

Yaya absolutely hated murdering perfectly beautiful roses. She made screaming sounds on behalf of the flowers as she pulled them from their stems until Tally swatted her and told her to go work on bouquets that didn't talk.

For the impending Gomez/Goldberg wedding, Tally had initially planned to stay out of the way until after the ceremony. Kayla had been handling the planning from the beginning and the clients really liked her. Tally double-checked all of Kayla's prep lists and had been cc'd on all the vendor emails her new wedding planning account executive had sent to the clients during the process, but Tally couldn't take credit for having planned the wedding. Kayla did all the heavy lifting, with Tally double-checking her work. And Kayla had missed nothing.

Go figure that Ariel's parents would turn out to be the problem for her destination wedding weekend. The bride's mother was a judge somewhere in Florida and it was obvious on the one Skype call she'd participated in with the wedding planners that she had a very high opinion of herself and thought wedding planning was beneath her. As a result, Tally and Yaya were up murdering roses the night before the wedding because it had taken all-hands-on-deck at the events to counter the mother-of-the-bride's efforts to ruin them.

Kayla hadn't been expecting the coming storm because Ariel Gomez and her fiancé, Steven Goldberg, had been pleasant to work with. They'd been easy to handle at their events, too. The couple was thrilled with their welcome party. The rehearsal dinner had gone really well, too, except for the fact that Ariel's mother showed up super late and missed some of it.

Ariel and Steven had taken their guests on a sunset dolphin cruise before their rehearsal dinner. The dinner would be held on the deck at The

Wharf at the Jekyll Island Club Hotel. The dolphin tour left from the pier where The Wharf was located and most of the guests arrived early to have cocktails while they waited for the boat to depart. The sunset cruise was scheduled to leave the dock at 6:30 p.m. but Ariel's mother – call me "Judge Gomez or Your Honor" – hadn't arrived yet. Ariel's father was there on time, but he and the scary mother had been divorced for years so he was no help at all.

When she still hadn't arrived by 6:45 p.m., Captain Adam, who was running the tour, asked Tally what she wanted him to do.

"It's a private charter so I don't mind waiting a bit more. But your clients were specific about where they wanted us to be to get sunset pictures and if we don't leave in a few minutes, that's not going to happen," he warned her quietly. The guests around them were enjoying sangria and rum punch and seemed oblivious to the ticking clock, as they should be.

"Let me check with the bride and groom," Tally said and headed off to find them.

She ran into Steven first. He was a seemingly reasonable real estate agent who had been a good wingman to Ariel during the wedding planning. He'd gone along with almost everything the bride wanted and had only put his foot down when she started upgrading the upgrades.

"Ariel's mom isn't here yet. If we're going to get the sunset pictures, we need to leave in the next couple of minutes. What do you want to do?"

"Let's go," Steven said without even thinking about it. "God only knows what time that witch will show up."

Tally cracked up. She agreed completely with his description of his soon-to-be mother-in-law, but she wouldn't have expected the groom to vocalize it.

"You wanna run that by your future wife first?" Tally asked. "You have to sleep next to her for the rest of your life."

"Nope, I'm going to tell her. You go tell the captain he can shove off."

And that's exactly what happened. Tally and Kayla agreed that Tally would stay behind on the dock so that somebody was on hand to deal with the judge when she finally arrived.

After the boat left, Tally checked in with the manager at The Wharf and found there was absolutely nothing she needed to do to help – all the floral centerpieces had been delivered by Jekyll Flowers that morning and the tables were set and looked great. The wind was unfolding the napkins and Tally wandered through touching them up, and then finally took a seat and worked on clearing email while she waited.

***

Judge Gomez rolled in more than an hour after she was supposed to have been there. To say she was shocked she had been left behind "without so much as a courtesy text" from her daughter was an understatement. She was pissed. No, furious was a better word.

Tally was glad she'd stayed behind instead of Kayla, or her favorite new account executive would have probably quit. The way the mother-of-the-bride spoke to Tally was nothing short of abusive. But the fact she kept using the words "lack of courtesy" after she'd shown up at her own daughter's rehearsal dinner an hour and fifteen minutes late really irritated the wedding planner.

"Your honor, I'm sorry that you are upset the boat left without you, but the decision was made by the groom to get moving because otherwise, they were going to miss the sunset wedding photos they'd planned with their photographer," Tally explained when Judge Gomez stopped fuming long enough to hear anything she said.

"The groom decided?" the judge's voice became even more strident. "Did my daughter have no part in this? She is the bride!"

"The groom made sure that Ariel was in the loop on his plan," Tally said. She didn't want to put too much on the bride. Ariel would have to spend all day the next day with her mother, getting hair and makeup and pre-wedding pictures. Tally didn't want the judge to bitch at her daughter the whole time about missing the sunset dolphin tour and ruin her wedding day. And the way that Steven spoke about his future mother-in-law to his wedding planner indicated there wasn't much love lost between them already. She had a feeling he'd happily shoulder the blame for this one.

Judge Gomez was still griping to anybody at The Wharf who would listen to her when the boat returned to the dock about 30 minutes later. Tally felt sorry for the club staff whom the mother-of-the-bride had trapped, but she didn't try to rescue them and risk getting yelled at again.

Ariel and Steven were glowing when the group disembarked. The photographers had already sent Tally some teaser pics and she could see that the couple was going to be thrilled with the results. All of the shots were unbelievably gorgeous with a variety of different backgrounds that included the golden marshes, this historic hotel, and the Sidney Lanier Bridge. The bride looked stunning. The groom was handsome. And the witch wasn't in any of the shots with her resting bitch face. Perfect.

The bridal couple posed for a few shots on the pier with Judge Gomez before sitting down at their rehearsal dinner, where the mother-of-the-bride was seated conspicuously far away from the bride and groom's table. Tally and Kayla stayed until everybody had their dinner and then checked out with the bridal couple. They weren't needed on site any more for the night and neither of them wanted to hang around and get pulled aside by the mother-of-the-bride again.

Tally and Kayla said goodbye in the parking lot next to the historic pier. Tally was headed back to the shop to help Yaya, but she wanted Kayla to get to bed as soon as she could.

"I think you need to shuffle the hair and makeup schedule around," Tally told the younger planner. "Put Judge Gomez on the front end because she's going to be a nightmare. I can just feel it."

"Ugh," Kayla muttered. But she made a note on her clipboard.

"It's going to be fine," Tally reassured Kayla. "The bride and groom are happy campers. Tomorrow we need to keep the mother-of-the-bride from raining all over Ariel's parade. Maybe we should set up hair and makeup in separate rooms just to keep them apart."

"But that would separate the bridesmaids, too. And that wouldn't be fun," Kayla argued.

"It's your call," Tally told her. "I'm just trying to set you up for success. My idea might not be the best one. You've seen us do it both ways. Make sure you cc me on the final schedule you send out to the girls, and make sure you get text responses confirming receipt from everybody – including Judge Witch – tonight. Last thing we need is to get started two hours behind schedule."

Chapter 17

The groom's family had been very tolerant of the mother-of-the-bride's behavior through the first two days of events, but it was obvious the mother-of-the-groom had hit her limit when things got behind schedule on the wedding day. Despite Kayla's best efforts, Tally was needed on site all day, too.

Everybody had anticipated that Judge Gomez would be late, so there were bridesmaids on hand and ready to jump in the hair chair so they didn't get behind schedule. Tally and Kayla had planned it so there was enough time to do hair and makeup on the bride, both mothers, and all of the bridesmaids, with a little time cushion. But it wouldn't work if people didn't show up.

The bridesmaids took the bride down to The Pantry to get a bite to eat at one point and Steven's mother took advantage of her time alone with the wedding planner to vent. Tally was supervising hair and makeup while Kayla was running setup down in the historic Main Dining Room at the Jekyll Island Club Hotel. They didn't usually leave a staff member in the bridal suite all day. They'd check in with the bride before and after setup, and then again shortly before she was to go down the aisle, unless there was a problem. But the Gomez/Goldberg wedding was the exception to the rule.

"I've warned Steven that he better put his foot down early and often with that woman," the groom's mother fumed to Tally when the rest of the bridal party was out of the bridal suite. "She's a terror."

After the near fiasco on the dock the night before, Kayla had asked Tally to babysit the process upstairs for her because she was worried about what was going to happen to the schedule with the judge causing mayhem. It was a smart move and Tally chalked up another score for the new wedding planner.

"She can be taught," Tally thought in her best Robin Williams' "Aladdin" voice and giggled to herself. Kayla had turned out to be everything she'd hoped when she promoted her and gave her a big salary bump.

The wedding ceremony was scheduled for 5 p.m. at the Methodist church on Jekyll Island. The Methodist Church shared its building with the Catholics and the Episcopalians, too. There weren't enough Catholics residing on Jekyll to justify a full church and facility, so many of the locals attended services in nearby Brunswick or at a parish on St. Simons Island. But the Catholic Church was a stickler for rules, and they don't allow their priests to marry couples anywhere but inside an actual church. Therefore, the only option for Catholic brides and grooms on Jekyll Island was the Jekyll Island United Methodist Church where St. Francis Xavier Church in Brunswick held a mass on Jekyll at 7 p.m. every Saturday evening.

Tally wouldn't have thought the religious part would be such a big deal when she took on the wedding planning for Ariel and Steven. He was Jewish and they were only getting married in the Catholic Church to make her mother happy. No shocker there.

Since the actual church was shared by so many denominations, there were some pretty firm rules about scheduling weddings, christenings, and other special events. The latest ceremony allowed on a Saturday was 5 p.m. because everybody had to be cleared out by 6:30 p.m., before people started arriving for the Catholic service held at 7 p.m.

Generally speaking, blocking 90 minutes for a wedding ceremony would be considered complete overkill. Tally blocked an hour for all big weddings and 30 minutes max for elopements. She'd yet to run short on time by utilizing those basics Isabelle had taught her in Vieques. But it turned out the Gomez/Goldberg wedding, once again, was going to be the exception to the rule.

Tally knew there was a problem by 3 p.m. A big problem. Judge Gomez had finally rolled into the bridal suite a little after 1 p.m. and had been put straight into the first empty chair, which happened to be hair. The logic all along had been that if anybody ran out of time, bridesmaids would start doing their own makeup. Girls that age could generally make themselves, and each other, look fantastic in a pinch and Kayla and Tally were confident that the bridesmaids understood the assignment. She'd seen all of them looking at their phones, checking the time, repeatedly throughout the day with worried expressions on their faces.

"Is this her usual routine?" Tally had asked the maid of honor at one point when Ariel wasn't around.

"Yep. Some form of it. She's actually behaving better than usual," the bride's childhood bestie, Bianca, said. "I'd have expected her to throw a dramatic snit by now, or at least have cried off her makeup at least once so it has to be redone.

"So far, all she's done is order us around, and that we can handle," Bianca assured Tally.

The schedule called for everybody to be ready by 3 p.m. for pre-wedding pictures. The couple wanted to get all the formal shots over with before the wedding so they could actually attend their cocktail hour. They'd gotten sunset pictures the prior evening and wanted their wedding photos to be all about the historic hotel and Millionaires' Row.

But that was not to be. Just as the last bridesmaids were getting finishing touches, and the bride's hair was being pinned with the veil, Judge Gomez decided she didn't like the way her own hair had been styled.

"This isn't going to work," she told the hairdresser who had finished her updo an hour earlier. "You need to redo it."

Ariel, sitting in the hair chair getting her veil attached, rolled her eyes at her mother. "Seriously Mom, you look fine."

"Fine isn't good enough for your wedding day, is it?" she asked in an imperious tone.

Nobody said a word.

"I think not. You'll have to fix my hair when you finish with hers," she ordered the stylist who was already standing there with a horrified look on her face.

When the bride was finished a few minutes later, Tally pushed her out the door with the bridesmaids to do her first look photos and groups shots under the watchful eye of Kayla. Tally stayed behind to make sure Judge Gomez didn't get up to any more shenanigans. Her hair did look awful, Tally agreed. But it was exactly what she had asked the stylist to do. It looked just like the picture she'd brought with her as an example. The fact that she had a neck waddle that the updo didn't flatter or hide wasn't the stylist's fault. Tally made a note on her clipboard to make sure they charged double for "Her Honor's" fake, dark-red hair.

By 4 p.m., Kayla was sending panicked texts asking where the judge was and the stylist was in tears. Tally sent a 911 text to Yaya and was over the moon when her friend replied and said she was on the way. Yaya had owned a salon for years and did all the brides' hair and makeup, in addition to the flowers, for Vieques Weddings. She wasn't licensed to do beauty stuff in

Georgia yet, so they'd decided not to offer her services to clients. But this was an emergency.

Tally texted a heads up to Kayla and told her to let her know if anything had been forgotten in the bridal suite. She told her not to bring the girls back up unless she absolutely had to, and to tell Ariel everything would be fine and to enjoy the reprieve from her mother.

"That made her laugh," Kayla texted back.

Tally crossed her fingers as the tearful stylist slammed down her curling iron and announced "I quit and I am leaving. You are insane." Then she started stuffing all her supplies back in their cases.

Judge Gomez berated the poor girl while she scrambled to escape. Tally, having never witnessed such behavior from an adult woman, wasn't quite sure how she was supposed to handle it.

"Your honor, please don't curse at her," Tally had said in a firm voice, stepping between the frightened stylist and the harridan spewing hateful words at her.

"It's not my fault you hired this talentless garbage," Judge Gomez replied. "I've got easy hair. Anybody could fix it." That was when the stylist made good her escape from the hotel room, slamming the door behind her.

"She offered to fix it and you called her names. In two languages," Tally reminded the mother of the bride when they were alone together. "I've got a hair wizard on the way who can fix this. But you can't talk to her like that or she'll walk out the door and I'll follow her."

"You wouldn't dare," the judge said in a challenging tone.

"Watch me," Tally looked her in the eye. They continued to sit in silence. The standoff ended with the knock on the door of the bridal suite. Yaya to the rescue, Tally thought to herself.

Judge Gomez continued to be difficult when Yaya fixed her hair, but she let Yaya play with it til she was happy and then spray it in place so there was no changing her mind again. It was after 5 p.m. when she finally let Tally zip her into her over-the-top beaded mother-of-the-bride dress, and it was after 5:30 when her honor finally arrived at the church.

Kayla had been talking the bride off the ledge for almost an hour by then and Ariel was truly in a panic. Her mother would show up an hour late to her only daughter's wedding and somehow make it her daughter's fault if she missed seeing her go down the aisle. Steven had told his wedding planner, on no uncertain terms, that he would be standing at the altar waiting for Ariel at 5:30 p.m. If she left him standing there in favor of waiting for her mother, he told Kayla that he'd wouldn't get married.

Kayla had texted Tally in a panic – that edict had been handed down at 5:20. Tally texted back they were on the way and included a nasty picture of the mother of the bride snarling at her to lighten the mood. Kayla showed it to the groom and it had its desired effect. She sent a picture of Steven and his best man belly laughing back to Tally.

***

Ariel was escorted down the aisle at 5:55 p.m. Her mother had made her grand entrance at the last moment and been seated by the best man, and then her ex-husband had escorted their beautiful daughter down the aisle. Tally and Kayla looked at each other and laughed in the back of the church once the ceremony started.

"I swear to God, I thought the groom was going to leave. He's had about enough of Ariel's mother," Kayla whispered.

"That was the closest I've ever gotten to slapping a mother of the bride," Tally admitted. "She was unbelievable. I had to stop Yaya from killing her right before we left."

"Oh no, and Yaya had saved the day – although I still don't get what was wrong with the first hairdo. It looked great. She didn't, but that's how she looks," Kayla said, giggling.

"Yeah well, Yaya was still cleaning up the bridal suite when we left. And as we're going out the door, the judge says – within full earshot of Yaya – 'you should have just brought your Mexican in from the beginning.'"

"She did not." Calling a Puerto Rican a Mexican was really insulting. It wasn't as bad as calling them Dominicans, but close. "Ouch."

"Oh yes, she did. She was out the door at that point and I stuck my head back in to look at Yaya and she was going nuts. I was dying trying not to laugh. If ever we were going to take a client's mother to Horton Pond to feed to the alligators, this is the one."

"I want to help," Kayla volunteered.

"You can put the duct tape on her mouth," Tally whispered.

Tally and Kayla stood in the back of the church watching the ceremony. Thankfully, it wasn't a full mass and the Catholic vows were finished in about 20 minutes. The bride and groom went down the aisle and out the front of the church at 6:30 p.m. on the nose, and when they emerged into the daylight, Kayla grabbed them and ran them back around to the back of the church. There was a door that led to the sacristy and, if they wanted to get any formal photos in the church, there was no time for the bride and groom to greet guests. They snuck in the back way and Tally brought the rest of the wedding party around a moment later and then went back to clear the church. The minute the last guest was out the front doors, Tally shut them and signaled the photographer.

Despite a pushy member of the ladies' guild who stood next to Tally and tapped her watch, the photographer managed to get enough pictures inside the church to satisfy the couple. Kayla had left ahead of them, shepherding the parents to the reception immediately. They weren't being included in the church pictures because Ariel was too furious to face her mother and mad enough not to care if she was in the pictures. Steven went with the flow, just glad it was all almost over.

Chapter 18

The mother of the bride's delayed arrival at the wedding ceremony had set off an unintended chain of events that screwed up the rest of the night, but Kayla had done her best to shuffle things around so that nothing important would get skipped. Cocktails were supposed to have begun at 5:45 p.m. on the pool deck of the historic hotel, but the bride hadn't even gone down the aisle at that point. Unfortunately, that didn't mean the clock stopped on the reception that had been bought and paid for.

The harpist that Judge Gomez had insisted on importing from Orlando began playing to an empty pool deck at 5:45 p.m. She was booked for 90 minutes of cocktails, and when the guests didn't even arrive until an hour after that, she wasn't interested in extending her time for any price. Kayla texted that news to Tally while her boss was still dealing with pictures at the church and Tally had replied with a shrug emoji. She explained to all of her clients on the phone, and in the client handbook, that the wedding schedule was the wedding schedule, and vendors had been booked to work or perform for certain hours. A bride or groom's lack of punctuality would not change that schedule. If a bride went down the aisle late, that much of her reception got cut off on the back end.

Tally felt a little badly in this case because it was completely the mother-of-the-bride's fault that everything had gone sideways. Ariel and Steven were where they were supposed to be when they were supposed to be there. Her mother's infinite rudeness had screwed everything up. Kayla would spend the rest of the night trying to get all the important stuff done. It wasn't easy to get through a seated dinner, toasts, first dances, and other carefully-planned moments an hour faster than what had been intended. Tally made a note on her clipboard to update the client handbook to address badly-behaved parents and the potential consequences.

The wedding reception had been scheduled to end at 11 p.m. and nobody said anything to Kayla or Tally about changing it before the time came to shut things down. Unfortunately, the dance floor had only filled up about 20 minutes before everything was over. Dinner had started 90 minutes late and toasts had to be cut short after Judge Gomez gave a 15-minute prepared speech that wasn't really about the bride and groom. Steven gave the okay for Kayla to cut all the guys' toasts except the best man, but Ariel wanted her maid and matron-of-honor to both speak. Steven's parents stood together and gave a classy toast to the couple and sat back down in under two minutes. Tally wished, not for the first time, that his mom had been the mother-of-the-bride instead of "Her Honor."

Tally had already coordinated with the band to play the last song of the night right after the bride tossed her bouquet. When the clock struck 11 p.m. about five minutes later, they swung into "Closing Time" by Semisonic. It lacked creativity but the couple had selected it and it did deliver the message. When Kayla touched base with the bride and groom to make sure they understood it was time to toss the bouquet, Ariel got upset. The bride had had too much champagne and didn't want her party to end, so the wedding planner directed her conversation to the groom. Ariel stalked away as Steven was telling Kayla that he understood why things were finishing up and thanking her for a great wedding. She later told Tally that Steven looked seriously relieved to hear things were over.

Kayla keyed her radio and let Tally, who was standing by in the wings, know that it was okay to bring the lights up as soon as the music stopped. Both women were wearing headsets that allowed them to discreetly communicate across the ballroom. Tally gave Kayla a thumbs up and headed for the light switch panel by the threshold to the room where a member of the hotel staff stood waiting. As the last notes of "Closing Time" wound down, the lights came up and the party ended. That was when all hell broke loose.

It turned out that when Ariel heard Kayla say their reception was ending, she went to her mommy to complain. The same woman who was the sole reason that the couple hadn't had time to do the traditional Jewish hora dance where the gentlemen guests lift the bride and groom in the air in chairs. Kayla had checked with Steven before dropping that activity from the schedule. He and his parents had all agreed there wasn't time and that there weren't enough sober men to make the dance a safe activity anyway. Kayla said they'd been really good sports about it, so Tally wasn't worried. They were the ones who were Jewish after all, not the Gomez family.

But Ariel was really, really drunk when her reception ended and she wasn't going to go down quietly.

"Apple doesn't fall far from the tree," Tally thought but didn't say.

Ariel cried and claimed she had really been looking forward to doing "the chair dance." Tally was pretty sure Ariel didn't even know the real name of it, and the look on Steven's face when his new wife tried to cause trouble over the Jewish tradition told her she was right. But that wasn't the end of it because Ariel had involved her "Her Honor."

There were many ways that things could have proceeded from that point that would have seemed reasonable, but Judge Gomez didn't take any of those routes.

"Do you know who I am?" she asked Tally at full volume. She wasn't exactly yelling, but it sure wasn't an inside voice.

The music had stopped and most of the guests were at their tables collecting their purses and wedding favors after having had a wonderful time at the wedding. Her Honor's voice could be heard over and above everything in the historic hotel's ballroom and everybody else went silent.

"You will turn the lights off and the music back on," she demanded. "Or I will ruin you. I will destroy you. You will never plan another wedding in the United States by the time I'm done with you."

"You can threaten me all you want," Tally replied in a much softer voice that caused nosey wedding guests to creep a little closer to the bruhaha unfolding on the dance floor. "The bride and groom had a contract and we have fulfilled all the terms of it. The event ended at 11 and the couple was well aware of that."

While that might sound mean to someone who doesn't do event planning for a living, it was the typical policy of most venues for multiple reasons. First off, drunk couples frequently said they could afford the expense of the extra reception time when they couldn't, and it wasn't pretty when their credit cards were declined the next morning. Second, all of the event staff at the hotel had planned to be home by a certain time. Some of them had babysitters waiting. Some service staff had to be back at the hotel by 5 a.m. to finish setting up for breakfast for those same wedding guests. It was unreasonable to expect 30 or more people to readjust their lives because the mother-of-the-bride had a tizzy fit over her hair. And that was exactly what Tally told Judge Gomez in a soft but stern voice.

Then she turned to the bride and groom and thanked them and wished them a beautiful life together.

Ariel started sobbing loudly, but Steven ignored her and reached out to shake Tally and Kayla's hands. "Thanks. You guys are amazing. I'll give you fantastic reviews." He leaned in and used a softer voice to whisper, "Don't even worry about the judge. I'll handle her."

Then he turned to his bride and smiled. "Don't ruin all your makeup by crying – you still look amazing, babe."

"Really?" the drunken crocodile tears stopped immediately upon receipt of the compliment from her new husband. Ariel battled her wet eyes at her groom.

"Really. And I am dying to be alone with you," he told her. Then he picked up his giggling bride and swept out of the ballroom, turning to give his wedding planners a wink as he left.

"We aren't done here," Judge Gomez informed Tally and Kayla.

Tally watched Kayla turn a paler shade of white and it infuriated her.

"Actually, your honor, we are done here. You are not our client. Your daughter was. And her wedding is finished now. The groom just thanked us and told us everything was perfect. If you have further problems, perhaps you should take it up with him," Tally said. "But I'd wait til tomorrow morning to bother him. Let's go, Kayla."

The wedding planners turned away and headed out.

"Don't we need to do some cleanup?" Kayla asked.

"Normally, I'd say yes. But Mayra saw what was going on and she volunteered to have the night manager just stick anything we needed to take into a box we can pick up tomorrow. It'll all be in Mayra's office.

"We just need to get out of here before that crazy bitch comes after us," Tally whispered, and she wasn't joking.

She wasn't wrong, either. Just as the valet shut the driver's door on Tally's Jeep, Judge Gomez appeared on the steps at the entrance of the hotel, yelling something in her direction. Tally pretended not to see the mother of the bride, mouthed the words, "I'm sorry," at the valet and got the hell out of there.

Chapter 19

Mitch got a text from Tally around midnight, after she and Kayla got home. He replied that he couldn't call her right then and she replied that the wedding had been an even bigger nightmare than she'd expected and she was going to bed, with her phone turned off.

"Good idea," he texted. "You deserve a break. Can't wait to see you for dinner tomorrow night."

They had a date night planned. He was taking her to a restaurant on Tybee Island that one of the guys on his task force had recommended. Since Tally started planning weddings on the island, it was getting harder and harder for her to go out to dinner to relax because everywhere she went, she ran into vendors and their employees who were working on her weddings. It was well-known that she regularly hired bartenders and servers to moonlight at her welcome parties when the clients held them at private homes, so everybody wanted to get on her call list. That meant very few dinners on Jekyll Island could be had without having to talk business with somebody.

The drive to the restaurant on Tybee would be almost two hours each way, but it would be worth it if they could have all the alone time that they needed. Mitch was planning to propose to the woman of his dreams and he really wanted to get it right on the first try. Tally had said in the past that she hated public proposals and thought it was weird when a photographer jumped out. So, Mitch kept things simple and the only one who knew what he had planned was the restaurant manager who was in on it.

"I want to sleep til noon tomorrow," Tally texted.

"You should. Text me when you're up and we'll go from there."

"Sounds like a plan."

"I love you," Mitch texted.

"Not as much as I love you. Stay safe," Tally wrote back. Then she sent a blowing kiss emoji and turned off her ringer.

The Gomez/Goldberg wedding would go down in the books as one of the worst wedding experiences Tally had ever had, and that was saying a lot. All she wanted to do was go to sleep and stop thinking about it.

Chapter 20

Mitch was sitting in an unmarked car with a cop from the Camden County Police Department as he texted Tally. They were watching the suspect's vehicle across the street. It had been parked in front of another suspect's trailer for several hours. When the guy left, Mitch and his partner, Joe Moody, were supposed to follow him to make sure he couldn't backtrack. Other units were waiting down the road and they'd make the stop together when the suspect was far enough away from the house not to tip off the guy he'd just visited.

When the suspect finally left the doublewide trailer carrying a ginormous, stuffed-full hockey equipment bag, Joe radioed the team that was waiting a mile away with an update. If the intel the DEA had picked up was correct, that bag was stuffed with marijuana and fentanyl, an interesting combination. All of the members of the task force had been warned about the possible fentanyl exposure and told to take precautions when they exited their vehicles to take the suspect into custody.

While it certainly wasn't the first arrest Mitch had ever made, it was his first action with the task force. He was keyed up because it was his first time successfully catching a suspect while he was undercover. He'd done about

20 stakeouts in the past month and it was the first time that somebody he'd been watching for had actually shown up. It was a relief because he was starting to wonder if joining the drug interdiction task force had been a big, boring mistake. It sounded good when he had to tell someone what he did for a living, but lately it had consisted of entirely too much sitting and waiting with no success.

As the target pulled out of the driveway of the mobile home where he'd picked up the stash, Mitch and Joe struggled into their ballistic vests as quickly as they could without opening their car doors.

"Let's go," Joe urged and Mitch put the car in gear with one hand while he used the other to secure the Velcro straps on his vest. He cursed himself for taking it off in the first place and knew his dad would chew his ass if he told him about it. But it got uncomfortable sitting in it in the car for hours. And Joe had taken off his vest first.

"If Joe jumped off a bridge, would you follow him?" his dad's voice asked in his head.

The plan was to deflate the suspect's tires with stop sticks that other task force members had put across the roadway a couple of miles up the moment they learned the target was on the move. When the suspect stopped to figure out what had happened, the task force would take him into custody quickly. They needed to confirm what was in the duffle bag in order to proceed with the next step of the operation - taking down the supplier in the doublewide trailer. And that meant not risking that the first guy would have time to warn him.

Mitch waited until the suspect's older model black Honda Accord went around a bend before he started following it. The road was dark and isolated and the target would definitely notice the sudden appearance of the unmarked green Mustang behind him. A minute later, the rest of the task force up ahead spotted the Honda and went to work making the stop happen. By the time Mitch and Joe arrived, the Honda should have been pulling over with four flat tires if everything went according to plan. And the Mustang coming up behind it as it stopped would just appear to be another car on the roadway.

But that wasn't how it went down.

***

The suspect, a 23-year-old meth head who had already been locked up on drug and weapons charges multiple times, saw the stop sticks in the roadway too late to avoid them. But he saw them and instantly knew he was busted and panicked. The task force guys waiting on the side of the road knew he'd seen them because he tried to slam on his brakes before he ran over them, but it was too late.

The minute the tires popped, the suspect's car started fishtailing all over the roadway because of his speed. The driver, who realized what had just happened, tried to keep going but there were two big black federal law enforcement Chevy Suburbans pulled across the roadway 100 yards up, blocking that escape route on the narrow country road, with or without tires.

The suspect slowed to a stop about 20 feet before he got to the roadblock and could probably see the cops in SWAT gear that were in position behind both of the SUVs. But he made no move to get out of his vehicle. Mitch and Joe arrived a couple seconds later and stopped the Mustang about 20 yards behind the Honda, as they had planned.

Nothing happened for a couple of minutes while the task force team confirmed their next steps, and then officers wearing night-vision goggles started coming out of the bushes on either side of the road. Mitch and Joe opened their car doors and took positions behind them with their weapons drawn. They were just back-up in case the suspect ran their direction. The SWAT team would yank him out of the car. There were probably 30 guys surrounding the Honda who would actively be involved in taking the suspect into custody.

A federal agent with a megaphone yelled orders at the driver of the Honda. "Turn off your car, open your window, and show us your hands," he commanded.

Nothing happened. The windows remained up. The car was still running, although it sat on four flat tires.

The fed repeated the command two more times and got the same result.

The windows of the Honda were tinted too dark for the officers to clearly see what was happening inside the car. They knew there was only one person in the vehicle because Mitch and Joe had seen the driver get in the car alone. When the suspect continued to ignore the police commands, the task force moved to step two of the plan to take the driver into custody.

Two groups of SWAT officers assembled on each side of the Honda, with two men holding ballistic shields in front of each group. Then each group moved together as a unit to approach the vehicle. The plan was to smash the driver and passenger windows at the same time and yank the suspect out. The timeline had been escalated by the fact that the suspect had seen them and was probably warning his buddy back at the doublewide as they approached to arrest him. There was supposed to be another team hiding in the tree line by the trailer, just in case that suspect tried to make a run for it.

Mitch and Joe held positions behind their car doors and let the guys in the SWAT gear do their jobs. Mitch was crouched behind his door watching the teams approach the suspect's vehicle when gunfire suddenly erupted from inside the Honda. The suspect was shooting through his back window at the unmarked Mustang stopped behind him.

"Fuck!" Joe yelled as a bullet whizzed through the Mustang's windshield and grazed his left ear.

Mitch turned to see how badly his partner was hit when the next bullet through the windshield struck him in the head.

Chapter 21

Tally was deeply asleep when she heard pounding on her front door. The sound scared the bejesus out of her – it wasn't a normal knock - and she jumped out of bed to see what the hell was going on. She grabbed her phone as she left her bedroom, in case she needed to call 911. She didn't. Because there was a state trooper standing at her front door. But it wasn't Mitch.

It was a state trooper she didn't recognize, but she could see he was standing there with Bonnie, Mitch's grandmother.

Yaya came out of the guestroom, only half awake and belting her bathrobe. "What's happening?" she asked. Then muttered in Spanish about the time.

"Tally, there's been a shooting. Mitch is hurt," Bonnie said as soon as Tally opened the front door. "They came to get me to take me to the hospital and I knew you'd want to go with us. Hurry and get dressed."

Bonnie sounded remarkably calm given the circumstances, but Tally figured she'd been a cop wife, and a cop mother and grandmother, for too many years to let anything shake her.

"How badly is he hurt?" Tally asked, unable to move.

"We don't know. Just get dressed and I'll fill you in when you get in the car," Bonnie gave Tally a gentle shove in the direction of her room and then turned on her heel and headed to the state patrol cruiser that was parked, running, in Tally's driveway. She hadn't noticed it when she first answered the door. Her heart sank. This was all just too real.

"Get your act together," Yaya said, bringing Tally back to reality. "I'll help you." She tugged on her friend's arm and snapped Tally out of her daze.

Tally ran to her bedroom and pulled on the first clothes she found, leggings and a Jekyll Weddings uniform shirt. She stepped into flip flops that were on the floor outside her closet and grabbed a hair clip and her purse from the dresser.

Yaya handed her a sweatshirt and a pair of socks. "Put these in your bag. Hospitals are always freezing. Do you want me to come with you?"

"No, you stay here and hold down the fort. There's a farewell brunch at the hotel at 10 a.m. – will you go and back up Kayla? She was expecting me to be there. Everything is already loaded into the back of my Jeep."

"I got it. Nothing for you to worry about back here. Go to Mitch," her friend said.

Tally grabbed the items and stuffed them in her oversized bag. As a wedding planner, she could build an entire bride in a pinch from what was in her purse – bobby pins, tape, lipstick, chapstick, clear nail polish, and files, etc. She'd pull herself together on the way to the hospital in Brunswick.

But Mitch wasn't in Brunswick, Tally learned as soon as she got into the car with Bonnie. He'd been airlifted to the trauma center at University of Florida Hospital in Jacksonville.

"He was working an operation with the task force and he was shot," Bonnie said in a matter-of-fact way. "But he was breathing when they transported him and his dad said he was in and out of consciousness during transport."

"Where was he shot?" Tally asked, not really wanting to know the answer but needing to know.

"I'm not sure," Bonnie lied to her. Tally knew damned well that Mitch's grandmother probably knew every single detail but she was trying not to freak Tally out too badly before they got to the hospital.

The trooper hit the lights and siren the minute they crossed over the Jekyll bridge onto the causeway, and Tally looked away from the dashboard when she saw the speedometer top 100 mph. The siren and the fairly-constant radio chatter saved Tally from having to make much conversation with Bonnie, and the young trooper driving them didn't seem to want to say anything. Or maybe he was just afraid he was going to say the wrong thing.

When she looked back to see why Bonnie was so quiet in the backseat, she saw her boyfriend's grandmother clutching her rosary and praying. Tally was so discombobulated at that point that the only thing that she could think of was that she had no idea Bonnie was Catholic. She was pretty sure Mitch wasn't. She didn't remember their family ever going to church together.

Although the trooper driving them made the 90-minute drive to the hospital in less than an hour, it felt like forever. Tally had seen Bonnie typing on her phone a few times, perhaps texting. Nobody had tried to text or call Tally. Most notably, she hadn't heard anything from Mitch. And she was positive he would reach out to her if he was able. It wasn't a good sign.

Chapter 22

The emergency room was a brightly-lit zoo when Tally and Bonnie burst through the doors. There were cops from a variety of departments standing everywhere, talking quietly. When Tally and Bonnie arrived, the room went silent and everybody stared at them. Then Mitch's parents emerged from the group.

"He's in surgery," Roberta wrapped her arms around Tally and held her tight for a moment. "They think there's a good chance he's going to be okay."

"Where was he shot?" Tally asked.

Roberta paused and looked at Mitch's dad. Tom looked at Tally and then put a hand on her shoulder.

"He was shot in the head," he said softly. "But if you're going to get shot in the head, he got hit in the right spot. He was talking before they took him into surgery. That's a really good sign that nothing major was torn up by the bullet."

"Oh my God," was all Tally could say. She took a couple of steps back and felt dizzy. A hand reached out and guided her into a hastily-grabbed chair.

Tom knelt down next to the chair so he was eye level with Tally. "Stay strong, Tally. That's what Mitch needs from you right now. There's a very good chance that he is going to be just fine and that's what we have to hope and pray for. Even if he's not just fine, as long as he survives this, it'll all be okay."

Mitch's dad looked at her like she was supposed to respond but Tally couldn't talk. Her head was spinning.

"Can I see him or is he already in surgery?" she asked.

"They rushed him straight into the operating room," Roberta told Tally, sitting down in a chair that had magically appeared next to Tally's. She noticed Bonnie was sitting in another chair across from them that hadn't been there a minute ago, either. Mitch's older brother, Pete, a Glynn County police sergeant, was crouched next to his grandmother, giving her the details. She looked very, very old as she received the news.

Somebody handed Tally a bottle of water and she took a long drink. She looked around the room – the buzz was getting loud again – and counted more than 40 police officers before she gave up. Tom saw her looking around and filled in the details.

"Everybody's here," Mitch's father explained. "The crowd will get bigger as more people hear about the shooting. If you feel overwhelmed at any point, just let me know. They've got a small room for just family that you can hide in if you need a break."

Everything continued to happen around Tally, but nobody seemed to expect her to do or say anything. That was good because she felt numb. She shot off a text to her Aunt Etah and got an almost instant reply.

"I know. I'm on my way home," her aunt wrote.

"Thank you," Tally replied.

She scrolled through her phone for a few minutes but had to stop after she found news about Mitch's shooting on Facebook and Twitter. Most of the information wasn't correct, if what she'd been told at the hospital was true. But that was how she learned that Camden County Police Officer Joe Moody had been shot, too. Tally had encountered Joe the week before when she and Mitch met up while he was on duty. He was a nice guy with a wife and twin toddlers, if she remembered correctly.

"Oh my God," she said aloud as she read. Then she looked at the officer standing closest to her and asked a question.

"Is Joe alive?" she asked.

"He is. It was only a graze wound," the trooper she'd addressed replied. "He just needed a few stitches."

"Does his wife know?" she asked.

"Yeah, he called her himself when he got to the emergency room so she wouldn't freak out if she saw the shooting on the news. But they have little bitty kids and they both have ear infections so she opted to stay home with them rather than coming to the hospital since Joe is going to be fine," the trooper explained.

"Oh," Tally was surprised. "I guess that's good." If it was her, she'd be running to the hospital with both babies on her back if she needed to, she thought. Then she stopped herself. She didn't know what she would do if the father of her children had just been shot. She had no business judging Joe's wife's reaction and she felt guilty that it had even crossed her mind. She didn't even know the woman's name.

Tally sat quietly and when she noticed Bonnie fingering her rosary beads again, she silently joined Mitch's grandmother in prayer. Seven years of parochial school, followed by almost six years at St. Margaret's, had taught her how to pray. She just didn't do it very often. Tally was relieved to realize all the words she'd memorized so many years ago came back to her as soon as she needed them.

Chapter 23

Shortly before six o'clock in the morning, a doctor in scrubs and a mask came out to talk to Mitch's parents. They included her in the powwow in front of the nurse's station, and all the other cops in the room seemed to back up a bit to give them room for some privacy. It was a quiet way to show respect and Tally appreciated it.

The doctor explained that the bullet had entered Mitch's head just under the left ear and stuck at the lower back of his skull. While it didn't appear to have struck his brain, there was significant swelling and the risk of traumatic brain injury was high. But they wouldn't know how bad the damage was until after the swelling went down and Mitch woke up.

The doctor used a lot of specific medical terms to explain the damage to Mitch's head but Tally didn't hear anything after the first part. She felt woozy, but she managed to stay on her feet long enough to be included in the small group that was going to be allowed to go back to see Mitch in the Intensive Care Unit. He was still in recovery, but Roberta, Bonnie, and Tally were allowed to wait in the ICU til he was brought up. Tom opted to stay in the waiting room with all the other officers but he could badge himself back behind the magic curtain at any point to visit his son.

Mitch looked absolutely terrifying when the orderlies finally wheeled a gurney into the ICU room he'd been assigned. Most of his head was wrapped in gauze and only one of his eyes was visible. That eye was closed. Tally reached for his hand and the eye didn't open. That scared her.

Nurses followed the orderlies into the room to help transfer Mitch into the real hospital bed and get him hooked up to about a zillion monitors. Bonnie and Roberta kissed him and talked to him and squeezed his hand, and then they went out to give an update to everyone waiting in the emergency room. Tally stayed behind. She'd had enough peopling for one night. There was only one person in the world who mattered to her at the moment and she was already holding his hand.

Tally dozed off in a chair next to Mitch's bed, and they left her alone there, holding his hand. She woke up when her phone buzzed in her lap. It was Kayla.

"Oh my God, Tally. Is it true?" the text read.

"Yes. Mitch was shot," she wrote back. She would have liked to just call her friend and cry, but she didn't want to wake up Mitch and she was mindful of his family members wandering in and out of the room.

"Is he alive?" Kayla asked.

"Yes. But we won't know how bad the damage is for a while yet. I'm just sitting here with him. He hasn't woken up yet," Tally texted back.

It was a few minutes before Kayla replied. "Is there anything I can do?"

"Hold down the fort with the weddings. We've got two this week and they still have to happen and that means you're in charge of them. Call Yaya in a little bit and give her the update. She was there when they came to get me last night. She'll meet you at the brunch."

In one last text, Kayla said she'd take care of everything and then Tally shut her eyes again. She'd been squeezing Mitch's hand occasionally, praying for a squeeze back one of those times. But so far, he just lay there and didn't react to anything. It was freaking her out and she was sitting there rethinking everything she'd ever said to him and questioning herself.

Maybe she should have agreed to move in together when he asked her a few months ago even though she hadn't felt ready. She certainly felt ready now, she thought. The idea of losing him made her feel physically ill and she leaned over and put her head on the pillow beside the man she loved and let the tears go.

Chapter 24

Mitch woke up later that morning. He didn't make a lot of sense and the doctors quickly knocked him out again with painkillers and sedatives after he tried to pull at some of the wires and tubes attached to him. But he was awake at least briefly and he'd recognized Tally instantly.

"They want to keep him sedated until the swelling in the brain reduces," his mother explained. "It's driving me nuts, too. I want to hear his voice. But it's better to rest everything until the pressure has reduced some. That's the most dangerous part of this wound."

Tally nodded as if she understood, but everything sounded like Greek to her and nothing was making any sense. She knew Mitch was alive and that was about it. Between the wedding from hell – could the big blowup with the judge have really only been 12 hours ago - and no sleep, Tally was totally cooked. She was doing her best to pretend she was functional but feared the sleep deprivation was showing.

Mitch's family was in and out of the ICU – it seemed visiting rules were different when the patient was a wounded state trooper – and his sister-in-law, Robin, brought Tally an everything bagel with cream cheese and ordered her to eat.

"Look, just eat at least half of it. If his parents don't see you eating, they're going to freak out that you're not taking care of yourself. Bonnie has said at least 20 times that she wished Etah was here," Robin told her.

"Etah is on her way," Tally said.

"I know, honey. But you can't wait til she gets here to eat and sleep. If you don't want to go home and sleep, at least eat something so everybody stops worrying. They have enough to worry about with Mitch," Robin said.

It was a fair point and well taken. Tally ate the entire bagel and made a point to thank Robin for feeding her within earshot of her boyfriend's parents. Afterwards, she got up and went to the soda machine and bought a Diet Coke. Her activity seemed to signal that she was handling things better and it felt like everybody stopped watching her so closely. When she took a break to use the restroom, her appearance in the mirror startled her and then made her laugh. No wonder everybody was looking at her so funny. Her hair was out of control and she had makeup circles under her eyes. She cleaned herself up the best that she could and was pleased to see that Bonnie looked relieved by the improvement when Tally returned to Mitch's hospital room.

Chapter 25

Mitch woke up again that night and the doctors let him stay conscious a little bit longer so Tally could talk to him. Everybody else had gone home shortly before Mitch woke up, but Tally was spending the night on a cot they'd set up next to his bed. She was sitting on it scrolling through client emails that she couldn't care less about when she heard her favorite voice in the world.

"Hey beautiful."

Tally jumped up and wrapped her arms around him the best she could as he lay in the bed. She kissed him on the lips and on the part of his cheek that wasn't covered in gauze and she hugged him gently around the chest.

"Oh my God, I've been so worried. I love you so much and I don't want to lose you," she told him, her words tripping over themselves.

"I love you more," he told her in a gravelling voice. "You can't lose me."

"But I almost did," she said, and then she laid her head on his chest and began to cry.

"But you didn't," he tried to stroke her hair.

About that time, the nurse came in to give Mitch a few sips of water and put another dose of medicine into his IV that would send him back to LaLa

Land for the night. Tally was tempted to ask her to wait – she wanted to hear him tell her he loved her over and over again – but the doctors had said it was really important for him not to be awake and active until the brain swelling was under control. She didn't like it, but she also wasn't about to be the reason Mitch didn't get better.

She slept fitfully on the cot but staying the night was worth it when Mitch woke her up to say hi early the next morning. Tally only had a couple of minutes to chat with him before he was knocked out again, but he had seemed clearer than he had during their last conversation and that had to be a good thing, right?

***

Roberta relieved her that afternoon and Mitch's dad drove her home to Jekyll Island. She needed to shower and make some arrangements with Kayla to keep the weddings going. Then she'd drive back to the hospital in Jacksonville in her own vehicle so she could come and go as she pleased. She planned to stay by Mitch's side until he was released, but with no idea when that would be, she also needed to take her laptop and charging cords back with her. Kayla could only handle so much of the business on her own. Thank God that Yaya was there to run the flower shop. She really didn't need Tally's help for that. And if she ran short on hands, Kayla would jump in to help make bouquets. She and Tally had done it plenty of times before they were even in the flower business.

Tally grabbed files for events that were scheduled in the next month and put them into her laptop bag. Kayla theoretically had copies of all of the info contained in the folders, but Tally wanted to be prepared to answer questions if Kayla got stuck. She also took her company checkbook with her. Vendors would have to be paid even if her life was falling apart. She'd have to give Yaya or Kayla the checks to hand out so that she didn't miss payroll for the week. Some of her vendors were counting on her to help them make ends meet, and she would pay them on time no matter what.

She packed a fuzzy blanket to hide under in the cold hospital room and, at the last minute, grabbed a vase of extra flowers leftover from the Gomez/Goldberg wedding and took them with her to put in Mitch's room. She didn't remember the blooms being in her house before Mitch was shot and she suspected that Kayla or Yaya had put them there to cheer her up.

Chapter 26

Tally was over the moon when the doctors told Mitch's family that they were going to let him start to wake up completely on the fifth day after he was shot. Imaging showed the swelling was going down and, as long as they kept him calm and he cooperated with treatment, there was no reason to continue to knock him out. If things went well, he might be able to go home to finish his recovery in about a week.

Plans for Mitch's hospital release started a whole lot of drama that Tally hadn't been expecting. Mitch lived at Bonnie's house, so Tally had assumed that sending him "home" meant to his grandmother's house on Jekyll Island. But his mother, Roberta, had other plans for her youngest son's recovery. She wanted Mitch to recuperate in his childhood bedroom in her house, under her watchful eye. She'd already put the kibosh on Bonnie's plans to care for him when Tally heard about the disagreement. She waited until everybody was gone late that night to discuss the plans with Mitch.

"Hey babe, did you know that your mother and grandmother are fighting over which one of them gets to take care of you when you're released?" she asked him.

Mitch laughed softly. "No, I hadn't heard that. But it doesn't surprise me."

"Where do you want to go when they release you?" she asked.

"Your house?" He said it like a question and Tally wasn't sure if she was supposed to answer him or keep listening, so she didn't say anything. She didn't know if he was kidding.

"Could I come to your house?" Mitch asked again, clearly this time.

"Of course you can," Tally told him quickly. "But I'm not sure your mother will approve."

"I'm 30 years old and pretty sure that you're the secret to my quick recovery. I'll tell her that I'm going home with you and she won't argue with me."

"Sure, she won't," Tally laughed. She decided to let Mitch handle things with his mother and sent a text to Yaya warning that they might have company arriving soon.

The next day, Etah arrived back in the country and went straight to the hospital from the airport to see Tally and Mitch. When she got to the hospital, she texted her niece and Tally met her at the entrance. Seeing Etah was a huge relief and Tally wrapped her aunt in a ginormous hug.

Etah hugged her back and held on. Eventually, she let go and looked at Tally's face.

"You look awful," her aunt said. Tally laughed and wiped her eyes. Etah handed her a tissue from her purse and Tally blew her nose.

"Thanks," Tally said and threw the used snot rag into a garbage can. "You look pretty good for a lady who just got off of a plane."

"That's not my point and you know it, young lady," Etah scolded her. "Bonnie was right. You needed me to come home and take care of you."

"I'm doing okay, Etah. Considering everything."

"Considering everything that's happened, you are doing great," her aunt agreed. "But we all need some love and support from our family and friends at times. This is definitely one of those times."

Etah wasn't wrong and Tally didn't argue with her. But then she remembered her conversation with Mitch the night before.

"Mitch wants to come home to our house when he's released from the hospital," Tally told Etah.

"Oh really? What did Bonnie and Roberta have to say about that?"

"I have no idea. I don't think it even occurred to either of them. They've been too busy arguing over which one of them was going to take care of him."

"Oh my. Yes, I can see that," Etah chuckled. "But he's a man now, and if he wants to stay with you, he should. I'm only going to be home for a few days and if he arrives before I go, that's fine with me. You two could stay in my room so you have the king-sized bed. You're not going to want to bump him in your sleep."

Her aunt was being practical but Tally was mortified. She didn't discuss the details of her love life with her aunt, and openly discussing sleeping with Mitch in her aunt's bed horrified her beyond measure. The look on her face made Etah laugh.

"Tally, you're an adult. The man you love is recovering from a life-threatening injury. Let's not stand on ceremony and pretend that you guys aren't an established couple. I don't care what you do with Mitch, just do it carefully so Bonnie can't claim that you broke him."

Tally was horrified by her aunt's directness. But she appreciated it all the same. She didn't want to have to worry about what people would say and she didn't care what anybody thought. Mitch was the only man she had ever loved this way and she intended to stick as close to him as possible while he recovered.

"Look, I'm going to head home after I visit with Mitch for a bit," Etah said. "I'll go see Bonnie and test out the waters. I'm pretty sure she'll like the idea more than Roberta's house since he'd be so close by at ours and she can visit him constantly. We can get Bonnie to work on Tom so he can convince Roberta."

"Do you think that will work?" Tally was skeptical.

"No, I don't, actually. But I also think they both realize he's a grown man and if he wants to stay with the woman he loves, they shouldn't try to stop him."

"And you're going to tell Bonnie that?"

"Of course not. I'm going to let his father tell Bonnie and Roberta that. I'm staying out of the line of fire on this one."

"Gee thanks," Tally said with a hint of whine in her voice.

To be honest, she wasn't thrilled with the whole idea. As much as she loved Mitch, she was in the middle of spring wedding season, she had just opened a flower shop, and the idea of having to take care of a sick man too was more than daunting. Plus, Yaya was temporarily living in her guest room. Something in her facial expression tipped off her aunt to what she was thinking.

"Pull up your big girl panties, Tally. This is real life. So far, you're handling it pretty well from what I've heard. Being a state trooper's wife isn't easy and you just got a really early taste of the ugly part."

"No kidding," Tally agreed. "It makes me wonder if I really want to marry a trooper."

"No, it doesn't, or you wouldn't still be sitting at this hospital," her aunt said.

Tally had to smile because Etah was right.

Chapter 27

The man who shot Mitch was dead. Tally hadn't even thought to ask about the gunman – she just assumed he'd been arrested. But that's not how it worked when a bad guy opened fire on law enforcement officers.

Mitch didn't remember most of it. He remembered stopping the Mustang behind the suspect's vehicle and the rest was blank until he woke up in the hospital. He'd had to get a copy of the incident report and a friend who had been there to help him understand what all he'd missed.

"How many guys shot him?" Mitch asked Joe Moody, who had brought him cookies from his wife and get-well cards colored by his twin little girls.

Joe had never lost consciousness after the bullet had grazed his head and he remembered every detail of what went down. He'd been having nightmares about watching Mitch get shot. His wife had suggested that hanging out at the hospital with his friend who had survived might help with his sleep. Mitch was doing much, much better and from what Tally had told Joe's wife, the patient was getting bored and restless.

"Everybody shot him," Joe said. "All the guys in the SWAT groups on both sides of the Honda opened fire. You know how it goes. If one guy on a team opens fire, everybody…" he stopped and looked around as if suddenly realizing the door wasn't closed.

"Total clusterfuck," Joe continued in a softer voice. "Amazing none of the LEOs got hit in the crossfire. They lit that Honda up. The dashcam video from our car is insane."

"Wow," Mitch said softly.

"Yeah."

"I don't remember seeing you get hit," he told Joe.

"That's because your own gunshot to the head was so much more stupendous than my graze wound. You scared the hell out of me, buddy."

"Tell me every detail you remember," Mitch pleaded. He felt desperate for information. "I just remember stopping the car and taking cover behind the doors."

"We weren't there for very long," Joe explained. "The task force SWAT guys assembled behind the ballistic shields and approached the car from both sides, pretty fast, when the driver ignored all the commands.

"They were about to smash the window and pull him out of the Honda when the driver opened fire on us with an AR-15 through the back window of his car."

Mitch tried to remember but it wasn't coming to him. He hated that blank spot in his memory.

"There were three shots initially, and the first one got me," Joe said. "It was just a graze wound though. It hurt for a second, and then I wasn't sure I'd actually been hit. I reached up and touched the side of my head and my hand came away all bloody and so I knew something had happened. But it didn't really hurt at first thanks to all the adrenaline."

"Lucky bastard," Mitch remarked.

"No kidding," Joe agreed. "I dove into the Mustang for more cover - not sure why, should have dove for the trees – that asshole started shooting again. I don't remember how many shots there were, but I know he didn't get to unload the entire 30-round magazine in his rifle because SWAT turned him into Swiss cheese. Since they couldn't see into the Honda, they all just started shooting until they ran out of ammo."

Mitch couldn't help laughing. "I hate it when that happens," he joked.

Joe smiled. "Everybody was reloading when the commander told them to cease fire. They determined that there was no movement in the Honda and the suspect had likely been shot," Joe smirked. "That would be an understatement. Dude was so dead that you couldn't recognize him. I heard that some of him was in pieces.

"He was pronounced dead at the scene. But I was already gone by then and so were you. They transported us both to Jax in the same helicopter not long after the gunfight," Joe explained.

"I don't even remember the medevac," Mitch said.

"It wasn't a medical airlift," Joe cleared up the confusion. "The state patrol chopper monitoring our operation picked us up. The ambulance crew that was staged with the task force sent paramedics to take care of us on the flight but it's all a blur in my memory, too. I don't think you were ever conscious during it."

"We need to get those pilots a thank you present," Mitch suggested.

"Already done. Found out what their favorite booze was and sent a bottle to each of them with a note of thanks from both of us, and a Tupperware of cookies from my wife and kids, the day after they rescued us."

"Your wife is the best, Joe. Please tell her thank you."

Joe had taken Mitch home with him for dinner one night while they were doing surveillance in Camden County. Carly Moody had been a gracious hostess and he'd looked forward to getting to know his partner's family better.

"You can tell her yourself when she comes to see you – she wanted to come today but we didn't have a sitter for the girls. She'll be here later this afternoon or tomorrow, I'm sure. I just came first because I had a doctor's appointment here," Joe explained.

"What did the doc say about your noggin?" Mitch asked. Both men had gauze wrapped around their heads and looked like something out of a zombie movie. They'd had a good laugh about it when they first saw each other.

"Said it's as good as it ever was. The headaches should go away – they're already better than they were a couple days ago – thought my head was going to fall off that night."

"It could have been so much worse. You're a lucky man," Mitch told him.

Mitch and Joe had been assigned to work together most of the time since they'd joined the task force. They were the youngest guys in the group, but Joe had seven years on the job already. He was a veteran compared to Mitch and the rookie deferred to him for most decisions.

Both of them had grown up in the counties where they currently worked, and they'd graduated from their respective high schools just a year apart.

"I thought I recognized the name Durham. Did you play football?" Joe asked the first night they worked together.

"Me and all three of my older brothers played for Glynn Academy. I think there was a Durham on the varsity team for 10 years straight. You played too?"

"Sure did. And I remember the coach warning us about you and your brothers."

"Seriously? That's hilarious."

"Yeah, absolutely hilarious til ya got hit hard by a Durham. You're still built like a Mack truck," Joe laughed. "I should start hitting the gym with you. Follow your workout routine."

"Anytime. But usually, I just run and swim in the ocean. I only go to an indoor gym when the weather is awful or I don't have any time."

"I never have any time," Joe admitted. "The twins are a handful and Carly started working from home again when they were six months old. The house always looks like a toy box blew up, and when I'm home, I've got kids on both my ankles if I'm not holding them. The 'terrible twos' are a real thing, my man."

"Walk around with toddlers on your ankles and you've done your leg workout," Mitch joked. "Play airplane enough and you've done your upper body, too."

"Funny guy."

"Did we get the supplier?" Mitch asked out of nowhere, remembering that Joe had been debriefing him when they got off topic. The whole operation had been about getting the supplier, not the guy they ended up killing.

"Oh hell no," Joe couldn't help laughing.

"The first guy warned him?"

"Maybe. But he probably heard the gunfire and got the hell out of there," Joe explained. "It was a clear night and Facebook warriors are claiming they could hear the gunfight five miles away. Not possible. But our target certainly could have heard the boys unloading hundreds of rounds into his buddy just down the road."

"What about the team that was supposed to be set up at the doublewide?"

"They were getting positioned when the shooting started and they high-tailed it up the road to back us up. Commander just about shit when he realized it and sent them back to arrest the guy in the doublewide.

"The dude in the trailer was long gone before anybody got there. He didn't even bother to lock his door," Joe added.

"Did we get any narcotics in the trailer?" Mitch asked.

"Nope," Joe said. "The dogs went nuts but there was nothing actually left in there but some residue. Remember that shitty-looking little travel trailer parked beside the mobile home? He took it with him when he rolled out of there. Guess that's where he was keeping stuff. Or he got it loaded up that fast. They haven't found him yet. He's probably holed up with somebody around here, but he may have just squeaked by and gotten far enough away that he was outside the perimeter before we even started looking for him."

"So he could be in Mexico," Mitch said.

"Or Vegas."

"Right. We have no idea," Mitch sighed. "What's next for us? Are we still on the task force?"

"Probably. If we want to be. But first you have to go through so many debriefings," Joe warned. "So many interviews with investigators. I think they're sending people over here today to talk to you. Your dad has been blocking them since you were shot but the initial stuff can't wait any longer. The suspect is dead so it's not a huge rush, but they really want to get the supplier, too."

"Understood." Mitch was a little annoyed that his father had played big bad trooper on his task force investigation team, but he didn't expect anything less. "I really want to get out of here soon. Hey, can you do me a favor?"

"Of course."

"Call that restaurant in Tybee and apologize for me. The manager has to think I totally flaked or got cold feet or something. I still want to take Tally to Tybee to propose to her," he told his friend.

Joe had been the one to recommend the proposal spot in the first place, it was one of Carly's favorites.

"Yeah, I'll give them a call when I leave here and explain. I'm sure they'll set it all up again when you're feeling up to it. When do you want to propose?" he asked.

"As soon as possible."

Chapter 28

Mitch was released from the hospital four days later, and he went home to Etah's house with Tally. Because Etah was leaving the same morning that Tally's boyfriend was due to be released from the hospital, the two of them set up the master suite for the wounded trooper together.

"This way he'll have TV in the bedroom," Etah said. Tally didn't have a television in her room. "And that beautiful view of the water to inspire him. And easy access to the outside shower."

"I really appreciate it, Aunt Etah," Tally told her and gave her a hug.

"I'm not doing this for you, honey. I'm doing it for Bonnie. She's mad as a wet hen that he's not coming to her house, but she's thrilled he's not going to be over in Brunswick. She's even promised to bake him cookies that aren't gluten free," Etah announced proudly.

Bonnie had gone on a gluten-free baking kick the year before and nobody was happy about it. She still made old-fashioned Chex mix and trail mix for her law enforcement sons and grandsons, but the demand for her cookies had dropped dramatically even though she denied it.

Tally had promised Mitch she would be at the hospital in Jacksonville before noon. He would be released sometime after that. Just as she was getting ready to leave the house, his dad arrived on her front porch. He was in his trooper uniform.

"Hi Tom," Tally welcomed him into the house and gave him a hug. "I was about to head to Jacksonville to pick up Mitch."

"I know. He told me. I was thinking you might just wanna ride down there with me instead of taking your Jeep."

"Why?"

"There's a lot of ceremony involved when a wounded law enforcement officer is released from the hospital after he's been shot. Pure chaos, actually. The whole task force will be there, as well as a bunch of Mitch's trooper friends. He'll be rolled out of the building with a lot of fanfare and there will probably be television cameras," Tom explained.

"Oh wow."

"Yeah," he continued. "So I'm thinking we should keep your Jeep and, more specifically, your license plate off the radar and just go in my patrol cruiser. That way you don't have to pay for gas either," he joked. But Tally knew he was dead serious about keeping her vehicle incognito.

"Um, sure. I'll ride with you. Just give me a minute to powder my nose and grab my bag and we can take off," she said.

"Take your time. I'm going to head over to see my mom – Bonnie opted out of joining us to go get him – just shoot me a text when you're ready to leave."

"It'll only be a minute and I can walk over to her house," Tally said. "I'm not the one who is wounded. And I need to move after all the time I've spent sitting on my butt in Mitch's hospital room lately."

"Either way, I'm ready to go when you are."

Chapter 29

Mitch's dad had not understated the fanfare at hospital when his son was released. Tally saw news crews from the local stations in Jacksonville and Savannah set up outside the doors when they arrived and by the time Mitch was rolled out, there were more than 100 officers from multiple law enforcement agencies outside cheering for him.

The volume doubled and several people started whistling when Mitch stood up from the wheelchair and waved to everybody. His head was still partially bandaged, but he walked the few steps left to the door of his dad's patrol car on steady feet and took shotgun. Tally stood by, ready to shut the door, but photographers moved in to get some close-up shots of the hero. Mitch had a big grin on his face that Tally tried to match but she was uncomfortable with the cameras given the situation. She was relieved when Tom gave her the signal to shut the door so they could leave. She jumped in the back of the Georgia State Patrol Dodge Charger and sunk as low as she could in her seat without looking weird.

"That was a lot, wasn't it?" Mitch asked, turning his head to get a look at her. "You okay?"

"I'm fine," Tally smiled at him. "I'm just glad you're coming home. I'm sick of this hospital and I missed you."

"Careful what you wish for," Mitch joked. "You might be saying you're sick of me in a few days."

"And that's fine," his father interrupted. "Your grandmother would be happy to have you spend some time at her house. And you know your mother would love it if you came home for a few days with us, too. She's still really mad you chose Tally's house over ours."

Mitch groaned aloud and rolled his eyes.

"I'm not saying she's right, son. I'm saying that's how she feels. And your mother is the one that I have to close my eyes around when I sleep so I'm reminding you that you should spend some of your recovery time at home letting her spoil you."

***

Mitch dozed off as soon as the patrol car pulled onto I-95. Tom and Tally stayed quiet so as not to wake him, and she texted Yaya and Kayla an update, promising to pop into the flower shop the next day if Mitch didn't have any problems overnight.

"The flower shop is fine," Yaya texted back. "But there's a crazy bride on the island looking for you."

"What? Who?" Tally asked.

"Brenda Fogel," Kayla texted back.

"No way," Tally wrote.

"Do you know her?" Kayla texted.

"Unfortunately," Tally wrote back. "She was a Vieques client who had two different grooms. She's totally bonkers. Ugh."

She realized she needed to give her staff some direction because it wasn't fair to dump Brenda on them without an explanation. Tally figured the crazy woman was probably engaged, again.

"I can't deal with this and Mitch today," she texted the girls. "One of you please call her and tell her that I'd be happy to meet with her tomorrow afternoon at the shop at 2 p.m. Otherwise, I'm not available this week. Do not tell her about what's going on in my life – she's cray and she doesn't need to know anything."

Kayla volunteered to take one for the team as long as she didn't have to meet with the woman herself. She also wanted to know the full story behind it because Yaya kept laughing and wouldn't tell her anything. Tally replied that she would explain Brenda later and promised she wouldn't make Kayla meet with her, along with some emojis. Tally silently hoped she would be able to keep her promise as she turned off her phone's screen.

There was so much going on and it was only Tuesday. First, there was Mitch to consider. Then she also had an elopement on Driftwood Beach on Friday and a mid-sized wedding at a private waterfront villa down the street from her own house on Sunday. Kayla had taken the lead on handling the clients and prepping – the welcome bags for the Crabb/Taylor wedding were all stuffed and waiting in tubs with spreadsheets for the hotels, thanks to Yaya pitching in with extra hands. The girls had been sending her pictures to keep her updated and the latest ones showed all the prep tubs were ready for the next three events.

Tally couldn't help laughing. That was more prepared than she ever was when she did things on her own. Kayla was amazing and she thanked God again that Yaya had decided to make the big move. What if she hadn't been here to pick up the pieces after Mitch was shot? Tally couldn't have done it without her and the early numbers showed the flower shop was going to be a success.

Tally rested her head on the back of the seat as Mitch's dad took the exit onto Route 17. It felt like things were coming at her from every direction and she was exhausted.

"Looks like Mitch isn't the only one who needs a nap when we get home," Tom said in a soft voice, looking at her in the rearview mirror.

"Don't give me ideas," Tally replied without opening her eyes.

Chapter 30

Nobody was waiting for them at her house when they arrived and Tally was thankful. While she loved Mitch's family and enjoyed being around them, Tally and Mitch didn't really live together and him coming home to her house for the first time with everybody there would have felt weird.

The doctors had given Mitch some pretty heavy pain medication before they'd sent him home so that he wouldn't feel miserable on the drive. His dad had to wake him up after they stopped in Tally's driveway, and it took a moment before he was clearheaded enough to get out of the car.

Tally ran up the steps and unlocked the front door. She stood in the threshold as Mitch and his dad came slowly up the stairs. She could tell he was leaning on Tom a little for balance, but she didn't know if that was from the headwound or the pain medication.

"Come in and make yourselves comfortable," Tally told the men when they got to the porch.

"I'm going to go back and unload his stuff that's in my trunk and bring it in," Tom told her as he went out the door again.

Mitch walked straight through the house and out onto the front deck. He stood at the railing and inhaled deeply, smelling the sea air and the pluff mud and everything else that made Jekyll Island unique.

"Nice to be home?" Tally asked him.

"So nice," he said and then bent to kiss her. It was a long, slow, deep kiss and Tally had completely forgotten that Mitch's dad was still there until Tom cleared his throat to get their attention.

Her face flushed bright red. "Oops, sorry," she mumbled, stepping back from Mitch.

Tom laughed. "Don't let me interrupt the healing process or physical therapy or whatever this is," he joked. "I just need to head out now."

Mitch laughed and Tally was mortified. She wasn't used to having a family who knew everything around all of the time.

"I'll tell your grandmother to text Tally to see if you're awake before she comes over later, but you know her. You guys probably don't have to worry about cooking dinner for a few days. Check out your refrigerator when you get a chance," he suggested.

Tally `got bottles of water for both of them, and then she and Mitch sat side by side on their favorite bench on the front deck for a while, just watching the water and not talking. She was so happy to have him holding her that nothing else mattered. Her phone was inside on the countertop and she was pretty sure it was going nuts. But everything that mattered in the world to her at that moment was right beside her and she wasn't going to move until he did.

Mitch started drooping after about 10 minutes, so Tally suggested that he check out Etah's bedroom. They'd put fresh sheets on the bed that morning and Etah had put away some of the stuff she would have usually left out on bedside tables and dresser tops. Tally had moved the Apple TV from the living room into Etah's room so that Mitch could keep himself entertained. He wasn't required to stay in bed, but the doctor warned that he would need a lot of naps for the first few weeks of recovery while his head and the parts of his brain that had been impacted took time to heal. The stitches had come out before he left the hospital and he still wore bandages on his left lower jaw, where the bullet had entered, and on the back of the left side of his head, where the bullet had been removed.

"Let's get you to bed, hero," she said.

"Don't call me hero. I didn't do anything except get shot. That 'hero' business makes me uncomfortable," Mitch told her.

Tally understood how he felt but his dad had explained it to her. "You were shot in the line of duty, Mitch. That makes you a hero whether you like it or not."

"But the bad guy got away."

"The bad guy was turned into a human lawn sprinkler by the task force SWAT guys," Tally corrected him, using a phrase she'd picked up from other cops at the hospital. "The other bad guy got away. And you guys will catch up with him eventually. That's not your problem right now. Your job is to get better."

He started to argue with her but thought better of it. She was right. And he was exhausted from the car ride home.

Tally walked him into Etah's bedroom and showed him where she'd stashed the pajama bottoms and shorts and t-shirts that his grandmother had brought over for him a day earlier.

By the time she brought him a glass of lemonade and some of the hope-fully not gluten-free chocolate chip cookies she found in a Tupperware on the counter, Mitch was snuggled into the bed and already falling asleep. Tally started to back out of the room but he saw her.

"Don't you dare leave with those cookies. Did you bring me one for each hand?" he asked her.

Tally sat down on the bed next to him. "I brought you two for each hand because you have been so good today," she joked. "But Bonnie made them so they're suspect until one of us has tried them. I'll let that be you since she's your grandmother."

Then she got serious. "I'm so glad you're going to be okay, Mitch. I love you so much and I have been so worried." She cuddled up against his side.

"I was scared, too, Tally," Mitch admitted, putting a strong arm around her. "I hated the way they kept knocking me out at the hospital. The only good part was knowing that every time I woke up, you were sitting there holding my hand."

When Mitch finished the cookies, he curled up and fell asleep almost immediately. Tally extricated herself from the legs that had her pinned to the duvet and pulled the bedroom door shut as she left the room. She took the empty cookie plate with her. Mitch needed a good nap for sure, but Tally didn't have time to rest. She had a million unopened emails to answer and she hoped one of them would explain why her certifiably-crazy former client was on Jekyll Island.

Chapter 31

Brenda Fogel had been a super-annoying client on Vieques Island the first year that Tally worked at Vieques Weddings. She and her first fiancé – Tally thought his name was Brad but she wouldn't swear to it – had come to the island on a planning trip not long after she was first hired, and they were the first clients that she took to see venues on her own, without Isabelle.

Tally had set up the visits on a tight schedule that allowed her new clients to see both hotels and villas that were big enough for their wedding group. Everything started out just fine – the bride and groom had fallen in love with Casa de Cristal as soon as they saw the glass house on the island's hillside – but it went to shit quickly after that. As Tally texted property managers to cancel the rest of their appointments, the bride and groom got into a disagreement about who would stay at the wedding villa with them.

It was a stupid argument, Tally thought. The house was an architectural unicorn and had been featured in any number of design magazines. There was a viewing window into the swimming pool from the gym underneath it that was kinda cool, but it also had a bunch of annoying things about it that made it a lousy wedding venue, in her opinion.

For example, in order to keep the open, all-glass concept throughout the home, the bathrooms were structured like public restroom stalls. There was no real privacy. All of the light fixtures in the home were modern and funky but permanent – meaning you couldn't move them around if you wanted to move the tables. There was a large dining room table in a bad place for guest-flow out to the deck, but it couldn't be moved out of the way because the guests would all run into the light fixture that was permanently mounted just eight inches over the table.

It was a cool house to stay in but it was difficult to accommodate a large wedding group. It would be even harder for the guests staying in the house the day of the wedding because there were so few walls that everything they needed to hide would have to be stashed in their bedrooms. Tally thought the couple's argument about who would get to stay there should have been over who HAD to stay there, but it wasn't. And it escalated. It was horrible to watch.

Brenda was pretty in her own right, but when she got angry, she screwed up her face in the most unattractive way possible. Tally noticed the groom turned his back on his future wife a lot and she wondered if he was trying to avoid getting that look, too. She reminded Tally of Ursula, the witch in the "Little Mermaid."

After the arguing went on for more than a few minutes, Tally tried to redirect her clients to another venue, thinking that something else might solve the problem. She pointed out that there wasn't enough parking at Casa de Cristal so they would have to pay for valets at the bottom of the hill, and a shuttle to run the guests up and down the steep driveway. The bride said they didn't care and they definitely wanted the villa. The groom disagreed.

Tally suggested that they go look at some other big villas that one of their families could stay in and they could use that for the rehearsal dinner. Casa de Cristal was up in the hills and boasted an incredible panoramic view, but wouldn't it be amazing to have the rehearsal dinner the night before at a villa that had a completely different view of Vieques? Nope, not interested.

To this day, that villa tour with Brenda and her fiancé was the most awkward client planning experience Tally had ever had. But it got worse before it was over.

The couple booked Casa de Cristal for their wedding week and locked it down with a deposit before they left the island. But when Tally dialed in for their scheduled wedding planning call a week later, Brenda was alone. She told Tally that she and her fiancé had split up and their wedding - 18 months out at that point - was cancelled.

It was the first cancellation call Tally had received and she tried to react appropriately. She was so glad they weren't doing a virtual call where she'd have to control her facial expressions, too, because that was probably more than the newbie wedding planner could have done at that point.

That was when it started to get weird.

"But I want you to keep the wedding date for me for now," Brenda had said.

"You think you two are going to make up?"

"Absolutely not," Brenda said in a haughty tone. "I wouldn't marry him if he were the last man on earth. But I love that villa so I'm going to get married there. I just have to find the right groom."

"Huh," was all Tally managed to reply.

"The deposit was on my credit card – do we need to do anything with the house contract and the names on it?" Brenda asked. "I just know my family will love staying there when I get married."

You aren't engaged, Tally thought, but didn't say it aloud. This was one she was going to have to discuss with Isabelle before she did anything else. They were under contract to the bride and the groom. If she swapped partners before the wedding, there would probably need to be a new planning contract. Ay yay yay.

Brenda would have liked to start her planning for the new wedding ceremony to the unknown groom at that very moment, but Tally wasn't going to go there until she got counsel from the person who actually owned the business and was under contract to this whacky woman. She lied to Brenda and said she was getting an emergency call from a bride who was on the island and promised to get back in touch as soon as possible. When she hung up the phone, she felt like she'd run a mile. Then she started laughing. She couldn't make this shit up if she tried. It would be great material for a wedding planning book someday. Or a stand-up comedy act.

The couple's initial planning deposit was non-refundable. Isabelle explained to the bride that the contract wasn't transferable, but in the interest of keeping things pleasant, and because Brenda wasn't altering any of the original plans other than who she was marrying, Isabelle agreed that she would only charge the same wedding change fee that she would have been charged if the bride and her original fiancé had changed the date. Really, the only thing that had been decided was the venue so Vieques Weddings wasn't giving up much. However, Isabelle told the bride on no uncertain terms that Vieques Weddings wouldn't start planning her new wedding events until she actually had a verifiable groom.

"I don't know if this is a normal woman having a nervous breakdown or a crazy woman inventing an imaginary groom, but the last thing I want to do is have to cancel all the contracts later for a wedding that never really existed," Isabelle told Tally. "We can keep Casa de Cristal reserved in case she actually finds a victim, but don't start booking caterers and music. We know we'll end up cancelling them later, and that's not fair to the vendors."

Brenda hit the ceiling when Tally told her they couldn't start planning the wedding without a groom. Tally forwarded the series of email nastygrams she received to Isabelle and her boss let the nutty bride know, on no uncertain terms, that her generous offer to carry over the non-transferable contract would be revoked if she continued to disrespect the wedding planning team. The harassment stopped for a few months. But then Brenda was back.

It started with an email to Tally from Brenda that explained she was engaged, again, and ready to plan her big day. She said her new fiancé did not know that she'd booked the villa with another groom initially, and she didn't plan to tell him. In fact, she wanted to bring him to Vieques and pretend to fall in love with Casa de Cristal for the first time while he was there with her.

Tally sat at her desk dumbfounded. But she was sharp enough to forward the message to Isabelle before she replied. A few minutes after she hit 'send' on the forward, she heard Isabelle hooting in her office.

"Hey Tally, come in here," Isabelle called.

"You rang?"

"Did you see this?" Isabelle was still laughing.

"Yep, read it before I forwarded it to you." Tally was leaning on the doorframe with her arms crossed. "How would you like for me to respond to this?"

"You can tell that crazy biotch that you will do a one-hour max imaginary villa hunting conference call with her and her 'new fiancé' but we are absolutely not planning a fake venue tour that takes us days to make happen unless she wants to pay us another wedding planning deposit in full under a new contract."

"Um, okay. Would you mind writing that email to her? She scares me." Tally wasn't kidding.

"Fine. I'm happy to respond to her for you," Isabelle said in a snarky tone and then began dramatically typing.

"Dear Brenda," the wedding planner read along as she wrote. "While we're happy to help you plan a wedding with your substitute fiancé, there's no way we can commit to doing a fake villa tour that would take up our time and the valuable time of all the villa property managers who have to be on site to let us into the venues.

"Given the unusual circumstances, Tally can do a conference call with you and the new groom (does he have a name, dear? You didn't mention it in your email) to look at venue options the way we would do it with any clients who didn't travel to Vieques to do it in person. You can choose Casa de Cristal, again, and then we're all up to date and we can start planning the new wedding.

"If you insist on doing the villa tour in person, we're going to have to write a new planning contract and collect a new deposit first because we never agreed to repeat the same services without payment. Congratulations on your new engagement!" Isabelle read. She was typing so hard that Tally thought a key might break. "CC Tally. And boom, send."

Tally hadn't said a word while Isabelle was having a tizzy on her keyboard, but when her boss finished sending the message to Brenda, she couldn't help herself and she burst out laughing.

"What?" Isabelle asked with a straight face.

"I've just never seen you lose your shit that way before," Tally said, giggling. "That was really, really funny."

"Well, Brenda is really, really crazy," Isabelle countered. "I'm going to match crazy with crazy and see how it goes because taking a professional tact obviously won't get us anywhere with this bride."

"Does that mean you're going to plan her wedding?" Tally asked hopefully.

"Not a chance. She's all yours. This is good training for you. She might be the nuttiest client you ever work with here. She's definitely the most batshit that I've encountered at this stage of the planning process in my more than 30-year career."

"Isabelle," Tally whined. All that did was make Isabelle laugh.

"I'm totally not rescuing you from this one, babe," her boss said. But then she got serious. "If you have real problems or she turns nasty, I'll shut her down for you in a heartbeat. But if I had to put money on it now, I'd bet she won't end up marrying this guy anyway so none of this will actually matter. We will not transfer the contract to a third groom."

"Fabulous."

Chapter 32

Isabelle was right. Brenda's second engagement lasted only a few weeks before she messaged Tally wanting to change things up again. Isabelle responded to that email, too, explaining that she wasn't willing to continue to plan wedding after wedding under the initial contract. She said that she would notify Casa de Cristal that the deposit should be returned – she'd get the whole thing back since it was still so far out – and Brenda should consider their current contract finished.

When they'd made team t-shirts at the end of the wedding season with all the silly memories and inside jokes, one of them was "Don't Be a Brenda." Tally had never expected to hear from her again, nor had she wanted to. But now Brenda was on Jekyll Island. Tally fervently wished that t-shirt had survived Hurricane Maria.

Enough time wasted thinking about Brenda, she thought. Tally sat down at the dining room table, where she would be able to hear Mitch if he needed her, and booted up her laptop. She was so far behind in responding to emails that it was entirely possible she had an email from Brenda explaining her visit. Or a warning message from Isabelle. She started at the top and read through everything she'd received over the past week, including the ones she'd only glanced at while she was still at the hospital with Mitch. Nothing related to Brenda.

She crafted a potential client email response to send to everybody who hadn't gotten the usual immediate response to their inquiry over the past 10 days. Tally apologized and explained she'd been off island handling a family emergency and offered them specific dates and times she was available that week if they wanted to set up a free initial wedding planning consultation. Two of the potential clients responded within minutes to book their appointments and Tally was pretty sure she'd hear back from even more brides before the end of the business day. She was getting a good reputation and those quick responses gave her the kick of enthusiasm she needed to keep digging through her backed up email. She didn't plan on doing any calls that day because she wanted to be available if Mitch needed anything. But she was going to have to get back to a semi-normal schedule as quickly as possible because it wasn't fair to keep dumping everything on Kayla and Yaya.

Yaya had sent her several wedding flower bids to approve and Tally reviewed each of them and signed off on all of them. Then she sent a message to Yaya.

"Looks like you've got the hang of the pricing. You don't need to run bids past me anymore unless you have questions or need help," she texted.

"Woohoo!" Yaya replied, followed by a series of creative emojis. Tally snorted. She was so happy to be working with her friend again that Yaya could get away with being a smartass.

"You gonna be here for dinner?" Tally texted back.

"Nope, I'm staying with Kayla tonight. We decided you and Mitch needed the place to yourselves."

Tally felt badly that her boyfriend had displaced her bestie. She hit the speed dial button for Yaya.

"You didn't have to do that," she said as soon as her friend answered. "I wouldn't have let him stay here if I thought you'd feel put out. I'm so sorry."

"Don't be sorry, girl," Yaya said in a soothing voice. "I don't feel put out at all. The sleepover was Kayla's idea and I accepted her invitation. We're going to make guacamole and pico and watch bad wedding reality TV while you and Mitch do whatever you do when your boyfriend survives a bullet in his head."

Tally sighed. "Are you sure?"

"Seriously?"

"Thank you, Yaya. Thank Kayla for me too."

"You're on speaker. She can hear you," Yaya replied.

"Thanks for the warning. What if I was calling you to bitch about Kayla?" Tally teased.

"You never bitch about Kayla because she's perfect," Yaya said. "Have you even looked in your fridge since you got home?"

Tally realized she hadn't. She'd gotten lemonade for herself and Mitch from a pitcher on the counter and dispensed ice cubes from the front of the fridge, but she hadn't actually opened it. She got up and walked over to check it out.

"Holy moly," she said when she saw the cleverly packaged and wrapped goodies on every shelf. "You guys are the best."

"It wasn't just us," Kayla piped up. "Bonnie did most of the cooking, we just made the silly labels. She said to tell you to tell Mitch that nothing was gluten free."

"Thank goodness," Tally laughed.

"So you should be all set for a few days," Kayla said.

"I'm planning to come into the shop tomorrow – if Mitch shouldn't be alone, I'll ask Bonnie to come over. Did you make that appointment with Brenda?" She didn't really want to hear the answer but she had to ask.

"Yep. She picked up on the first ring when I called her back. She'll be here at 2 p.m. tomorrow and she cannot wait to see you again."

"Nooooooooooooooooooooooooooooooo," Tally wailed.

Both women on the other end of the phone started laughing at her but Tally wasn't kidding. She was dreading a rematch with the craziest bride she'd ever met.

"Ugh. Okay. Thanks for setting it up," she said, but didn't mean it.

"I cannot wait to hear this story. Yaya won't tell me anything," Kayla complained.

"Yaya was never unlucky enough to meet her on Vieques. But I'll explain it all to you tomorrow when I come in at noon," she promised and signed off after thanking them, one more time, for having everything ready for Mitch's return. Not having to worry about meals took one big thing off her plate. She didn't usually cook for herself when she was home alone. Tuna fish on crackers and sometimes peanut butter on graham crackers, if she happened to have them, was about as creative as it got if she didn't have a to-go container of leftovers from an event waiting in her fridge.

Chapter 33

Bonnie stopped in at 5 p.m. with more food.

"I got thinking about what Mitch liked to eat when he was having a bad day when he was younger and I remembered that he loved my macaroni and cheese. So I whipped some up," she told Tally as she swept into the house holding a casserole dish with potholders.

"Okay if I set this on the stovetop?" Bonnie asked.

"Sure," Tally said as she walked over to Etah's bedroom door to shut it before they woke up Mitch. But she was too late.

"Hey Gram," she heard Mitch call.

Bonnie dashed past Tally into the room and went to her grandson's bedside. "Hey baby," she said and then gave him a careful kiss on his bandaged head. Tally left them alone and used the time to clean up the paperwork scattered all over the table. Bonnie came back out of the room a moment later, shutting the door behind her.

"He said he'll be out as soon as he uses the bathroom," she told Tally. "Doesn't he look just wonderful compared to last week?"

Tally agreed that Mitch looked a lot better, but she was still very worried about him. It was too soon to know if there was any long-term brain damage and he wasn't totally in the clear yet. He definitely didn't have his balance fully back. Tally just wanted to be careful not to celebrate Mitch's recovery too soon. Sort of like declaring a wedding was a success before the entire event was over was bound to bring on something horrible at the end of the night.

Mitch was wearing pajamas pants with rubber duckies on them and a state police academy t-shirt when he joined them at the dining room table a few minutes later.

"Are you hungry?" Bonnie asked before Tally could.

"I'm starved," Mitch said.

Bonnie was already out of her chair and getting a plate to dish up some of the still-warm macaroni and cheese. It was her best friend's house and Etah had kept everything in the same cabinets for the last 30 years so it wasn't surprising that Mitch's grandmother knew her way around.

"Would you like some, Tally?" Bonnie asked.

"Sure, that sounds great."

Tally got up and went to get Mitch's medicine. He was due for a dose of the painkillers and the doctor had warned not to stop those for a few more days or the pain would likely send Mitch back into the hospital. She had a feeling that between the pills and the cheesy noodles he was shoveling into his mouth like he hadn't been fed in a week, Mitch was going to pass out pretty early. That was good because she needed to get to bed early, too. But it was also good because she'd have more time to work after Mitch conked out. She was multiple blogs behind her usual schedule and she needed to get caught up while it was quiet and nobody was bugging her. They were her cheapest and most prolific marketing tool, too.

Mitch was charming and funny while he ate his macaroni and cheese, and Bonnie sat across the table from him and glowed just watching her grandson.

"I've got to go into the flower shop for a few hours tomorrow," Tally told them. "Any chance you're free to come hang out with Mitch in case he needs something?"

"Absolutely," Bonnie said at the same time Mitch objected.

"I don't need a babysitter."

"Yes, you do," Tally told him firmly. "The doctors said you shouldn't be alone for the first five days while you're still taking all the heavy-duty meds, and we're going to follow their orders. At least we are if you're going to be staying here."

She gave Mitch a stern look she didn't mean but he caught her meaning.

"Okay fine, Gram, you can come hang out with me tomorrow afternoon," he told Bonnie in a defeated tone.

"If you stop acting like I'm the neighborhood menace, I might bring you shrimp salad and Key Lime pie," his grandmother promised.

"Well, why didn't you say that first?"

"You're cruising for a bruising, Mister," Bonnie told him. "You're lucky that you already look like somebody beat you up this week or I'd go borrow a wooden spoon from Etah's crock over there and remind you who's in charge."

The image made all of them laugh, and Bonnie held her hand up like she was holding a wooden spoon to make a point.

"Oh my gosh, I'd forgotten your legendary wooden spoons," Tally guffawed. "We could hear the boys screaming from over here."

"That was such baloney," Bonnie argued. "They used to run away and stand at the top of the stairs yelling so that one of their parents would rescue them. Or I'd get tired and give up. I didn't deliver half the swats those boys deserved because they got too fast for me."

"You got me once in the car," Tally recalled. "You used to keep a wooden spoon in the glove compartment."

"Tally," Bonnie said in a conciliatory tone. "In the future, if you ever find yourself carpooling four boys and their friends back and forth on the Jekyll causeway every day, I'd be willing to bet you will also carry a wooden spoon in your glove compartment."

Tally thought about it and looked at Mitch and saw he was smiling.

"Probably," she agreed.

Bonnie stayed to visit for more than an hour after they finished eating. Mitch beat her at two games of backgammon and then declared himself done for the night. He wanted to take a shower in the outside shower before bed, and his grandmother took that as her cue to leave.

Mitch could shower, but he wasn't supposed to be alone when he did it, just in case he got dizzy. He also wasn't allowed to get his head wet yet or shave, but that didn't stop him from dragging Tally into the Etah's big outside shower with him two minutes after his grandmother left.

"Is anybody else coming over?" he asked.

"I don't think so," Tally replied. "I locked the front door."

"Good," Mitch said. And then he turned on the water in the big shower with a conveniently located bench in it. "I missed you and I want to be alone with you."

"Me too," Tally agreed.

She didn't end up doing any blogging that night, but she also didn't get to bed early.

Chapter 34

Tally snuck out of bed early and went out to the kitchen to commune with the Nespresso machine. She patiently waited while the machine brewed a quad-shot espresso for her and then took it to the dining room table so she could wake up while she blogged. She finished her first coffee and her first blog at the same time, then she took a break to get dressed and get her act together while Mitch was sleeping.

She was dressed and almost caught up on work life when Mitch woke up. Tally delivered breakfast in bed and gave him his medicine. Then she helped him figure out the Apple TV remote so he could get caught up on all the bad shows he'd missed in the past couple of weeks. She didn't understand his fascination with watching "LivePD" and "Cops" – it would be like a wedding planner watching "Say Yes to the Dress" for fun - but she found the shows for him and kept her opinions to herself. He fell asleep after about 30 minutes, when the pain meds kicked in, and Tally pulled the bedroom door shut so that Bonnie wouldn't blow him out of bed again when she arrived with lunch.

Tally had her laptop bag packed and was waiting when she saw Mitch's grandmother coming across the street with a wicker picnic basket, shortly before noon. She opened the door and welcomed her, holding a finger to her lips to indicate that the patient was sleeping. Bonnie got the message and air-kissed Tally as she blew past her into the house. Tally waved goodbye and headed directly out the front door. She debated taking her Jeep because she wasn't a huge fan of golf carting – that was more Aunt Etah – but the golf cart needed to be driven on at least a weekly basis if they wanted to keep it running well, and she hadn't driven it since before Mitch was shot. The top speed on the island was 35 so it wasn't like driving her Jeep was really going to get her anywhere faster. It just delivered her with much better hair than the open-air golf cart.

***

She was glad she'd taken the smaller vehicle when she arrived in Beach Village and saw that the parking spaces were packed. Spring break, she thought to herself. Tally wedged the golf cart into a space that wasn't really a space just behind the flower shop and startled the girls when she burst in through the back door.

"Hey girls," Tally called out. "Why isn't this back door locked?"

Yaya looked at her with a guilty face. "We've been processing flowers all morning and it's a pain in the ass to have to remember to grab my keys as I'm going in and out to the dumpster."

"Fair enough," Tally agreed. She hated processing flowers, too. "But remember to lock it back up after you're done because we've had enough weird and wonderous stuff happen to this company and the people who are important to me over the past year. I don't feel comfortable taking any chances."

"There's no crime on Jekyll Island. Nobody even locks up their bikes," Kayla said.

"Tell that to my hydrangeas from the first big wedding I did here," Tally snarked. An ex-girlfriend of Mitch's was serving time behind bars for that incident.

"She has a point," Yaya agreed.

"Would it be easier if we installed a keypad lock so you don't have to mess with keys at the back door?" Tally asked.

"Absolutely," Yaya answered quickly.

"Okay, we'll do that. As soon as Mitch is feeling well enough to install it."

Kayla groaned but Tally laughed. "I think he's going to bounce back pretty fast just to have an excuse to get out of backgammon with his grandmother. If I had to guess what's going on at my house right now, I'd wager Mitch is pretending to be asleep while Bonnie hovers."

Chapter 35

Kayla and Yaya left Tally alone for the first 15 minutes she was there. A customer came in to order Mother's Day flowers and mentioned having seen the social media promotions about a discount for Jekyll residents.

"Score!" Tally mouthed to Kayla, who grinned in response as Yaya took the order at the front counter.

When the customer left, it was no holds barred. Kayla sat down on the table next to Tally's laptop and pushed the lid closed.

"You MUST tell me about Brenda Fogel now. I'm dying of curiosity," Kayla wailed. "And you promised!"

"Oh my God. I'd almost forgotten she's coming this afternoon," Tally lied.

"You're meeting with her here."

"Actually, I'm not. I think I'll treat her to a beverage or ice cream from the Jekyll Market and we'll sit outside at one of their tables to talk. She's crazy and if she's here to go nuts, I'd rather she did it in public. We don't have any cameras in here yet. Leigh has them all around the market for security."

"You're serious?" Kayla was shocked.

The young wedding planner had been expecting – no, looking forward to – another story about a crazy bride whom Tally had planned a wedding for in Vieques. But the way her boss was behaving, it looked more like she thought she might have a stalker.

Tally explained Brenda's history with Vieques Weddings to Kayla, with Yaya chirping in to add details. They called Isabelle partway through the gossip session and put her on speaker. She couldn't come up with either of Brenda's previous groom's names, either.

"Do you need me to look it up? It's in the dead files. Might take a while to find it," Isabelle said. The girls could hear her rustling papers through the phone.

"Not necessary, Isabelle. This is an entirely new company and I do not plan to work with her on anything. I only agreed to meet with her because she showed up on Jekyll in person. If she'd emailed me or called ahead, I would have put the kibosh on it."

Tally and Etah reminisced about the crazy conference calls with Brenda and the first and second grooms.

"I was so glad when the second groom backed out. I didn't want to plan it at all," Tally admitted. "She was absolutely whackadoodle."

"She seemed nice when she came into the shop," Kayla observed.

"Yeah, that's how she seems when you meet her. We thought she was pretty normal until the venue tour when she turned into Ursula up at Casa de Cristal," Tally explained. "Be polite, but don't tell her anything. Don't check date availability or anything else. We're not working for this nutball. I have enough stress with the clients who aren't certifiable."

Tally loved what she did. Planning weddings was a happy job and most of the time, she could stand back at the conclusion of a complicated event and feel satisfaction that she'd troubleshot the problems and given the wedding couple the best day she possibly could. But every once in a while, she got a client that made her seriously question her life and career choices.

Yaya and Tally were still spilling the tea on Brenda when the subject of their gossip opened the front door of the shop. At 1 p.m. A full hour early.

"Why am I not surprised," Tally grumbled. But then she pasted a smile on her face and went out front to welcome her former client.

Chapter 36

A completely sane-looking woman with a normal smile greeted her and approached to give Tally a hug. Tally cringed inwardly but let Brenda embrace her.

"Hi Brenda, you look fantastic. What brings you to Jekyll Island?" Tally asked when she was able to take a step back.

Then, before Brenda could answer, Tally cut her off.

"You know what, let's pop next store for a coffee – I'm desperate for some caffeine," she placed a hand on Brenda's arm and turned her around. Then she steered her right back out the door while Kayla and Yaya watched from the back with amused expressions on their faces. Tally fervently hoped they would keep the volume down when they burst into hysterical laughter after they left.

It was a zoo inside Jekyll Market – definitely spring break. Tally grabbed a Diet Coke out of a nearby cooler and gestured to Brenda to choose something.

"I'm fine," Brenda said.

Tally put two bucks on the ice cream counter and caught the eye of one of the girls working behind it. She got a thumbs up that she was good to go, and so she and Brenda avoided the backed-up line of tourists seeking ice cream cones and made their way to the door.

***

Once outside, Tally led Brenda around the corner and chose a high-top table for them to sit at. She didn't want Brenda to be comfortable. She wanted this to be quick and over.

"Okay," Tally said as she sat. "Thanks for indulging me. I needed a break from the shop. Tell me why you're here on Jekyll Island. Vacation?"

"I want to work for you."

"What?" Tally was sure she hadn't heard her correctly.

"I want to work for you," Brenda repeated. "When Isabelle cancelled my contract after the second engagement ended, we exchanged several emails. In one of them, she suggested that if I really wanted to plan weddings every day, I should consider going into the planning business. I thought about it long and hard and decided that she was right. I would be an excellent wedding planner."

Tally sat quiet. She didn't know what to say. She'd remembered joking with Isabelle about Brenda being a bride who wanted to be a wedding planner, but neither one of them had ever suggested they might have a job for her. Certainly not Tally. She worked for Isabelle back then.

"So, when I finally realized that advertising and marketing wasn't my bliss, my therapist agreed it was time for me to take the plunge into something I'm passionate about. And I'm passionate about weddings. I've planned like five for myself now, and I did the last three without professional help because I knew I needed a groom first before I could call you guys back again," she chuckled as if she recognized how crazy she'd been.

"I reached out to Isabelle but didn't hear back from her, and when I called around the island to try and find her, I learned that you guys were both gone and Vieques Weddings was shut down," she continued. "So, I filled out the new client inquiry form on the old company website just in case somebody was still checking that email, and I got what was probably an automated response from Isabelle that referred me to your new destination wedding company here in Georgia."

Brenda sounded proud of her detective work, but Tally just felt trapped. There was no way she was ever going to work with this crazy woman in any capacity. Not as a client and certainly not as an employee. Even if she wasn't as crazy anymore – and that was questionable because who travels for a job interview that isn't scheduled – Tally got the heebie jeebies just thinking about having to deal with her. She caught herself looking around for an escape route as Brenda shared the details of the faux weddings she'd planned for herself. She even had a binder of imaginary weddings she'd planned as a portfolio.

Tally knew she had to be direct and let the woman down easily because she didn't need any problems.

"I'm really flattered, Brenda. You've done a lot of work," Tally said as she looked through the binder Brenda had practically shoved at her across the table. "I wish you had called me before you took the time to come all the way here, though. Where are you living these days?" She couldn't remember where the former client was from at the moment.

"I'm ready to move to Georgia if you'll hire me," she replied.

"Unfortunately, I'm not hiring right now," Tally told her. "We're a really new company and I've brought everybody that I can afford on board the team already. We don't have a place for you."

"I could start out as an intern," the mid-30s advertising executive suggested. "I know a lot more than your average intern and I could teach the others a lot."

Oh, dear God, Tally thought. But what she said was, "I'm sure you have a lot to offer, but we just don't have a place for you. And we probably won't in the near future."

"But this is what I want to do," Brenda said with a determined look. "I thought about it for a long time and now that I'm here, I think you should give me a chance."

"I can't, Brenda. And I don't want to do that right now. I thank you for coming, but I'm not hiring and I would never hire a former client if I was, just to avoid conflicts of interest," Tally was totally making it up as she went along. She'd never had to deal with something like this and pausing their conversation to dial a lifeline and get help from Isabelle wasn't the right thing to do. Even though she really wanted to.

Brenda stared hard at Tally as if trying to figure out if she was serious. To fully convey her message, Tally put the cap back on her Diet Coke bottle and slid off her stool.

"I've got to get back to work now. It was great seeing you and I hope you'll enjoy the rest of your stay on Jekyll. It's a neat place and there's lots to see and do," she said as she started to slowly back away from the table.

When it dawned on Brenda that Tally was seriously blowing her off, her facial expression suddenly changed. She stopped looking like a normal, pleasant woman and took on the visage of Ursula. It didn't help that she had her hair in an updo that sort of resembled the cartoon witch, too. Tally had a flashback to the pool deck at Casa de Cristal when Brenda had the throwdown with her first groom and cringed at the thought of what was coming.

"You must be joking," Brenda said in a loud voice. "You're just walking away from me?"

Tally stopped in her tracks, well aware that she was being watched by a number of people passing by on the sidewalk and sitting at other tables outside Jekyll Market. She considered returning to the table to try to talk calmly with Brenda but she knew from prior experience with this woman that reason was impossible. Instead of engaging in a verbal battle on the sidewalk, Tally opted to walk away. Anyone who judged her for doing that would have a far worse opinion of her if she stayed to get screamed at in public.

"How dare you!" Brenda screeched as Tally turned the corner to return to her shop. "You don't know who you're fucking with!"

Tally kept walking, hoping nobody associated her with the foul-mouthed harridan making a scene. She opened the door to Jekyll Flowers and went in. She was glad there weren't any customers there.

"Kayla," she called into the back room. "Is the back door locked?"

"I think so."

"Please double check and make sure it's locked." Tally locked the front door and dropped the blinds in the front window of the shop. Then she scooted into the back room. She turned off all the lights and stepped behind the wall that obscured the messy area where they assembled flowers.

"What the hell?" Yaya asked, coming out of her own office, which didn't have windows and had gone entirely dark thanks to Tally.

"Shhhhhh," Tally held a finger to her lips.

Yaya looked at her friend like she had lost her mind. Tally was crouched down and appeared to be hiding. So, she squatted down and dashed across the entry into the back, careful to keep beneath the counter out front so she couldn't be seen. She squatted next to Tally.

Kayla followed Yaya's lead and joined them.

"Who are we hiding from?" Kayla asked.

"Brenda Fogel."

Yaya burst out laughing and Tally shushed her, putting a hand over her mouth and pointing towards the front of the shop where they could clearly see Brenda with her nose pressed to the glass, trying to see if anyone was inside.

"Wow, she's scary," Kayla whispered. "What does she want?"

Tally held a finger to her lips and watched silently as Brenda finally gave up and walked away. She had a feeling the crazy bride was sitting on a bench just outside her eyeshot waiting to pounce when she left work. When she was sure nobody could hear them, Tally told Yaya and Kayla about Brenda expecting to get a job with Jekyll Weddings and how she freaked out when Tally said no.

"She really is nuts," Kayla said as it sunk in that the definition of "crazy" for this former client was very different than the average bride.

Yaya got serious as she stood back up. She muttered in Spanish to herself and extended a hand to her boss.

"Tally, she's loca and if she comes back, we should either beat her up or call *la policia*. If we were in Vieques, I would handle it differently. But you live with a state trooper now."

"Not exactly. We don't live together."

Yaya and Kayla looked at each other and rolled their eyes knowingly. Their boss blushed.

"Well, he's broken anyway. I don't want to bother him with this," Tally admitted. "I feel like I've been one problem after another since I moved back here. I mean, good grief, he was just shot and lucky enough to survive it. The last thing he needs to deal with is crazy bride drama."

"No, the last thing he needs is Brenda hacking you to little pieces in the flower shop," Yaya said. "Do you still keep a machete handy? I can bring mine in if you didn't bring one home."

Yaya's face said she was dead serious, and she was freaking Kayla out, so Tally had to intervene.

"Yaya's kidding," Tally said. "We don't subscribe to Viequenses justice here. No vigilantism, even if it would have worked back home. But I appreciate you wanting to get my back. I will tell Mitch about Brenda when I get home but I don't think she'll come back again to bother us. If she comes back into the shop for any reason other than to buy flowers from the fridge, please ask her to leave."

"I'm not going to be here that much this week anyway, so if I maintain a low profile, she'll probably lose interest and go away," she added. "If either of you is here alone, keep the doors locked."

Yaya looked at her skeptically but Tally shrugged. There was a tense moment of silence between the besties and then Kayla interrupted it.

"Well, you guys were right about her being completely batshit. If she really thought you were going to hire her on Jekyll after her multiple grooms in Vieques, she's the craziest bride I have ever encountered," the 25-year-old wedding planner said.

They turned the lights back on in the shop a few minutes later, but they kept the door locked and the blinds drawn. If anybody knocked, they'd see who it was before opening up. Meanwhile, they needed to review the lists and schedules for the Friday elopement and the beach wedding on Sunday. Everything was ready to go for the Crabb/Taylor events, but the bride and groom who were having the big wedding at the house a few doors down from Tally had sent a list of questions and changes via email. Kayla wanted to review them with her boss and be clear on all the answers before she sent the couple a reply.

It was almost 4 p.m. when the planners decided to call it a day. Tally needed to get home to Mitch and she didn't want to leave anybody alone in the shop with Brenda on the island. When Yaya saw that Tally had driven the golf cart, she insisted that she and Kayla follow her home just to make sure she didn't have any problems.

"Look, Tally. You can't hide with no doors. Just let us follow you home and keep an eye on you. We both want to see Mitch anyway if he's awake," Yaya told her in a voice that said she wasn't giving her friend an option.

Chapter 37

Yaya needn't have worried about Tally's safety at home because it looked like half the law enforcement officers in Georgia were parked in her driveway. Tally pulled the golf cart onto the lawn. Kayla turned around in a neighbor's driveway and pulled up at the curb.

"It looks like he's busy," Yaya said from the passenger window of Kayla's SUV. "We'll come see him tomorrow."

"I'm not sure what's going on. I know he had to do a lot of interviews with investigators about the shooting but I thought most of that got done. These are probably just friends here to see how he's doing," Tally said. "You should come in."

"Uh uh," Kayla said. "No thanks. I'm no badge bunny."

"Me either," Yaya added.

Tally rolled her eyes.

"Have a good night and we'll talk to you tomorrow. Give Mitch our love," Kayla said and then pulled away without giving Tally an opportunity to respond.

Tally grabbed her overloaded laptop bag from the golf cart and made her way to the porch, muttering under her breath.

She was startled when the front door suddenly swung open and Mitch's dad appeared in the threshold.

"Hey Tally," Tom greeted her and grabbed her laptop bag from her hand. "Let me take that. Come on in. Welcome home."

She couldn't help smiling at Tom Durham's enthusiasm. His grin was infectious.

"So, who all is here?" Tally asked. She could see a group of about 12 men, mostly in uniform, surrounding Mitch outside on the front deck.

"It's guys from his academy class who are assigned to posts in this area. They brought him some gag gifts for being the first one in the class to get shot."

Tally's jaw dropped. "Seriously? Isn't that a little dark?"

"Cops have warped senses of humor, Tally," Tom said. "You should have figured that out by now. When a trooper gets wounded in the line of duty and is expected to recover, there's always a lot of teasing involved. If he wasn't expected to be okay, they wouldn't joke. Coming over here and giving him a hard time is one way they help Mitch understand that he's going to get through this whole thing."

"I think I have a lot to learn about being in a cop family."

"Being a cop wife isn't an easy way of life, Tally," Tom said. "You know that. But now you've been through what will probably be the worst experience and closest call ever, so in a sense, you can handle anything else because nothing will ever be as bad as this shooting was."

"God, I hope so."

"Me too," he agreed. "Now you go out and say hi to everybody – they all want to meet the woman who snagged Mitch. They shouldn't be staying too much longer anyway. He's wiped out."

Tally did as she was told, feeling a little bit like Alice in Wonderland in her own house. She supposed she'd have to get used to men in uniform wandering in and out, and patrol cars blocking her driveway, if she married Mitch.

Chapter 38

Brenda didn't reappear at the shop the next day, and by the weekend, the girls had let down their guard a bit. Kayla had held down the fort all week while Tally bounced back and forth between Mitch and the shop. So Tally offered to deal with the Sunday beach wedding on her own so that Kayla could grab at least a full 24 hours off. She'd been covering for Tally for weeks, helping to juggle brides, and she worried she was going to burn Kayla out.

"Seriously?" the look on Kayla's face when Tally told her to take off reflected how badly she needed down time.

"Go, before I have a chance to change my mind."

"Tally, I don't want to dump this on you."

"Are the tubs prepped? Welcome bags delivered?" Kayla nodded.

"What about the flowers?"

"Ready to go except for the bridal bouquet – going to do that tomorrow since it's tulips," Yaya said.

"Ugh, tulips," Tally made a face. Tulips were super pretty in a vase but they didn't hold up very long in a bouquet.

"I'm available to help out with the wedding on Sunday if you end up needing extra hands," Yaya volunteered. "Isn't the venue next door to your house or something like that?"

"It's three houses up from us but on the same street. Which means we should pre-think where we put our cars and warn the neighbors so they don't hate us the next day," Tally said. "If we need to get out to run get something or drive to a hospital, we don't want all our cars to be blocked in. I'll ask Bonnie if we can just back our Jeep and golf cart into their driveway."

The Durhams' house faced Beachview Drive and backed Aunt Etah's house, across the street on Tallu Fish Road.

"Smart thinking," Yaya said.

Yaya and Tally locked up the flower shop and went home to Etah's house to make dinner. Mitch had napped after losing lots of backgammon games to his grandmother and was feeling a little perkier.

"Somebody stopped by for you today," Mitch said.

"Who?"

"A former client. Hang on, I have her card." Tally and Yaya looked at each other and locked eyes.

Tally shook her head slightly, signaling to her friend that she hadn't told Mitch about Brenda.

"Here," he pulled a card from his pocket and flipped it across the counter to Tally.

As she looked, her eyes widened and her jaw dropped.

"What?" Yaya asked.

"Did you look at this card?" she asked Mitch.

"Um, no. Should I have?"

Tally smacked the card down on the counter so that they could see what had left her speechless.

The card looked exactly like Tally's business card – with the Jekyll Weddings and Jekyll Flowers logos. But instead of her name, it had another name. Brenda Fogel, Wedding Planner.

"You have got to be shitting me," Yaya scoffed. "Anybody else need a drink? I need a drink." She stomped around the counter and found a bottle of Captain Morgan in the cabinet. She got out glasses and started making cocktails.

Tally took hers and drank half of it through the straw before she set it down on the dining room table and sat down. She took a deep breath before she spoke.

"Un-fucking-believable," she muttered.

"You do attract the weirdos," Yaya agreed.

"Shut up. The last one was Mitch's ex."

"Hey, how did I get pulled into this? I'm wounded."

They all laughed. Tally finished her Captain and Coke in two more big sips and went to refill her glass as Mitch got serious.

"Okay, so she's bonkers. And she's impersonating an employee of your business. I'm not entirely sure where we are on the law with this. Certainly, there would be civil ramifications if you chose to go that route, but I don't know if what she's done thus far is criminal. We should talk to my dad about it. She'd have to actually do something that indicated she was trying to defraud somebody, if I understand it correctly. Not sure whether business cards would be considered crossing the line."

"It's creepy," Yaya said.

"I totally agree," Mitch nodded. "I think we need to give state patrol a heads up right now, even if she hasn't done anything else, just so Tally has something documented. Why would she do something like this?"

"It's a long story," Tally said. "Do you want a drink?"

"Nope, just had a pain pill," he recognized that she was trying to change the subject. "Spill it, Tally. And from the look on Yaya's face, why am I the last to know about this psycho?"

Tally and Yaya told Mitch the sordid story over dinner, stuffed peppers that Bonnie had left warming in a crockpot on the counter. Mitch kept having to ask them to stop laughing because he couldn't understand them, and Tally almost choked to death on a piece of pepper when Yaya was describing her crawl across the shop's back room to avoid Brenda peeking through the window.

"And you didn't tell me about this why?" Mitch was trying not to sound annoyed. He wasn't laughing.

"Because I forgot."

"How could you possibly forget this whole thing?"

"When we got home, it looked like all the cops in the entire state were having a party at our house. It slipped my mind in the moment."

"Understandable," Mitch allowed. "But it's been a few days."

"And in that time, I've done four potential client calls, and countless other things, after work because we're scrambling to make weddings happen with me out so much," Tally explained.

"I'm sorry." Mitch felt terrible for mucking up her schedule at the wrong time of year.

"Stop it. Don't be dumb. I just meant that I'm sure I would have told you the story at some point in the near future, we just haven't had much sit around and chat time. I guess I didn't file Brenda in the important category."

"I get it."

"You probably should have told him," Yaya said, throwing Tally under the bus.

"Thanks."

"C'mon Tally, I told you don't be driving the golf cart while that crazy bride is on this island," Yaya pointed out. Tally flipped her the bird.

"Excellent point," Mitch agreed. "If you'd told me about this, we'd have been keeping the blinds shut a heck of a lot more, too. And I would have told the guys to keep an eye out.

"Fortunately, you have the security system I installed for you after the last nightmare, and you will start using it again. Somebody got lazy," he said the last in an annoying sing-song voice.

"Fine," Tally wasn't going to argue because it would be stupid. He wasn't wrong. She didn't bother turning the system on and she didn't like having the cameras running all the time. It icked her out. But if there was something weird going on, she wouldn't take chances to stand on principle. "I'll use it."

"I'm not going anywhere for another week or so," he pointed out. "So you don't have to keep it armed all the time. But we should turn those exterior cameras back on in the front and the back."

Tally made a face, but she didn't argue. They'd both had some close calls in the past year and she definitely didn't want to take unnecessary chances.

Chapter 39

The welcome party for Jessica Crabb and Marshal Taylor had a fun golf theme. The groom had played on the University of Georgia golf team and competed on Jekyll Island numerous times. The gentlemen in the wedding party would all be golfing in the afternoon. They would end up at Tribuzio's Grille on the golf course clubhouse that served as a 19th Hole.

Tribuzio's, a family-owned restaurant, had done a beautiful spread on their patio facing the golf course, with tons of blackened wild Georgia shrimp and other favorites of the groom, who'd been coming to the island for years with his family. They usually stayed on St. Simons Island next door, but they always golfed on Jekyll. The bar set up on the patio outside featured signature cocktails such as a "Happy Gilmore" and a "Sam Snead."

Interestingly, the bride wasn't into golf, at all. But Marshal and Jessica had explained to Tally on their first planning call that he got to make all the decisions for the Saturday party and Jessica got to make all the decisions for their wedding on Sunday. Tally had figured it wouldn't stick, but it did. Jessica's contribution to the theme was a cute Lilly Pulitzer golf dress with new Michael Kors tennis shoes.

Tally had given Kayla Sunday off instead of Saturday because Kayla had done all the golf party planning with the groom, and she had come up with the décor. Some of it looked simple but Tally knew from experience that it would be better if the person who created the plan executed it.

***

Interestingly, there was less detail required for her work at the wedding setup the next day. The house that Jessica and Marshal had rented had been built for entertaining. The two big decks were triple the square footage of the interior, and both levels had been retrofitted to also hold a tent, in case of inclement weather. That wouldn't be a problem this weekend, Tally knew. But it was good to know it was there – and how to work it with the cranks – if the heavens suddenly opened.

The wedding ceremony would be on the beach in front of the house – timed out perfectly with the tide schedule so that the bride and groom could get married with their feet in the wet sand and still accommodate dry guests on the beach. Then cocktails and dinner were being catered on the deck by a local restaurant. Dinner was to be a traditional lowcountry boil with shrimp, crab, crawfish, sausage and likely several other things found in local waterways. It would be served buffet-style and cleared early because the bride and groom were far more concerned about dancing and drinking than eating. They'd been clear about that with Tally and Kayla. They'd paid for an extra hour of the DJ and the bar so they could party until midnight, but they understood the house's location on a residential street meant the music would have to be turned down for the last hour of the party.

It wasn't a big group – only 50 guests – so it wouldn't be too bad. Everybody except the wedding couple was staying over at the Jekyll Ocean

Club and the hotel was running shuttles to and from the wedding venue to make life easier. The bride and groom had tried to book the Jekyll Ocean Club for the ceremony and reception, but their space was already booked out for a big tennis tournament that was in town. The date was more important than the actual venue to Jessica and Marshal – weirdly enough, it was also the wedding anniversary of both his parents and her parents, although they weren't married in the same year.

Working with that, the theme of the wedding and reception was "tradition." Jessica was wearing an updated version of the gown her mother had gone down the aisle in, and side-by-side pictures of both brides were on the table next to the guest book. They'd had big posters made out of both set of parents' cutting-the-cake pictures to display on stands on either side of Jessica and Marshal's wedding cake, which was stylistically supposed to be a combination of the two cakes. Jessica and her bridesmaids carried bouquets that were modeled after the ones that her future mother-in-law had carried. They were mostly yellow carnations and they were hideous. Jessica knew they were ugly but she thought it was hilarious. Tally wasn't sure it was the greatest idea but it was in-theme so she didn't argue with the bride about it. Besides, the picture of the groom's mother's wedding party holding the same hideous flowers on the favor table was hysterical. She looked forward to watching guests look at it and do a double-take. Not all ideas were good ideas.

The party on Saturday night went smoothly, and Kayla helped Tally load up all the supplies she'd need for the wedding day before they said goodnight. Yaya took all the flowers home with her in the Jeep because they'd get beaten up in the open golf cart. Kayla had promised she would follow Tally to make sure she got home okay. But when the girls got out to the six-person golf cart she'd left parked behind the shop that morning, they found two of the tires – left front and right back – were flat. It was hard to tell what happened in the dark, but Tally didn't think it looked spontaneous.

"Well fuck a duck," Tally muttered.

Kayla shook her head when she saw it. "Forget it. Load into my SUV and I'll take you home. We'll tell Mitch about it and let him decide next steps. You have a wedding tomorrow. Want me to come in and help? This sorta changes things up a little bit."

"Nah, just help me get all this stuff to the house and we'll switch it into the back of my Jeep in the driveway. This is weird but the timing could be coincidental."

Kayla gave her a look that said she didn't agree.

Chapter 40

"It's not fucking coincidental," Mitch said angrily and grabbed his phone. A second later, "Dad, it's me. I think somebody slashed the tires on Tally's golf cart behind the flower shop. Can you have somebody go look?"

His father must have replied because Mitch nodded in agreement and then said "thanks" before hanging up.

"What did he say?" Tally asked.

"He said he was on his way to my grandmother's anyway and he'll swing by Beach Village to see if he can tell what flattened the tires. And he said to be careful here."

"Okay."

"Did you activate the cameras like we talked about?"

"Um, no."

"Now would be a good time," Mitch suggested.

Yaya was sitting at the counter trying her best to disappear as she felt the tension climb in the room.

Tally spared her additional agony and pulled up the security system app on her phone to turn the exterior cameras back on.

"Front and back, please," Mitch said in a soft but assertive tone. She knew that sometimes he struggled not to use his trooper voice on her. Then again, sometimes she liked it.

This was not one of those times. "Okay, it's on. Front and back."

"Thank you."

The three of them ate dinner – leftover macaroni and cheese and stuffed peppers – and then Mitch flipped channels while Tally reviewed all of her lists for the next day. She had papers spread all over the dining room table when Tom knocked on the front door. Tally hopped up to let Mitch's dad in.

"Hi Tally," he greeted her, but he wasn't smiling.

"Come in, Tom. What did you find?"

"Somebody doesn't like you very much."

"Uh oh. I was hoping I was wrong."

"Nope," Tom said. "Somebody tore the hell out of those little tires. I don't know what they used but they didn't know what they were doing. Made a huge effort for something that should have been simple."

Tally didn't really care about Brenda's tire slashing skills, but she didn't want to be rude to Tom. Southern gentlemen had a way of slowly delivering information that required you to hold your tongue while they spilled the entire can of beans before they got to the actual point.

"Crap," Tally blurted. "Sorry."

"I'd say worse if it was my golf cart," Mitch said. "The cameras back there won't help us because the whole area is so dark. We should install some exterior lighting behind the shop."

"Great idea, Captain Hindsight," his father snarked.

"It's not his fault," Tally intervened. "We've only been in the shop for a few weeks. He's been busy installing new locks and signage and everything else for me in his free time, and then he got shot. So you can't blame him for me slacking on security."

"I think this is the first time something like this has ever happened on Jekyll Island, at least in my memory," Tom said.

"It happens on St. Simons Island," Mitch tried to soften the blow.

"That's not Jekyll," Tom sternly corrected him.

"I'm sorry. This is the second time that I've brought problems to the island that became yours to deal with," Tally felt genuinely bad that her own problems were going to sully the crime-free record of the beautiful state park.

"This isn't your fault," Tom, Mitch, and Yaya all said at the same time, speaking over each other. Then they all laughed.

"You just attract the nuts," Yaya said. "You attracted crazy in Vieques too. It's a talent of yours."

"Gee, thanks," Tally said.

The doorbell rang and Tom turned to let in two more troopers. He introduced them to Tally and Yaya and they sat down at the table to take a report. The women tried to describe Brenda in as much detail as possible, but she wouldn't be hard to find if she hadn't left Jekyll.

"Do you know where she's staying?" Tom asked.

"I didn't ask her," Tally said.

"Do you have her cell phone number?"

"I do." Tally reached for her phone, scrolled, and read off the number.

"It won't matter if we can't get a warrant for it and I'm not sure we have enough probable cause at this point – gotta make some calls." Tom started dialing.

"Hey dad, take a look at this," Mitch handed Tom the business card that Brenda had handed him earlier that day. He explained about the woman who had stopped by for Tally and left her business card.

"Our fingerprints are going to be all over it, but so are hers because she wasn't wearing gloves," Mitch said.

Tom asked Tally for a Ziplock baggie and then put on gloves before taking the business card from his son. He dropped it in the bag and then took a close look at it before handing it to one of the other troopers who was already filling out a form to attach to it.

"I take it you didn't hire this person?" he asked.

"Absolutely not. She's a former client from hell that showed up wanting a job earlier this week. It's a long story – she had two different grooms," the troopers all looked at each other strangely. "But that's not important now. She tried to get me to hire her and when I didn't, she threw a screaming fit outside Jekyll Market."

"Then the market will probably have it on their security footage," Tom said.

"Probably," Tally agreed. "But no, I didn't hire her, I never offered her a job or even looked at her resume. We sorta fired her as a client a few years ago because she's crazy. Isabelle said something like maybe she should become a wedding planner – it was meant in snark – and this crazy bride took her literally. And she insisted I had to hire her. The more insistent she got, the more I wanted to get away from her."

"And then we all hid from her back in the flower shop with the lights off," Yaya added.

Mitch glared at Tally. "And you never thought to mention hiding in the back of your new business?" He looked really miffed.

"I didn't intentionally not tell you, it just didn't come up that night and I forgot about it. Brenda didn't come back to the shop so I forgot to mention it and never told you. But I meant to. And I should have," she said in a more appeasing tone.

Mitch raised one eyebrow at her. She gave him a pouty look and he winked.

"Has she ever threatened you?" Tom asked.

"Only when she was yelling at me for not hiring her and she threatened to put me out of business. I think maybe she sent some threatening emails to Isabelle back when we fired her as a client, but that would have been years ago in Puerto Rico."

Tally provided all the details of her recent interaction with Brenda, and an abbreviated explanation of her professional history with the former client, to the troopers and they took it all down on paper. It was the middle of the night and she was completely exhausted by the time they finished taking the report and left. Mitch hadn't made it through the entire interview. When he started looking droopy, his father ordered him back to bed. Yaya had already snuck into her bedroom by that time, and Tally was hitting the point of diminishing returns.

"Be extra aware of your surroundings for the next few days. Maybe she committed the vandalism and then left the island and you won't hear from her again. Or it could be a sign of escalation," Tom warned. "If she's staying on the island, we'll find her."

"I sort of hope you don't. I'd be happy to never ever have to see her again. Seriously."

"Either way, lock up tight when I leave and be more alert than you usually are until we figure out what's going on here."

"I will. Thanks for everything," she told Mitch's father as he let himself out the front door.

Tally felt drained. It was the middle of the night and she had a wedding the next day. She walked through the beach house turning off lights, and then went into Etah's bedroom to find Mitch completely zonked out with COPS playing on the television. She turned it off and hit the light switch.

She made sure she had two wake-up alarms set before she finally let herself curl up on the other side of the bed. Tally was asleep before her head hit the pillow.

Chapter 41

Tally slept well, and when she woke up to her first alarm, she found Yaya sitting on the front porch drinking coffee in her pajamas.

"Good morning," Tally greeted her, stepping out onto the deck with her own coffee.

"Beautiful day for a wedding," Yaya smiled.

"I love springtime here. Beach weather in the daytime and sweatshirts at night."

Yaya had her lists on the table in front of her.

"Have we found anything we forgot yet?" Tally asked.

"Not yet. But there's time. I think I brought all the flower supplies home last night."

"Mitch said we could use his truck if we needed it, because of the golf cart and all."

"Do you think we'll need it?" Yaya asked. "I figured we could just do two loads if we needed to. It's just a few houses away."

"I figured the same, just wanted to put it out there in the universe in case we needed another vehicle today."

"Gotcha."

Tally made lunch for Mitch, who was just starting to stir around noon, and then she joined Yaya and the setup crew down the street. None of the chairs could be set up for the ceremony until the tide dropped, but everything was staged as close as possible. Most of the decorating had been done at the house already thanks to Yaya's instructions to her team. The favor table was set up inside by the exit and the guest book was staged inside too, just in case the weather turned on them.

The bride and her girlfriends were doing their own hair and makeup in the master bedroom and Tally popped in to check on them. Everybody was happy and, she thought, slightly drunk. But nobody needed anything from her and she took the opportunity to run home and change into her wedding outfit before things went sideways. She'd learned long ago to get dressed for events as early as possible. If she put it off, something cata-strophic would happen that required the wedding planner's full attention and she might not be ready when the guests started to arrive at the venue.

Joe Moody was visiting Mitch, with his wife Carly, when Tally returned to her aunt's house. She saw them through the glass door and set an alarm on her phone – she would only be able to chat for a few minutes because she didn't want to risk being late getting back to the wedding venue – but she was excited to finally meet Carly.

"I was starting to wonder if you really existed!" Tally called to the woman sitting on her couch.

"Same here," Carly replied, getting up and heading toward her.

The women embraced.

"I feel like I've known you forever," Carly told Tally.

"Yeah, it's weird."

"It's that cop wife life thing."

"I'm still learning that," Tally gave her new friend a meaningful look.

"I'll give you the cheat sheet," Carly promised.

The two couples sat and visited for about 30 minutes before the alarm on Tally's phone went off and she took her leave to get ready for the wedding.

"It's a royal blue wedding," she explained to her guests.

"What does that mean?" Joe asked.

"Everybody except the bride is supposed to wear royal blue. Including our staff."

"Why?" he asked.

"Because that's what the clients wanted," Tally shrugged and laughed. "I've been doing this so long that few things inspire me to ask 'why' anymore. That's kinda sad. But it's not our first royal blue wedding, so at least I didn't have to run out and buy something like last time." She rolled her eyes.

***

When Tally returned to the living room a little while later in a blue dress, Mitch was telling Joe and Carly about her golf cart tires.

"Hey Tally, I forgot to tell you that Dad called and said they hadn't found a Brenda Fogel registered anywhere on the island. And there were about 40 unidentified rental cars in and out of the gates yesterday," Mitch said.

"This place really redefines 'gated community,' doesn't it?" Joe chuckled. "Cameras and a pay booth at the gate. That'll discourage most miscreants."

"There's no crime on Jekyll," both Tally and Mitch said at the same time. Then they laughed.

"Jinx, you owe me a Coke," Mitch said first.

"Speaking of that, do you need anything from me before I take off? Bride goes down the aisle in an hour and I need to go make sure everything is on track," Tally explained and held up a hanger with a dry cleaning bag. "And I'm taking Yaya's royal blue dress up to her, so I need to get going."

"I'm good. Joe and Carly brought me dinner and they're going to stay and hang out for a little bit longer. Then I'll just watch TV til you get home. Bonnie is home, too, if I need anything," Mitch said.

Tally thanked the other couple and she and Carly exchanged cell phone numbers. She kissed Mitch goodbye and then left for the wedding without further ado.

Chapter 42

The Crabb/Taylor wedding was nearly perfect. The weather was good, the tide was low, the wedding party was where they were supposed to be when they were supposed to be there, and the vendors were ready to go early. The ceremony was romantic – and seamless – and all the chairs were stacked back up on the catwalk before the tide came in.

Jessica and Marshal had warned their wedding planners that they had a party crowd, so Tally wasn't shocked when the caterers had to send a runner for more booze during the buffet dinner. Caterers tried to guess what they needed to bring but, frequently, the wedding groups surprised them. Die-hard vodka/tonic drinkers might spend an entire destination wedding weekend sucking down rum punches.

The bride and groom appeared to be a little drunk when Tally went over to warn them the toasts were about to begin, but it turned out that Jessica and Marshal were in great shape compared to their wedding guests. Tally thought, not for the first time, that any guest giving a toast should have to pass a breathalizer first. Legally drunk? Sit down, nobody trusts you.

Tally had the pre-planned list of guests who had been invited to give a toast. The first person on the list was the best man, Marshal's older brother,

Johnny. She handed him the microphone and reminded him to begin by introducing himself.

"Hey everybody!" Johnny said into the microphone much too loudly. "You guys know me, but if you don't, I'm the groom's big brother."

It sounded like there were significantly more than the actual 50 wedding guests in attendance when all of the groom's friends began hooting, stomping on the floor, and banging on the dinner tables.

Johnny's toast was a hot mess, full of obscenities and inappropriate references. Tally watched the bride put her hand over her face and turn crimson at least twice before she hooked an arm around Johnny and guided him back into his seat as she rescued the microphone. The bride's father was no better – actually, he might have been worse. He was so drunk that you would have sworn he was speaking a different language when he gave his toast. But the maid of honor took the prize.

She took the microphone from Tally and began her toast by announcing, "I had him first, ya know." Then she launched into a long and convoluted story about how she had dated Marshal in high school but then Jessica met him in college. The way she phrased things left everyone in the audience wondering how serious things might have been between the maid of honor and the groom, and Jessica was not smiling. She hadn't want to hear her groom declared her best friend's "sloppy seconds" at her own wedding.

Tally went over to the DJ and consulted him on the remaining list of "must play" songs. They chose one guaranteed to get all of the wedding couple's friends back out onto the dance floor. Then Tally rescued the microphone from the maid of honor, who was in the process of telling a story about going to the Homecoming dance with the groom. She caught a grateful look from Jessica as she brought the speeches to an end and the first beats of the Black Eyed Peas "I Gotta Feeling" came up on the sound system. As predicted, the drunk bridesmaids rushed the dance floor squealing, dragging some of the groomsmen with them. Disaster averted, the bride followed her friends, pulling her groom by the hand with a smile on her face.

***

The bride and groom cut a small wedding cake an hour later, and Tally and Yaya helped themselves to some of the royal blue cupcakes topped with the couples' new monogram – MTJ. Tally snagged a couple bottles of water and the wedding planners scooted up the back stairs to the upper deck that had emptied out when the dance floor filled.

Tally and Yaya parked themselves on a built-in bench along the railing with a good view of the dance floor and watched the bridal party get their groove on to the "Grease" remix that was on every wedding playlist ever made.

"This was an easy one," Yaya commented.

"It's not over yet. Don't jinx us," Tally warned. "I'll call Isabelle and tattle on you."

They both giggled but it wasn't an idle threat. Tally was very superstitious.

She texted Mitch to see how he was feeling and he replied that his dad was there hanging out with him.

"Let's do the upstairs teardown before we go back down," Tally suggested. "Nobody is coming back up here tonight." It was almost 11 pm and many of the older guests had left after the cupcakes were served. The DJ had already lowered the volume on the music and while everybody was still having fun, the energy level of the group was visibly dropping.

Tally blew out candles in tall glass vases – the better to keep them lit in a breeze on the deck – and carried all the vases over to the table by the staircase. She pulled two plastic tubs out of a guestroom where she'd stashed them during setup and carefully loaded the vases back into their cardboard boxes within the tub. By the time she was finished, Yaya had almost finished picking up all the little royal blue plastic crystals that were sprinkled all over all the flat surfaces.

"I hate shit like this," Yaya mumbled, dropping a handful of the crystals into a Ziplock bag. "It's tacky and a pain in the ass."

Tally rolled her eyes – almost every bride had something little and annoying in her décor – and held out her hand for the bag. She put it in one of the tubs and left them stacked at the top of the staircase for the teardown crew to load.

"Next weekend is going to be worse. Rainbow water beads for that big gay wedding at Jekyll Ocean Club," Tally pointed out.

"Nah, that's okay because we're at a hotel. They're doing most of the cleanup. I'll just tell them to dump the beads after the event unless you want to try to reuse them," Yaya said.

"How much are they per pack?"

"We bought cases so it ends up being about 35 cents a vase, I think."

"Fuck it, toss them. They'd be a bigger pain in the ass to store than they're worth," Tally determined.

"We always kept them in Vieques," Yaya said. She wasn't arguing, just making sure Tally remembered.

"Yeah, because we couldn't buy them on Vieques. We had to order them from the real world and have them shipped in. So we kept them because we didn't make a profit on them until we'd used them a few times. Here we are charging them for all the materials, plus a markup."

"We could put them in arrangements in the front window for the next week – add a nice pop of color," Yaya suggested.

"If you want to deal with the mess, go for it. That's your baby." The flower business was proving to be quite profitable out of the gate and Tally was trying to let Yaya make most of the important decisions. She was the one who had to fill the window with sellable arrangements from wedding leftovers, not Tally.

Chapter 43

On Monday morning, Mitch's brother, Pete, showed up at the flower shop with his older son, Nate, to pick up Tally's golf cart.

"Mitch called me," Pete said by way of explanation after he knocked on the back door of the shop.

Tally watched as Pete and Nate loaded the wounded golf cart onto a trailer.

"We're just going to change the tires, but it's easier to do it at my grandmother's house," Pete explained. "And that way Mitch can sit and pretend to supervise my work."

"Oh, I see how it is," Tally laughed.

When she got back to the house in the early afternoon, her golf cart was sitting in her driveway with four inflated tires. It also appeared to have been freshly washed. She found Mitch and Pete sitting on the back deck with beers.

"The cart looks great. Thanks. How much do I owe you for the new tires?

"No cost. Dad had extras in his garage. We put the new ones in the back and old ones in the front. You should be good to go for a while unless you piss off somebody else," Pete joked.

Tally gave him a look but kept her retort to herself because of the kid standing next to him.

"And you washed my golf cart, too? I feel spoiled. Thank you so much, Nate," she handed Mitch's nephew a five-dollar bill.

"Where's my tip?" Pete asked.

"Ask your wife," Mitch suggested and his older brother laughed.

"I'm going to go in and change and get a glass of wine. I'll bring you guys out some munchies when I return."

"Good woman," Pete said.

"Your grandmother made it all. I'm just putting it in serving dishes," Tally admitted.

She wished she could take a long shower but she didn't want to be rude, so Tally changed clothes quickly and returned to the deck with a tray full of snacks that included Bonnie's Chex mix and a plate of celery filled with peanut butter and raisins. Yuck, she thought.

"Ants on a log!" Pete laughed when he saw them. "That's the best."

"Oh wow," Mitch agreed. "I haven't had these since I was a kid."

"Well, Bonnie left a whole Tupperware full of them in the fridge, so please help yourselves. I'm not eating them. Not my thing," Tally said.

That wouldn't be a problem because Mitch and Pete were already scarfing them down.

"She brought over some of her pimento cheese too," Tally told them. "I was thinking we could have pimento cheese sammies and soup for dinner tonight."

"Sounds good to me," Mitch said.

"You staying for dinner, Pete?" Tally asked.

"I can't, but thanks for the invite. Nate and I are expected at Bonnie's for dinner and I need to get over there before she starts ringing the bell for me."

Bonnie's bell was legendary. She would stand out on the porch and ring it when she wanted her boys to come home. It could be heard on the beach and at every house on the street. Depending on the weather, sometimes the sound carried a lot farther.

They said goodbye to Pete and Tally walked him out.

"He's looking good," Pete said.

"Yeah, he is. So much better."

"You're part of that," Mitch's brother told her.

"Not sure I can take any credit, but I do love him," Tally said in a serious tone.

"Can't think of another girl I'd rather have my little brother in love with."

"Aw," Tally blushed. She was far more used to being teased by the Durham boys than receiving compliments.

She locked the door behind Pete and went to the kitchen to refill her wine glass. She brought it out to the front porch with her and sat down next to Mitch.

"How are you really feeling?" she asked.

"Tired. But the headache is gone. I haven't had a headache in two days."

"That's amazing."

"I know. I feel good enough to go into the office for some debriefing and paperwork tomorrow, I think," Mitch said.

"Could you put it off for a couple more days?"

"Probably. Why?"

"Because Yaya and I decided today that from now on, the flower shop will be closed on Tuesdays. At least until we can afford some full-time clerks to give us a break. She and I need a full day off from that at least once a week. And Mondays never work because we're always playing catch-up from everything we ignored during the previous wedding," Tally explained.

"Makes sense," Mitch agreed.

"And so I was hoping to spend this Tuesday with you."

"Aha," he said. "I suppose that could be arranged. What do you want to do together?"

"I was hoping to spend the entire day in bed cuddling with you," Tally said in a husky voice.

Mitch smiled at her. "Why do we have to wait until Tuesday?" he asked.

"We don't."

Chapter 44

Yaya took the Jeep before Tally and Mitch were awake on Tuesday morning to go apartment hunting on St. Simons Island. She was looking on Jekyll, too. But there were a lot more options for a lot less money on the next island over. She wouldn't mind the commute – the view from the four bridges and two causeways between Jekyll and St. Simons was well worth the effort. But spring was the wrong time to be looking for an affordable place to live on the coast of Georgia. Tally and Etah had told her she was welcome to stay with them as long as she liked, but Yaya had a feeling that if she moved out, Mitch might stay after his convalescence and she didn't want to be a factor that played into that decision.

She left a note on the kitchen counter for Tally and shut the door quietly when she left the house. They really needed some alone time and she wondered if it would be too rude to put a "go away" sign on the front door. Probably.

Tally woke up long before Mitch and read the note from her houseguest as she made coffee. Then she sat down at the dining room table with her laptop to catch up on email and see what was happening in the world before he got up. There was an email from Brenda Fogel. She felt her stomach drop.

"Hi Tally! I'm really looking forward to my first day working for you tomorrow. Should I meet you at your house or the office?" it read.

She's delusional, Tally thought. This chick is genuinely crazy.

She wondered if she should wake up Mitch and tell him about the email, but ultimately decided it could wait. Brenda's imaginary first day wasn't for another 24 hours. She printed out two copies so she'd have them.

Tally quickly responded to several potential clients, offering them dates and times for a free consultation on their wedding plans, and then moved on to client emails.

The big gay wedding group would be arriving on Jekyll Thursday so she started with emails from those grooms. She made some notes in their file, responded to both of them in one email. Tally kept referring to their event as the "Big Gay Wedding" because that was their theme. It was the title on their wedding invitations, it would be on signs at the entrance to their reception, and the phrase had been worked into their ceremony in several places.

Tally had hoped they'd make her life easy and use the same kind of rainbow roses she'd used for the Noahide wedding on Driftwood Beach, but it was not to be. The grooms decided rainbow roses were tacky. But putting a rainbow-colored variety of water beads in vases holding white roses was not tacky, according to the couple's style guide. Tally didn't think the Wizard of Oz wedding cake was tacky, just misplaced. It was cool and belonged at an 8-year-old's birthday party. At least they were going to get some interesting pictures out of it. The inside of it was rainbow.

She caught herself returning to the email from Brenda, over and over. It was creepy. Really creepy. She called Yaya and told her about it and her friend said it gave her goosebumps, too. Tally wished her luck house-hunting but told her to be super-alert in case she encountered the crazy former client.

When Mitch finally poked his head out of the bedroom just before noon, Tally practically pounced on him with the email.

"That is creepy," Mitch agreed after he'd read it. Tally made him coffee and put a piece of his grandmother's blueberry coffee cake on a plate in front of him while he texted his dad.

A few minutes later, he looked up. "Dad said they're going to send a detective over to talk to us later today."

"There goes our day in bed," Tally sighed. "Should I respond to the email from her and tell her to go rot in hell?"

"Let's wait and see what the detectives have planned first."

"I don't want her showing up at the flower shop tomorrow for some kinda of blowup," Tally told him. "Or here. I don't know what's worse."

"I know."

"She's crazy."

"Obviously. But she hasn't done anything criminal yet," he reminded her. "At least not that we can prove. I know we think she slashed your tires, but that's not enough. We have no evidence linking Brenda to it directly."

"So we do nothing?" she was getting frustrated.

"No, that's not what I said. She's escalating, too, if all of this is her. We just need to sit back and wait for her to do something that will get her locked up."

"Let's hope she doesn't decide to steal our flowers," Tally said, feeling a little bit of déjà vu.

"Ha!" Mitch laughed. "I was more concerned about the Jeep tires. Those are expensive to replace."

It was warm and sunny out and Tally spread towels on lounge chairs on the front deck for her and Mitch. She hung her pink wireless speaker off her chair and turned Pandora to Yacht Rock. She watched Mitch cringe at a few of the songs, but figured it was good for him. He'd never had any sisters. Time to get used to living with a woman. She wasn't giving up her angry chick CDs yet, either.

She went into her bedroom and came out wearing her yellow polka dot bikini. It was truly looking worse for the wear and she made a mental note to find a new, better one online. Mitch wouldn't notice the difference, but she knew it was his favorite bathing suit.

***

When the detectives arrived less than an hour later, Tally pulled on a coverup over her bathing suit before she answered the door. She invited the troopers in – they were both in casual clothing and she wondered if they'd come in to work just for this and had interrupted a day off, or if that was how they dressed all the time. She'd ask Mitch later.

The men all sat down at the dining room table and Tally poured glasses of sweet tea before joining them. They both knew Mitch and his dad, and they introduced themselves to Tally as Detectives Andy Johnson and Ted Johnson, no relation. Tally wasn't sure which one was which.

The detectives asked questions about her past relationship with Brenda and tried to pick every detail she knew about the woman out of her head. She really didn't know that much. But she stepped away to call Isabelle and see what she might have on hand.

Isabelle answered on the second ring, as if she'd been expecting to hear from Tally. Her former employee updated her on what had happened to her golf cart and the weird fraudulent business card and Isabelle was glad she had taken the time to hunt down Brenda's old file in the dead files box.

She'd already scanned it and said she was emailing it as they spoke. Tally thanked Isabelle and hung up.

When the email arrived, she handed her phone to one of the detectives and he forwarded the file to himself and some of his colleagues. Then he handed the phone back to Tally and told her to look through Brenda's file quickly and see if anything stood out.

Every client file was the same. They asked the same questions of every client regardless of the size or scope of their contract. Much of the information played into some aspect of what the company was providing in services. It was the handwritten notes that were the most interesting. Tally hoped there would be something helpful in Brenda's file.

Tally recognized her own handwriting on the forms that Isabelle had scanned in. That info would have been added to the online file after the conference call but the original version was much more enlightening. Tally had written "WTF?" in at least three places in the first few pages of the file.

The phrase "no groom = no contract" was written at the top of the first page and "cancelled per Isabelle" with a date at the bottom. Exactly what Tally had remembered.

"All her work contact info is there, but she said she doesn't work there anymore. If she ever did. I have no idea what's true," she told the detectives. "That was her home address in Virginia at the time of the contract but it's been several years. And we did everything via email. She told me she was moving here when she showed up and demanded a job. I didn't ask how far she'd gotten in that process so I don't know if she's already moved to Georgia."

That was a horrible thought and it was the first time it had occurred to Tally. Her goosebumps suddenly got goosebumps.

"Well, that's enough to get us started," the detective she thought was Andy said. "We'll be back in touch later today to let you know what, if anything, we found." He started to stand up and gather his things. His partner stood up with him.

"Should I reply to her email?" Tally asked. "I would like to avoid another public screaming match. And if she shows up at the flower shop, that's inevitable."

"Can you not go into the shop tomorrow?" the other detective asked.

"Only if we stay closed. Otherwise, Brenda might encounter Yaya and end up in the hospital."

Mitch snorted trying to hold in a laugh.

"Email her back and reiterate that you don't have a job for her and that you're not available to meet with her anywhere and then we'll see what happens. It doesn't sound like this woman will give up very easily," the detective she thought was Ted suggested. "Forward it to me when you hear back from her and then we can gameplan next steps."

They said goodbye to the detectives and went back into the kitchen.

"It's always an adventure with you, Tally," Mitch said in an amused voice.

"I never had a run-in with the police in my life before I got involved with you, Trooper Durham," she replied in a huffy voice as she carried used glasses and plates to the sink. "Maybe you've brought me some bad luck. Suddenly, everybody wants to ruin me."

"Ouch!" Mitch said, stopping Tally in her path. She thought his head was hurting but he was holding his chest. "That's like a knife to my heart," he said dramatically. "The very suggestion that all of this could be my fault. You're killing me, Tally."

She rolled her eyes at him and continued to clean up the kitchen.

A few hours later, after some playtime, a nap, and a long outside shower for them both, Mitch and Tally dressed to go out to dinner. She wore a short sundress and he rested his hand on her butt as she carefully applied a fresh bandage to the back of his head. The bruising and scrapes on his face had healed and, if it weren't for the bandage and the whacky way his hair was growing in around it, nobody would know he'd recently been shot in the head.

It was his first venture out of the house for anything other than a doctor's appointment and Mitch was looking forward to it. They were going just down the street to Driftwood Bistro because they had the best fried green tomatoes on the island and Mitch had a craving. Tally didn't care what they ate as long as it didn't arrive at her home in a casserole dish. She appreciated all of the food that family and friends had brought over but she was eager to eat something that didn't taste better the second time it was microwaved.

Before they left for the restaurant, Tally sat down at her laptop and replied to Brenda's message.

"Hi Brenda. You don't work for me and you never have. You are not welcome in the flower shop or at my home. If you show up tomorrow, we will have to call the police and have you arrested for trespassing on my property. Best wishes to you in your other ventures. Our business is concluded," Tally wrote.

She blind copied the message to the detectives and hit send, mentally crossing her fingers that the email would solve the problem, not make it worse.

Chapter 45

Brenda never replied to Tally's email, so everyone was walking on eggshells in the flower shop the next day. Tally was strung so tightly that she'd snapped at everybody, including Laurie, the mail carrier.

"As much shit as our clients send, you'd better be nicer to her," Yaya warned Tally.

"I know." Yaya wasn't wrong. Laurie was a lifeline for them.

"What's wrong with you?" Yaya asked.

"I'm waiting for the other shoe to drop."

"And you're stomping all over everybody who might help you catch it while you wait for it."

"I'm sorry."

"Then change up your attitude, *chiquita*. Your mood carries everyone in your business. When you're in a bad mood, we're all in a bad mood," Yaya warned.

"Seriously? That's a bit extreme."

"Well, you're a bit extreme and that's how it works around here."

Tally pondered that while she walked over to Ameris Bank to make a deposit. Yaya was right. She might as well have hired the crazy bitch if she was going to let Brenda's dark shadow ruin the whole day. Tally stopped in Jekyll Market and picked up some treats before she went back to the flower shop.

"You're right," she told Yaya when she got back. "Chocolate to make up for me being a jerk. I'm sorry."

"What did she bring us?" Kayla called from the back and then poked her head out front a moment later.

"Chocolate shortbread straws," Yaya read from the package.

"Yum! You're forgiven, Tally," Kayla said. She grabbed several of the locally-made cookies and disappeared back to her desk.

"I'm not as easy as she is," Yaya warned.

"I have Jack Daniels for you at home," Tally winked.

"See, you do know the way to my heart."

***

The detectives - "Johnson & Johnson," Tally called them in her head – stopped by the flower shop late in the afternoon to check on them.

"I haven't heard anything back on that email, and she didn't 'show up for work' today, thank God," Tally told them.

"That's good news. We tried to find an address or employer for her but just hit a lot of dead ends. She didn't rent the car from the agencies at the Jacksonville or Savannah airports, we've checked all of them. It's almost as if she doesn't exist, but we know she does," the older of the two Johnsons, Andy, told her.

"And we ran the fingerprints we found on the business card and only got two sets, you and Mitch. She must've been very careful when she handled it to give to Mitch," the younger detective added.

"Freaky," Kayla commented from her desk.

"No kidding," Tally agreed.

"Just keep your eyes open," Andy advised. "I noticed you parked the golf cart out front – that's smart. Lots of businesses have security cameras on the front side of their businesses. That's how we got these pictures of your friend, Brenda."

"She's not my friend," Tally muttered.

"If she was, we wouldn't be here," the detective agreed.

He pulled some printed images out of a file folder and showed them to Tally. Cameras had perfectly captured Brenda's Ursula face as she screamed at Tally's departing back in front of Jekyll Market.

"You can keep those," the younger detective – Ted – told them. "Maybe show them to the other business owners here in Beach Village and give them a heads up so they can keep an eye out for her. Show Bonnie and your other neighbors, too. Anybody who might encounter her on Jekyll."

"Great. We've got 200 wedding guests arriving on the island starting tomorrow for a Big Gay Wedding at Jekyll Ocean Club," Tally told the detectives.

"Show their desk staff and security, just in case she decides to make trouble for you. We've made sure to put up something in the Jekyll Island Authority breakrooms. They can't stop her unless she's doing something wrong, but if anybody sees her on Jekyll Island, they're supposed to alert the state patrol," Andy explained.

The island's population was tiny and the staff of the Jekyll Island Authority was bigger than the number of residents most of the year. Tally was impressed by their thinking. If Brenda was on the island, somebody would spot her.

Chapter 46

On Thursday morning, Kayla delivered the last of the welcome bags to the guests who would be staying in Crane Cottage, a beautifully restored home on Millionaires Row on the historic side of the island. The Jekyll Island Club Resort offered brides and grooms a neat dichotomy of options for their guests because it had two distinctly different sides with vastly different accommodations. The historic Jekyll Island Club Hotel, built by the likes of the Goodyears, Pulitzers, and Morgans in the early 1800s, was on the river side of the mile-wide island. The brand-new, modern Jekyll Ocean Club had opened on the beach side just a year earlier and was designed more in the style of a W Hotel, with muted lighting and a too-cool-for-school vibe in the lobby. Guests could pretty much choose which century they wanted to stay in.

Tally had planned her first wedding in Georgia at the Jekyll Ocean Club, just as the facility was opening, and it was a total success. She'd done a few more since then, but nothing as large as the Big Gay Wedding was going to be on Saturday.

Oliver Loomis and Simon Teller's wedding was one of the ones she'd saved from the Vieques Weddings slate of clients that were cancelled after

Hurricane Maria. Tally had reached out to the grooms after the storm and given them the option to continue their planning with her on Jekyll Island under the same contract or cancel their wedding altogether because nobody knew when Vieques would recover. Oliver and Simon lived in Atlanta, so as soon as Tally gave them the Jekyll Island option, they hopped in the car and came to check it out.

Tally had shown the grooms everything else on the island before she took them to the Jekyll Ocean Club. She had known that was really the only option for them – they wanted an uber-modern décor and upgrades on everything that just weren't possible in the centuries-old buildings on the historic side of the island. The grooms were just about ready to give up when they walked into the Jekyll Ocean Club.

"Is our date available? I need to know before I take another step," Simon stopped in the threshold and told Tally dramatically.

"It's available," Tally said. At that point, the ocean side of the hotel had only been open for a couple of months and they had loads of open wedding dates because the hotel had changed management mid-construction and the new bosses hadn't wanted to start taking large event bookings too far ahead.

"We'll take it," Simon said.

"We haven't even toured the hotel yet. This is the just the front desk."

"I don't care. It's the only thing remotely close to what we wanted," he said in a voice that dared Tally to tell him he couldn't have it. But she wasn't going to do that.

"Let's walk around the property and then we can have lunch on the patio and decide what you want to do," she suggested.

"That's a good idea," the other groom, Oliver, agreed. "Simon gets dramatic when he's hangry. But he never remembers to bring a snack."

"Duly noted," Tally said, and made a note on her clipboard. She wasn't kidding. The right notes to herself would mean she'd have a candy bar in her purse on their wedding day. Maybe two. Whatever it took to avoid a tantrum.

The Loomis/Teller wedding had been fun to plan, with Simon upgrading the upgrades on everything and Oliver complaining about the budget but not meaning it. Oliver hadn't told his fiancé "no" on anything and there were no upgrades left to request by the time Simon was done planning. The rental equipment company was bringing in lit, Lucite highboy tables for the Astor Roof Deck on top of the club and to use at the end of the pool deck. The bar they were setting up atop the hotel would also be lit in much the same way – it was coming from the same rental company. The hotel had its own highboy tables and a bar that were included in the wedding costs, but to make Simon happy, everything had to be "upgraded." It was fine with Tally – she was paid a percentage based on the cost of the overall wedding weekend – but it did make the planning a little bit more complicated to orchestrate so she earned every penny.

The color scheme for the wedding was largely rainbow, but Simon wanted neon lighting everywhere they could reasonably add it for the reception. And he wanted it in a few places that weren't very reasonable, too, like the bathrooms. The hotel had been more accommodating than Tally expected. They'd agreed to have their landscapers change the color of the bulbs for all the landscape lighting that was visible from the roof or pool deck for a small fee, and the general manager and Tally had chatted about having the wedding photographers get some really good pictures of it lit up so that they would be able to show it to future potential clients. The venue was really a flexible space but not every bride could imagine how it would look once it was decorated, lit, staged and ready to go. The more pictures they had to look at as examples, the better. Tally made a note to ask the grooms if the hotel could use the pictures on their website. Her own contract already included that clause, but she had a feeling the Jekyll Ocean Club would want to use them, too.

The wedding had a ton of little details, like the neon bathroom signs Kayla had tracked down at a vintage film prop rental place in Savannah. But the Jekyll Weddings team was more than ready. Executing a wedding at a big hotel was so much easier than setting up everything at a private home like they had a week earlier.

Even though the Loomis/Teller wedding was four times the size of the Crabb/Taylor wedding, the Big Gay Wedding would be far less physical labor for the wedding planning staff than the 50-person beach wedding had been. Nobody had to haul chairs around because the hotel staff would do it if Tally gave them the schedule. When they arrived at the hotel with all of the flowers, they could pull up out front and use the hotel's luggage carts to carry it inside. All the flower boxes and prep tubs could be hidden in the back at a hotel so Tally's team didn't have to inconvenience wedding guests by hiding supplies in the rooms they were staying in. Everything was easier at a hotel than a private venue and Tally was always more relaxed going into those wedding weekends.

Simon and Oliver had chosen three different live musical groups for their wedding – a harpist for the ceremony, an acoustic guitarist for cocktails, and a band that had traveled to Jekyll from Atlanta to play the wedding. The grooms knew one of the band members and the performance was his wedding gift to them, but they still had to pay for the whole band's accommodations and expenses, which added another hefty chunk to the budget. Oliver wouldn't say no to Simon on anything and Tally just smiled as she watched her fee skyrocket, too. She loved gay weddings.

Isabelle had claimed that gay men were her favorite weddings and Tally would have to agree. They had the biggest budgets – double income, no kids – and many of them had spent their entire lives dreaming about marrying a man but never thought they would be able to. The legalization of gay marriage made it all possible and most of the gay couples who'd hired them on Vieques had hosted big bashes. Jekyll didn't attract the gay clientele in the same way the little Puerto Rican island had, but Tally felt certain that she'd be able to use the pictures from Simon and Oliver's events in her marketing materials to lure more gay clients to the gem of the Golden Isles.

All of Simon and Oliver's events were being held at the Jekyll Ocean Club or they were providing transportation to the venue so that everybody could get really drunk and nobody had to drive. The hotel ran shuttles between the oceanfront hotel and the historic hotel accommodations on the other side of the island, and they'd promised to keep them going on the wedding night until the last of the after-party guests had departed.

Kayla and Tally met at the hotel on Thursday afternoon and were impressed by the welcome setup in the grooms' suite. The boys were due to arrive within the hour and management was more than ready.

"Everything about this wedding is over-the-top. We wanted to meet their expectations from the outset," Olivia Reynolds, the resort's food and beverage director, said with a smile.

"Yeah, but wow," Kayla said, unable to find a better word. "This is amazing."

A small chocolate fountain bubbled on the sideboard of sitting area in the grooms' suite. There was a display of delectable cake and cookie bites beside it for dipping. There were skewers of berries and a bowl of freshly whipped cream, too. Tally spotted bottles of champagne in ice buckets staged at least three places in the room.

"Okay, I'm hungry. Let's go," she told Kayla, only half joking. Tally wanted to skedaddle before the grooms arrived or she'd miss dinner at

Bonnie's house. Once they had ahold of her, she'd be trapped greeting all of the arriving wedding guests. And that was Kayla's problem tonight, not Tally's.

Kayla stayed behind at the Jekyll Ocean Club when Tally jumped in the golf cart to run back to the flower shop. She'd promised Yaya that she'd check in to see if she needed help before she called it quits for the day.

Chapter 47

Yaya had been invited to join them at Bonnie's for dinner, but she'd begged off. Tally didn't blame her. She didn't get much alone time in the house since Mitch arrived, and with all of his friends and family stopping by all the time, it felt pretty crowded these days. The girls drove home from the shop together and then Tally ran across the street to try and get some of Bonnie's mini crabcakes before Mitch and his brothers ate them all.

She hadn't seen Mitch's two oldest brothers very often since she'd been back in Georgia. They were both divorced, and neither of them had children, so they weren't at their mom's house with the kids all the time like Pete and Robin were.

Tommy, named for his father, was almost 10 years older than Mitch. He and Frank were considered Irish twins because the second Durham baby arrived barely 12 months after the first. Pete came along a few years later, and then Mitch was a surprise baby when Tommy was in the 5th grade. He and Tally were born the same summer.

Pete was a sergeant with the nearby Glynn County Police Department, and Tommy and Frank were state troopers, like Mitch and their dad. They were both assigned to posts in Atlanta, and they'd shared a house there together ever since Frank and his wife split up. Mitch went to visit them in Atlanta for boys' nights more than Tommy and Frank came to Jekyll Island, so it was an occasion when all four of the Durham boys were under the same roof at the same time. It had happened several times lately, because Tommy and Frank raced down lights and sirens after Mitch was shot in the head, and then stayed for several days until he'd gotten the all-clear from the doctors. But those hadn't been fun family dinners while they were waiting to find out if their little brother would be okay.

Now that Mitch was recovering just fine, his older brothers were back to harassing him like usual. Their latest schtick was giving him a hard time for failing to duck after his partner was shot.

Bonnie's house was a total zoo when Tally arrived.

"Did you actually stick your head up higher after Joe was shot?" Frank was asking Mitch as Tally walked in. "That's what I heard."

"You're such an asshole," Mitch replied. Then, "Stop it, you guys," when he saw Tally arrive. "Hey babe, how's the wedding going?"

Tally said hello to everybody, hugged the appropriate people, and then unapologetically helped herself to several mini crabcakes from the platter on the coffee table before she sat down next to Mitch on the loveseat. She'd been sharing meals with Durham boys her entire life. It was eat or be eaten.

When Bonnie got up to finish dinner preparations in the kitchen, Roberta, Robin and Tally went with her to help. They made quick work of it, pulling pans of baked beans and macaroni out of the oven to put beside the big platter of fried chicken on the buffet.

Halfway through dinner, Tally's phone vibrated.

Caller ID showed it was the general manager of the hotel calling so Tally excused herself from the table and went into the front hallway to answer it.

"What's up?" she greeted Mayra, hoping upon hope that her wedding guests were behaving themselves.

"Last I heard, everything was great over at Ocean Club. This is something else. Is it a bad time?" Mayra asked.

"Never for you. Whatcha need?" Tally asked, relieved.

"I got a resume for the open wedding planner position here at the hotel, and the applicant claims she's currently employed by you."

"I only have two employees. Kayla and Yaya. Who ya trying to poach?"

"That's what I thought," Mayra said with a sigh. "I'd never heard you mention this Brenda woman."

Tally groaned aloud. "Of course, that's who it would be. You won't believe this one." She stepped outside onto the porch to give Mayra a brief rundown on Brenda.

By the time she finished explaining about the multiple grooms, she and Mayra were both laughing.

"So, she's just completely bonkers?" Mayra chuckled. "That's a new one. I've never had half the couple keep the date and look for a replacement to marry."

"It's nuts."

"Never a dull moment with you, Tally."

"Hey, this isn't my fault," she defended herself. "But I'm sorry that she's doing this to you. Total waste of your time. Seriously, try not to piss her off when you turn her away. We think she slashed the tires on my golf cart."

"She didn't!"

"Somebody did. Two of the tires were shredded to pieces a couple nights ago outside the shop while we were at an event," Tally explained.

"I've never heard of anything like that happening here." The hotel manager sounded shocked.

"Nothing like that has ever happened on Jekyll before. I'm mortified that I attracted this to the island. They're probably going to kick me out of the citizens' association," she joked.

"Her resume says she worked for you in Vieques, too," Mayra told Tally.

"You're joking! She never worked for us down there. She was just a bad client. Can you email me a copy of her resume? I should probably give copies to the police and Isabelle."

The whole situation made Tally livid, but Mayra was amused.

"You have to laugh about this, Tally. Otherwise, it'll make you crazy. It's great material for a wedding planner tell-all someday."

"Could you hold off on responding to her until after the wedding this weekend?" Tally asked. "I don't want to set her off."

"That's an excellent idea. You've got a huge group over at Jekyll Ocean Club. No reason to rock the boat on this property while that's underway," the hotel manager agreed. "How are things going with the Big Gay Wedding grooms?"

"The welcome setup in their room was to die for. Kudos to Olivia," Tally said. "Kayla said the boys were happy as clams at check-in. She's handling their welcome party tonight and if anything is less than stellar, I'll hear about it. These grooms are genuinely fun guys so unless we forget something they have already paid for, I think they'll be pretty easygoing during their events," Tally predicted.

"Are you trying to jinx us?" Mayra sounded perturbed.

"Nope, just saying that I wasn't worried about tonight."

"Well, bite your tongue and keep those thoughts to yourself. I don't want to hear how well it all went til the last guest has left the island."

Tally rolled her eyes but didn't argue with Mayra. They said goodbye and before she returned to the table, she popped off a text to Kayla warning her to keep an eye out for Brenda at the welcome event. Her former client was popping up everywhere and it seemed like nothing was off limits.

When Tally returned to the dinner table, Mitch was filling in his brothers on the whole backstory of how she met Brenda.

"So she had a wedding planned, she just needed a groom?" Tommy asked. "That's creepy."

"Can you say big red flag?" Frank joked in a knowing tone. Then he and Tommy high-fived each other on something that was apparently an inside joke.

"Yeah, yeah, yeah," Tally said. "It's all fun and games til the crazy bride stalks you from Puerto Rico to Georgia and starts handing out your business cards."

Then she sat back down at the table and told them all about the resume Brenda had given to Mayra.

Chapter 48

The Big Gay Wedding's welcome party had been a complete success, but Kayla was frowning over her clipboard when Tally arrived at the flower shop the next morning.

"What's up, buttercup?" Tally asked with a grin. She'd slept well and was in a great mood.

The flower shop looked more like an actual business and less like the construction zone that it had been for the past few months. All three women were wearing uniform t-shirts with shorts. Kayla appeared to be double-checking her prep tubs for the reception and Yanira was working on flower arrangements. Tally thought it looked like all was right in the world.

"Simon was a little pissy with me this morning because their breakfast wasn't sent up to their room. Remember how they submitted all those breakfast orders ahead for every day? Anyway, I called to see what happened and the front desk said that the order had been cancelled," Kayla said.

"That's weird. But so was ordering several days of breakfast before they'd even checked in. Oliver said Simon read about it in some wedding magazine. Anyway, the hotel is probably just confused. Talk to somebody about it in person when we're over there today."

"Are you going with me to help load shuttles?" Kayla asked hopefully. The wedding guests would all be boarding open-air trolleys for afternoon tours of Jekyll and nearby St. Simons Island.

"Sure, why not? Then I can hear all about how fabulous the welcome party was."

"It was pretty great. Those fire dancers were the bomb. I got some awesome pics for us."

"I'm so glad the weather played ball," Tally said. It was dicey to let clients spend a lot of money on something that could not be moved inside if the weather didn't cooperate.

"Me too. I've got the coolers loaded for the trolleys and the boxes of snack bags to hand out as they board. I figured we'd add the ice to the coolers over at the hotel so we can lift them," Kayla explained.

"Good idea. Working smarter, not harder. I like it."

Tally followed Yaya into her office and the women reviewed three pending flower bids that needed to be sent out before the end of day. Yaya didn't need her approval anymore, but she was getting backed up and wanted Tally to help expedite the stuff on her desk. Word of mouth had gotten them quite a few weddings that weren't using their planning services, and a few from nearby St. Simons Island. Yaya's work station was piled high with flower catalogs, bridal magazines, and client files. There were also lot of ribbon snips and other detritus from her working on bouquets at her desk while she talked on the phone.

When they were finished with the flower bids, Tally told Yaya about the call she'd received from Mayra and forwarded a copy of the bogus resume to her and Isabelle.

"What's the end game here?" Yaya asked.

"What do you mean?"

"She's not doing all of this to get a job. She has to know, in whatever rational part of her brain still exists, that you're never going to hire her after all of this. So, what does she get out of it?" Yaya asked.

"I have no friggin idea. Maybe she wants to put me out of business."

"I don't think so. If she was trying to hurt you, she wouldn't be pretending to work for you. Imitation is the sincerest form of flattery. I just wish we knew somebody who knew her in real life – outside of weddings – that could tell us what's going on," Yaya said.

"The state police have been investigating and they couldn't track her down," Tally said. "I don't know how hard they tried, to be fair. But she's not easy to find online. She's not on social media at all, which I find suspicious. She seems more like the type who would have multiple accounts."

"Agreed. But don't you have a wedding event to get to?" Yaya asked. "Stop letting Brenda take up so much space in your head rent-free. You've got clients on the island."

"Ugh," Tally looked at her watch. "Yeah, we need to go in a minute. You're right. It's just hard to put her out of my mind and keep an eye out for her at the same time."

"I bet it is."

"You should probably lock the front door while Kayla and I are gone, just in case Brenda shows up here," Tally suggested.

"Girl, I hope she shows up here when nobody else is around. I'll take care of the problem once and for all," Yaya declared.

Tally started to reply with a quip but stopped herself. Yaya was serious.

"Just don't get caught," Tally wasn't kidding either.

That was when Kayla interrupted.

"You ready to go?" she asked Tally from the doorway.

"Sure."

"Do you guys need help loading?" Yaya asked.

"Nope, it's already in the Jeep. But thanks," Kayla said.

"I like this girl," Yaya told Tally.

"Me too."

Chapter 49

The party was in full swing at Jekyll Ocean Club when the wedding planners arrived, despite the fact that it wasn't yet noon. From the look of things, the grooms, and most of their guests, had taken advantage of the bottomless mimosas the hotel offered for breakfast.

Simon and Oliver were both visibly tipsy when they boarded the trolley and one guest had to bow out and go back to her room for a nap. Kayla gave the lady her cell phone number and offered to help her hook back up with the group when she was feeling better. They were headed out on an excursion that would last into the evening hours.

Tally was going back to help Yaya with flowers and Kayla would be on hand when the trolleys arrived for the rehearsal dinner at Reid's Apothecary. The restaurant was on the other side of the causeway, in historic Brunswick. The restaurant was solid and could be counted on to deliver, so the wedding planner wouldn't need to hang around after the toasts were finished. Kayla had wisely scheduled the toasts at the front end of the evening because the guests would have already been drinking for at least five hours by then, some longer.

Frankly, the busy, busy schedule the guests were on for the Big Gay Wedding was Tally's own personal worst nightmare – if she were a wedding guest, she would hate to be stuck with a group all day with no way to escape – but for the most part, Simon and Oliver's guests seemed delighted by the agendas for the weekend. Happy guests made for happy clients, and that was what mattered.

She spent the afternoon in the flower shop helping Yaya fill a zillion cylinder vases with a rainbow of water beads. They'd prepped all the flowers that were going in them, and then put several stems of roses into each of the vases. Ideally, they'd have a pastel rainbow by morning. Worst case, they'd have white roses in a rainbow of vases. And that was fine, too. There was no formal wedding party, so Yaya created boutonnieres and corsages for the grooms and their parents in short order. But when Tally left for the day, Yaya stayed behind to work on several pending bids that still hadn't been sent out.

***

Tally made it home in time for dinner and found Mitch out on the front deck grilling.

"You must be feeling a lot better," she said and kissed him hello. He smelled like he'd just gotten out of the shower and his hair was still damp.

"I am," he smiled. She noticed that he'd shaved completely for the first time since he was shot. "I'm starting to feel human again."

"Is that why you shaved?"

"Nope. I shaved because my dad gave me shit about showing up at Post with a scruffy face for the debriefing. Told me to grow the fuck up and buy a razor," Mitch reported.

"Ha!" she laughed. Tally didn't disagree with Tom, but she wasn't going to tell Mitch that. "Well, I think you look very handsome. And I like a man who can cook."

"I couldn't eat anything else that came in a casserole dish," he explained with an embarrassed look on his face. "I'm sorry, people have been so thoughtful and I don't mean to sound ungrateful. But I am really sick of the stuff in our fridge. So, I scoped out your freezer this morning and thawed us some steaks. Hope that was okay."

"More than okay. It smells fantastic. You have perfect timing," Tally said.

"Well, I might have cheated and asked Yaya to text me when you actually left the office."

"Oh, I see. You're in cahoots with my girlfriends now?"

"Is that a bad thing?" Mitch asked innocently and smiled. "That's what you get for loving a cop."

"It depends. Tonight, it was definitely a good thing because I'm starving. What can I do to help you finish making dinner?"

"I think it's all under control – I already made salad," he said. "Why don't you get changed and pour us both some wine?"

"I can do that." Tally left him on the deck to finish with the steaks and went back to her bedroom to change.

They enjoyed an uninterrupted dinner together and then Mitch filled her in on his doctor's appointment and a call with his sergeant.

"I'm not cleared to go back in yet, but the doctor said I should be approved for admin duty at my next appointment in a month."

"That's not so bad."

"I'm going to go nuts from boredom. I can't even go to the range to blow off steam because I'm not allowed to shoot yet," he complained.

"You just got rid of the headache," Tally pointed out.

"I get it, but that still doesn't give me anything to do except sit on my butt and eat."

"I dare you to say that in front of Roberta and Bonnie," she challenged him. "They both have huge honey-do lists of things that you could probably accomplish in your delicate condition. You know, like changing lightbulbs and smoke alarm batteries, and HVAC filters. All the fun stuff."

"Mom wanted me to come help in her garden." Roberta always needed help in her garden but they all benefited from the results.

"Sounds to me like you've got plenty to do to keep you busy. And we can plan cool stuff to do on my days off," Tally suggested.

"Speaking of cool stuff to do. Remember that restaurant I was going to take you to on Tybee Island? The one Joe recommended?" Mitch asked.

"Of course I do. But you got shot so we didn't go." She said it like that was a perfectly normal reason to cancel dinner plans. She was getting the hang of the cop wife stuff.

"Right. Well, anyway, I was thinking maybe we could try to go to dinner if you have a free day this week? I promise not to get shot again and screw it up."

"Sure. Sounds good. I could do Tuesday night if that works for you," Tally said.

"My calendar is wide open. Tuesday works. I'll make a reservation."

***

Tally worked on her blog after dinner while Mitch watched "Law and Order." She liked having him around all the time, and she'd almost trained herself to completely tune out the never-ending series of cop shows streaming in the background.

Kayla called Tally at 10 p.m. to say that the rehearsal dinner had been a success and the trolley captain had just reported having returned the same number of guests, plus one, to Jekyll Ocean Club. The unwell wedding guest had caught a ride over to the rehearsal dinner with Kayla.

The bar at Eighty Ocean, the hotel restaurant, was planning to stay open late to accommodate the wedding guests, but Kayla told Tally she didn't think the group would last that long.

"They're veteran drinkers, but nobody can go all day and all night. The front desk told me that Oliver and Simon didn't even stop in the bar," Kayla was laughing as she described it. "But the grooms said they were having a wonderful time when I checked out with them at Reid's Apothecary after the toasts. By the way, did I tell you the restaurant gave me the most amazing to-go charcuterie sampling to take with me? I meant to save you some but I ate it all."

"You suck."

"I couldn't help it. It was THAT good."

"Let's hope the reception food is just as good tomorrow night," Tally said. "Want to meet at the office to load at 10 am? God, these late start times still feel so weird to me. We always started setup by 8 am in Vieques."

"You're not in Vieques anymore, Dorothy," Kayla told her.

"Then what is Brenda doing here?" They both laughed.

"Seriously," Kayla agreed.

"Did you confirm their breakfast orders in person with the front desk?" Tally asked as an afterthought.

"Oh yeah, about that. Somebody specifically called and cancelled the breakfast order for all week, according to the front desk manager," Kayla reported.

"How weird is that? I think they've got their wires crossed."

"Well, I had the original order on my phone so I got it all sorted out and there's a huge red flag on the order that says it cannot be cancelled by anyone," Kayla explained. "I hope Simon and Oliver don't try to change up their wedding day breakfast. Cuz they're gonna be told no."

Tally laughed and thanked Kayla for doing such a great job keeping the trains running on time. She was starting to feel like she might be able to have a real life outside of work,

Chapter 50

"Helloooooo! Good morning wedding planners! We're getting married today!" Simon yelled across the lobby when he spotted Tally and Kayla arriving at Jekyll Ocean Club on Saturday morning.

Tally and Kayla laughed and applauded.

Simon and Oliver were going to spend the day on the beach with their guests to get everybody out of the way for wedding reception setup. Jekyll Ocean Club was catering it - hot dogs and hamburgers and veggie/tofu kebabs on the grill. There would also be a full open bar at the foot of the stairs to the beach, and a whole umbrella and lounge chair village set up nearer to the water for the guests. And don't forget the volleyball net.

Simon crossed the lobby with a bouncy gate and embraced Kayla. He was wearing a rainbow Speedo-style bathing suit with a Hawaiian shirt featuring engagement pictures of him and Oliver. It was quite the combination.

"You were so good last night. Thank you for shutting down that horrible toast," he said dramatically, kissing the younger wedding planner on both cheeks.

"You didn't tell me about a horrible toast," Tally said. "What happened?" She looked at Kayla skeptically.

"It wasn't a biggie," Kayla said.

"Wasn't a biggie? Oliver, did you hear her?" Simon's fiancé was approaching at a normal pace.

"Happy wedding day," Tally greeted Oliver. But Simon was not going to be derailed.

"She told Tally that Mark's toast was no biggie. Did he, or did he not, start naming everyone in the room that I had slept with?"

Tally's jaw dropped and she let a short laugh escape before she got control of herself. "Oh no," she managed to get out.

"But Kayla saved the day," Oliver put a hand on the younger wedding planner's shoulder. "I don't know what she said to him, but he sat down pretty quickly without making a scene."

"Seriously," Simon agreed. "He was only halfway down the list of people I'd slept with that are here. A lot more damage could have been done."

Tally didn't even try to stop her laughter. "My goodness, you guys have an interesting group of wedding guests."

"If you want to see it get interesting, hang around for the after-party at the pool tonight," Simon suggested with a mischievous look and waggled his eyebrows at Kayla.

"Stop trying to corrupt my wedding planners," Tally waved a finger at him. "Kayla's a nice girl."

Simon gave the women a "who me?" look and then got distracted by the arrival of the guests who had taken the shuttle from the historic hotel. One of them was wearing a giant inflatable pink flamingo costume. Tally and Kayla watched the boisterous group make its way outside to the beach catwalk and then returned to their mission of setting up the Big Gay Wedding. It was just another day at the work for the girls.

They had every detail they'd discussed with Simon and Oliver charted, and some of it was a little time consuming so they wanted to get that stuff done first. Gay men were easy on their wedding day in that usually, nobody needed to have their hair and makeup done, and they weren't that excited about the pictures. On the flip side, they weren't hiding in a bridal suite, afraid of running into their groom all day, so they were more likely to make nuisances of themselves at setup.

Tally figured they had about two hours of grace while the beach party got started, and then they'd begin to attract attention. The goal was to get things set up and be out of the venue with time to shower and dress before returning for the main event. If they had to stop to make polite conversation with the grooms or the guests, they wouldn't have time to shower. After hauling in and setting up all the decorations, flowers, and favors, both Kayla and Tally were sweaty, so they worked fast to make sure that didn't happen.

Chapter 51

The Big Gay Wedding was a raging success that night. Tally giggled as a conga line of guests, all wearing glow necklaces and halos, passed by them on their second lap around the room. Again, she and Kayla declined the invitation to join the conga line, and then they stepped farther away from the dance floor to avoid Round 3. It was a zoo with 200 neon-draped guests getting their groove on to the grooms' favorite band. The music was great and the wedding planners were enjoying themselves watching the fruits of their labor.

So far, so good, although Tally wouldn't say that aloud. The wedding ceremony was beautiful and the harpist looked really cool, but the venue had been breezy and Tally doubted the guests had heard much of the music. The grooms hadn't noticed the problem, so as far as the wedding planners were concerned, it hadn't happened.

Thanks to a really good acoustic guitarist, and the fact that all the guests arrived at the wedding pre-buzzed, people started dancing and singing during the cocktail hour on the roof deck, something that didn't usually happen until much later in the evening. Kayla said the photographer had gotten some really fun pictures of the grooms dancing to "Brown-Eyed Boy" while Tally was downstairs double-checking the placecards.

The trickiest part of the wedding reception, so far, had been trying to get everybody downstairs and seated for dinner. It was worse than herding cats. It was herding drunk cats. Once they were seated, Kayla predicted that nobody was sitting where they were supposed to be. Tally fervently hoped the guests were too drunk to remember what they had pre-ordered to eat on their RSVP card if they weren't at their own assigned seat. It had the potential to become a mess of epic proportions. But luckily, it did not.

Blessedly, everybody who was supposed to be seated at the grooms' table found their way there. And it was the first table to be served so everybody got exactly what they'd checked on their RSVP cards and there were no problems. Tally had learned early on in her career that if the head table was perfect, anything else could be fixed without the grooms even knowing about it. If there was a mistake at the wedding couple's table, they'd start looking closely at everything else around them and start to nitpick. Fortunately, that didn't happen.

There were a few snafus at the other tables – people who weren't where they were supposed to be and got the wrong dinner – but ultimately, everyone got fed. And from the look of the tables after dinner, most of the guests were too drunk to do much eating. The service staff spent most of the dinner hour running trays of cocktails back and forth to the tables. Kayla and Tally had eaten in the kitchen and the food was good, but Kayla rubbed it in and said it wasn't as good as the charcuterie she'd had the night before.

After dinner, Kayla took the mic and introduced the grooms' first dance. Then Simon and Oliver did a double mother-son dance and switched partners halfway through to dance with their new mother-in-laws. It was cute and thoughtful. Then the lights went out.

When the neon lighting came up a moment later, the DJ hired for just this purpose began pumping club music out of the giant speakers. Tally and Kayla walked around passing out the loops of neon for guests to wear. They had necklaces and bracelets and wands, and even some glasses frames. They'd pre-cracked and assembled it all while they were eating dinner so that everybody would start glowing at the same time. The effect would be lost if guests were too drunk to bother using the props.

The wedding planners took a lot of pictures of the reception for Tally's website – not a lot of clients requested neon weddings, thankfully, but they looked cool in marketing materials and it showed what Jekyll Weddings could do if asked. Tally had just parked her butt in a chair next to Kayla when the DJ stopped the music and announced it was time to cut the cake.

"What the?" Kayla asked, looking confused. It was too early.

Tally jumped up from her seat and headed to the cake table to make sure things ran smoothly. The timeline hadn't called for the cake cutting for another half an hour, and Kayla should have been the one to cue the cake cutting announcement. Obviously, a communication problem. But it wasn't the end of the world. They'd made sure the cake table was properly set up and the knives were in place before the guests were called to dinner. Hopefully, Simon and Oliver were having too much fun to notice the blip on their timeline.

Kayla was making a beeline to the cake table, too. She passed Tally and then came up short.

"Tally, look," Kayla whispered and pointed.

The grooms were standing at the cake table with Brenda Fogel. Everybody was smiling and it appeared that neither Simon nor Oliver had caught on to the fact that the woman handing them the cake knife was not on their wedding planning staff. Brenda certainly looked like a member of the Jekyll Weddings team – she was wearing a sleeveless navy A-line dress that was disturbingly similar to the one Tally was wearing. And she held a clipboard and appeared official, just like the real wedding planners.

Tally and Kayla locked eyes. Kayla looked scared. Tally was angry.

"Call Mitch now," Tally told the younger woman. Kayla nodded in understanding and headed out of the crowd of wedding guests so she could hear the phone.

Tally resisted the urge to jump in and out Brenda as an imposter, right then and there. But that would only mess up her clients' wedding and reflect poorly on her. So instead, she stayed a few rows back in the crowd and watched carefully as the cake cutting unfolded in front of her. Nobody had any idea that Brenda wasn't on her payroll and for the moment, she was okay with that.

If Brenda got through the cake cutting without anyone being the wiser, Tally would drag her out of the reception as soon as the music started back up. Wedding crashing wasn't a crime unless she was asked to leave and refused. Then it became trespassing. Impersonating a wedding planner wasn't a crime, either, as far as Tally knew, because it wasn't a licensed profession. Having the clients find out what Brenda had done would only hurt her company's reputation.

She watched quietly and kept her fingers crossed that nothing went wrong as Brenda gave the grooms instructions – bad instructions, Tally noted – on how to cut the cake. While Simon and Oliver were butchering the spectacular three-tiered Emerald City cake they'd paid several thousand dollars for to the hoots and catcalls of their friends, Brenda caught sight of Tally in the crowd and froze. Tally started making her way around the cake table. Brenda saw Tally coming and turned and started walking toward the exit. Just then, the room went dark and the neon lights came back up again, totally disorienting Tally. When she had her balance and focus back five seconds later, Brenda was gone.

As she stormed around looking for the interloper but not finding her, Tally realized she was going to have to find a business attorney and file a lawsuit against Brenda if she wanted the crazy to stop. There wasn't any other recourse as long as the wanna-be wedding planner wasn't breaking any big laws. She would have to go the civil route and sue her. She'd get a stay-away order against Brenda, too, while she was at it. She'd poo-pooed it when Mitch had suggested it and she was going to have to admit she was wrong. Ugh.

***

Tally found Kayla in the lobby talking to Mitch on the phone and updated them both. She took the phone and told Mitch to stand down whomever he'd been sending to the hotel – Tally would prefer it if the clients weren't alerted. It was more important than catching Brenda, she explained.

Mitch started to argue with her, but instead, compromised and agreed that he'd come with Yaya to pick her up after the reception. In the meantime, he'd stand down the state police and have them see if they had picked up anything on the cameras at the gate.

The rest of the reception passed without incident and drunk guests were already doing cannonballs into the pool at the after-party as Kayla and Tally cleaned up after the reception. They collected vases of weirdly-colored roses that they definitely would not try to sell in the flower shop the next day and put them in boxes to transport. The roses were a complete loss, but the centerpieces had looked cool on the tables, especially after the lighting change. Tally filed away a mental note to do it again for another client using a better color scheme.

When she said goodbye to the photographers, she discreetly asked that they send her shots of the cake cutting as soon as possible. She'd implied there was a problem with the cake that she needed to verify, but really, she wanted to be able to hand the police some good clear pictures of her new nemesis. And she wanted another look at Brenda's outfit. Because what she remembered was eerie. How could she have copied her?

When Mitch and Yaya arrived to pick her up 30 minutes later, they helped load everything that needed to go back to the shop into Tally's Jeep so that Kayla could head directly home. Brenda's presence at the reception had them all a little freaked out, and Tally asked Kayla to keep an eye out behind her, and to let them know when she got home.

Mitch backed the Jeep up to the shop and they got things unloaded in just a few minutes. Tally was almost starting to relax by the time they pulled into her driveway five minutes later. Then she saw the necklaces. Five glowing neon circles marking a path from her yard to her door.

"What the hell is that?" Mitch asked.

"It's from the wedding reception," Tally said softly. "The question is how did it get here."

"Could you have dropped them on your way out and we just didn't notice them when we left?" Mitch asked. Both women gave him a look.

"You might not have noticed them, but I would have," Yaya said. "Those weren't here when we left the house."

"It should be on your cameras," Mitch said. "Let's go see who the visitor was. Although I think we already know. But maybe we can get a look at her vehicle. That would be helpful for stopping her."

Tally bent over and started to pick up the necklaces as she passed them on her way into the house, but Mitch stopped her.

"Don't touch them yet. This could be a crime scene."

Chapter 52

The glow necklaces were the only evidence that Brenda had been at the house. She'd obviously noticed the cameras when she stopped by before and left the bogus business card with Mitch, because when she returned with the party favors, she had avoided them. It appeared she stood outside their range and threw the glow necklaces up onto the porch like frisbees.

"Points for creativity," Tally said when she saw the video clip on Mitch's phone. No cars went up or down the street right before or after the incident so they could only assume Brenda had parked her vehicle someplace nearby and walked over. She could have taken the bike path, the road, or the beach. There was nothing for police to work with on the security video, but Mitch clipped it and sent it to Johnson & Johnson with a note about what had happened anyway.

After she watched the video, Yaya dramatically declared that she was "done with everything."

She had to be in the flower shop in the morning, she announced, so she was going to bed. She stopped by the fridge to grab a spiked seltzer and stomped down the hall to her bedroom, muttering to herself in Spanish. Tally recognized a few obscenities.

"I get how she feels but I refuse to let that woman ruin my night," Tally declared as she watched her best friend go. "The grooms were happy and the Big Gay Wedding was a mad success even with a wedding crasher. It was the highest dollar event we've planned so far."

Mitch high-fived her and she giggled.

"Was it the most guests you've had?" Mitch asked.

"Nope, just the most expensive. You can do some serious damage when you start upgrading everything. Plus, all the live music they had adds up quickly. Which is good for my business."

"Show me the money?"

"Exactly," Tally replied. "Now that I have a real payroll to meet, I'm a lot more worried about the money. It's not just me that's depending on my success."

"That's gotta be stressful." Mitch hadn't really thought about that aspect of his girlfriend's growing business. All of his professional experience so far had been with employers who paid the bills with tax dollars and never seemed to have a problem paying overtime.

"I need a shower. I think I've been sweating since I saw that crazy woman at the hotel. I feel gross." She resisted the urge to sniff herself in front of him.

"You don't look gross," Mitch said and wagged his eyebrows at her.

Tally laughed. "How do you even do that?"

"Lots of practice."

"Okay, that's it for me. I gotta get out of this dress," Tally said then turned back to Mitch suddenly. "How did she know what I was going to wear tonight? Her dress was freaky similar to mine. Wait til you see the pictures."

"You and Kayla should have turned on your cameras when her bs began." Mitch sent another text to Johnson & Johnson about the dresses.

Every little bit of information might help because they had no idea what was going on with this mess.

"You're right, we should have filmed it. But it didn't even occur to me. I was too busy praying she wouldn't ruin the whole wedding and doing damage control in my head. Ugh, just thinking about it makes me start sweating again. This time I really am I'm going to go shower."

"Do you need somebody to wash your back?" Mitch asked as he followed her into the master bedroom.

Chapter 53

Simon and Oliver's wedding photographers had kindly sent the cake cutting pictures before they went to bed after the wedding and Brenda was able to forward them to the detectives first thing in the morning. Then, using those pictures, the state police checked through Jekyll Ocean Club's parking lot security videos and found Brenda in more than a few clips. She'd arrived at the wedding venue during the ceremony, according to the video. And gone back out to her vehicle at least once during the reception before the cake cutting.

More importantly, footage from the parking lot showed she was driving a white SUV. The plate numbers weren't readable on the security video, but the cameras at the gate would have captured it clearly. It would just take a little bit to find her car on the gate videos by approximating the time she left. The only thing more common than white SUVs on Jekyll were white pickup trucks.

Once the detectives had the plate number, the Jekyll Island Authority could set the gate to alert them if Brenda entered in the same vehicle again. Although Mitch was still out on sick leave, he called and bugged his buddies who were working in the area for information constantly. So, when Tally got home from the office on Monday evening, he proudly gave her an update on the investigation.

"They got the plate number off of a white Nissan Pathfinder, but it's bogus registration. The address is old. None of the motels in Brunswick recognized it and they're not going to go wider than that at this point," Mitch told her.

"I don't blame them. She hasn't actually broken any laws."

"Well, she may have. She's definitely skating the edge of stalking. It's like she knows what she's doing. Just enough to aggravate the hell out of you, but not enough to get locked up. They still haven't figured out who she is," Mitch reported.

"Really? That's so weird. We had all her old info. You can still find me at my old addresses if you search them."

"From the looks of it, none of the information you had in your file about her then was true. She wasn't from Virginia. Or at least they can't find any record of her."

"I guess it's not shocking. If I hadn't met the first groom myself, I wouldn't believe he ever existed now," Tally said. "It's all just so weird. I've heard of wedding-obsessed women, but most of them restrict that to hoarding obscenely expensive bridal magazines and making appointments to try on gowns at dress shops," she said.

"That's scary."

"Seriously. They wear fake engagement rings to go try on dresses, too," Tally explained. "So the salespeople don't suspect they're just wasting their time."

"Now that's just creepy."

Tally shrugged. "A lot of the little girls who played bride with their friends are my higher-dollar clients now. It's hard to satisfy a woman who has been planning her big day in her head for 30 years."

"You and Cheryl used to play wedding all the time on the beach," Mitch recalled. "I seem to remember playing the groom on a few occasions. But you both turned out normal."

"Normal is relative and both of us became wedding planners. Read into that what you like," she teased. "Neither one of us will be a bridezilla when our weddings days finally arrive. Heck, we might even elope."

"We?" Mitch smiled.

"Me and Cheryl," she replied with wide eyes and a straight face. They both laughed.

Tally explained that she figured she and Cheryl had gotten it out of their systems by ordering each other around on the beach while wearing toilet paper veils.

"I have some good news for you," Mitch changed the subject.

"I like good news."

"If you're still off work tomorrow, we've got dinner reservations at that place on Tybee Island at 7 pm," he said.

"Sounds good," she lied. Tally's energy tank was running on empty and she'd hoped for a down day together. But Mitch looked excited and she wasn't about to burst his bubble.

"I'm not going in to work tomorrow, but I do need to run a few real-life errands in the morning. Do you need anything from Target or Sam's Club?" Tally asked.

"Nope, I'm good. We should probably leave earlier than later tomorrow if we want to avoid rush hour traffic near Savannah." It was at least a 90-minute drive without traffic, probably closer to two hours if the driver didn't have a brass pass to get him out of tickets.

"That's fine," she agreed. "What time should I be ready to go?"

"How about 3:30ish?"

"I'll be ready," Tally promised.

Chapter 54

It was a little bit after midnight and almost all of Jekyll was asleep. Trooper Moe Hankin was on patrol and driving a lazy loop of the island for the second time, keeping an eye out for critters in the roadway. That was about the only thing he ever saw after midnight when he worked on the tiny barrier island.

He had been looking for the SUV that Brenda was spotted in, but he hadn't seen anything happening that shouldn't be happening on a normal Monday night in the state park. Several of the restaurants were closed on Mondays, and the rest of the island rolled up their sidewalks by 8 p.m. Even in high season, nothing was open after midnight. Jekyll was a family vacation kind of place, not a wild party spot.

Moe rolled past several of the oceanfront hotels – all of the major hotel brands had several properties on Jekyll - and drove through some of their parking lots looking for the suspect SUV. He marveled, as always, at the lack of lighting along the coastline. Nobody had bright lights because they would attract and misdirect nesting sea turtles who relied on the moonlight for guidance. Everything had a yellow or red tint to it, so white vehicles didn't necessarily look white.

Trooper Hankin had just entered the traffic circle in front of Beach Village from the south side when an explosion of light to his right grabbed his attention. He stopped his patrol car and got out to see what was happening. The sidewalk in front of the new flower shop was on fire.

He leaned back into his car and grabbed the radio to call for backup. Moe also requested the fire department as he watched the sidewalk in front of the new flower shop burn. The fire appeared to briefly chase the person who had started it, and then he watched as a woman stripped off her flaming clothing in the middle of the street and then stopped, dropped, and rolled.

The trooper grabbed a blanket from his trunk and raced over to the woman to make sure the fire on her was out. She was screaming but her words didn't make any sense. The flames on the sidewalk had already burned themselves out. So was the fire on the naked woman. Whatever the lady had been trying to do when she set herself on fire, she wasn't very good at it.

Trooper Hankin could hear sirens in the distance. It would be the fire department first. There was only one little firehouse on Jekyll but they were professionals and close by. The next closest state trooper had been patrolling on the other side of the causeway when Moe called for backup. It would take a bit for other cops to arrive. There would be another fire department responding from the mainland, too.

When the burned woman stopped squirming for a few seconds, he was able to see her face clearly. He instantly recognized her as the suspect with the SUV that he'd been looking for. He didn't see the white Pathfinder anywhere nearby but he recognized the suspect's face from the wedding pictures he'd been shown when he came on shift.

Moe knew he was making assumptions about what happened. But it looked to him like the naked lady now writhing and screaming in the street was the only person around on the otherwise quiet block. He hadn't seen her light the fire but he'd be willing to bet she'd burned longer than the sidewalk. She'd probably gotten the accelerant all over herself during her amateur bomb-making attempt. Moe would leave it to investigators to determine what-all had actually occurred and keep his opinions to himself when he wrote the report. He chalked it up to the lady being a nutjob in his little notebook. Moe hadn't expected to encounter this on Jekyll. In fact, he'd never done more than write a speeding ticket in the state park in the past.

State police troopers, Glynn County police and sheriff's deputies, and more than a few supervisors from each department swarmed the Beach Village, arriving lights and sirens in what was probably the most first responder chaos the residents had ever seen. There were no houses nearby to the shopping area, but the sirens screaming across the Jekyll bridge carried both ways across the marshes.

The residents' Facebook page lit up with speculation about what was happening while they waited for somebody who knew something to post details. Everybody tagged Jamie, the owner of At Your Service Jekyll Errand Girl, because her husband was a retired law enforcement officer and they lived in the marina next to the bridge. She always knew what was going on and was usually right on the money with the details. Her company's slogan was "if it's not illegal, we can probably do it." Jamie had her finger on the pulse of every aspect of the little island.

Trooper Hankin knew he was going to pull a lot of overtime on the paperwork for this incident. Within 30 minutes of his arrival on the scene, the burned woman had been transported over to the island's small airport where a medevac helicopter met it to fly her to a burn center in Jacksonville. A trooper, fortunately not Moe since he was first on the scene and they needed him for the investigation, flew with her because she was under arrest.

The burn victim, who was also the suspect, had been confirmed as matching the description of the woman known as "Brenda Fogel," who had allegedly been fraudulently representing herself as an employee of the island's one wedding planning company. Moe hadn't been notified when she returned to the island because she wasn't driving the same white SUV. Authorities found a different vehicle parked nearby with an arsenal of poorly-assembled Molotov cocktails in milk crates in the back.

The damage to the storefront and sidewalk was minimal and didn't deserve the kind of police attention the incident was getting, but they brought in the bomb squad for the SUV. Once the sun was almost up, several residents arrived and stood sipping coffee and watching from behind the Crime Scene tape. It was the most interesting thing happening on the island.

Chapter 55

Mitch's phone blew them out of bed about 10 seconds before they heard a distinctive police knock – bang bang bang bang - on the front door. It was just after 4 a.m.

He jumped out of bed and pulled on his pajama bottoms, then he grabbed his phone and gun off the bedside table before going to see who was there.

It was his father on the phone and Johnson & Johnson at the door. Mitch answered them both simultaneously and told his dad that he would call him back.

Tally grabbed a robe and followed Mitch out of the bedroom to see what was going on, flipping on light switches along the way. She hoped nothing bad had happened to one of his brothers. The last middle-of-the-night police knock at this house had been when Mitch got shot. Tally wasn't a fan of these wake-ups. The hashtag #copwifelife flashed through her head.

"Sorry to wake you folks up," Andy began. "We had an incident at the flower shop in the Beach Village."

"Oh no!" Tally cried. "What happened?" It hadn't occurred to her that the detectives were there for her.

"Brenda Fogel came back to Jekyll tonight," Ted began.

"What did she do?" Mitch asked.

"It could have been much worse than it is," the detective hedged. "She had made a whole bunch of Molotov cocktails and apparently planned to burn down the business. She also brought spray paint and wrote a nasty message to you across the front of the building."

Tally felt a little dizzy. "How bad is it?" She was picturing total destruction of the little space they'd so lovingly put together over the past month.

"She did some damage to the front window of the flower shop, and your sidewalk, but she did more damage to herself," Ted said. "Looks like she got a lot of whatever accelerant she was using – smells like plain old gas to me but they're testing it – anyway she got a lot of it all over herself while she was making the bombs.

"The first one she threw at your window bounced off of it and smashed next to her on the sidewalk. It set the sidewalk and Brenda on fire, but the shop is fine," he added.

"Is she going to be okay?" Tally wondered.

"Do you really care?" Mitch asked.

She shrugged in response and Andy saved the awkward moment by jumping in.

"She's got burns, but mostly to her extremities. She'll probably survive," he told Tally. "She's under arrest and in custody at the hospital in Jacksonville."

"Good," Mitch said.

"You are supremely lucky," Ted said. "She had enough ammunition to burn everything to the ground if she hadn't set herself on fire with the first one."

Tally's stomach dropped even further.

"We need you to look at some pictures real quick and just confirm whether this is the woman who has been giving you problems," Andy held his iPhone up to show the screen to Tally. "We already confirmed it's her using the cake cutting pictures so this is really just a formality."

"That's her." Tally nodded and looked away. Brenda's face didn't appear burned but she was still terrifying. She wore her Ursula expression in the picture.

"Okay, thanks. That's all we're going to need from you folks tonight," the older detective said.

"Do you need us to come down to the shop tonight?" Mitch asked.

"I don't think so, unless you really want to. Fire department is doing their best to wash the paint and fire mess off the front of the building and the sidewalk and the streets are going to remain closed off until the bomb squad is done processing her vehicle. The inside of the shop wasn't affected. I'd say go back to bed for a few hours and then deal with this unless you want to be in the early edition of the Brunswick News."

Chapter 56

Mitch went back to sleep for a few hours after the detectives left, but Tally couldn't. She really wanted to be at the shop – but she also knew it was better to avoid being part of the news story while all the first responders were still on the scene and the reporters were milling around.

Nothing like this had ever happened before on quiet Jekyll Island. It was a bad look for her little business. And it was the second time she had brought authorities into the state park because of crimes committed specifically against her. She wouldn't blame the other residents if they tried to vote her off the island. Jekyll Island Authority would certainly think twice about renewing her flower shop lease. Tally took an outside shower and watched the sun rise through the peekaboo window, but even that didn't cheer her up.

By 9 a.m., she couldn't stand it anymore, so she woke Mitch up to see if he wanted to go look at the damage with her. Yaya had spent the night at Kayla's after a movie, and she'd texted them both the news when she got out of the shower. It was their day off, anyway. But she wanted them to hear it from her, not the grapevine.

Mitch took a quick shower and Tally was waiting with coffee in a to-go cup for him when he emerged from the bedroom.

"Where's yours?" he asked.

"I've already had way too much caffeine today."

Mitch's eyes widened. He'd never heard her say that before.

When they left, Tally got into her Jeep and Mitch took his truck because he didn't need to hang around the shop all day. Plus, he'd gotten his driving privileges back, if only to run around on Jekyll, and he wanted to drive. He planned to head to the Post to get the inside scoop on everything as soon as his girlfriend didn't need him.

The detectives had been right about the courtesy of the local fire department. Most of the nasty writing on the front window was gone. Tally wanted to know what it said, and Mitch assured her there would be crime scene photos in the incident report. They could go over to the barracks and look at it. Her new hanging signs were probably toast, but she'd talk to the artist who did them for her and see if touch-up was possible. Maybe they could just repaint them.

Fortunately, the front window had not been broken and there was no damage whatsoever to the inside of the flower shop. There was a scorch mark across the sidewalk that would have to wear away over time, but Tally realized she had been very, very lucky.

"She could have done that at my house," the realization chilled her. "Oh my God, we're so lucky. The porch around the house is wood. Even if she hadn't broken the glass, she could have burned Etah's house down."

She unlocked the front door of the flower shop and turned on the lights, gesturing for Mitch to follow her in. She walked directly to the new Nespresso machine she'd bought as a treat for herself and her staff and started brewing a double-shot of espresso.

"I thought you said you didn't need more caffeine," Mitch reminded her.

"Now that I know the world is not coming to an end, I need coffee," she looked at him sheepishly.

"Can I do anything to help you before I go? I want to go over to the office and find out what kind of info they need from you or if what Johnson & Johnson got last night was enough."

"That would be great. I need to stay here for a few hours to figure some stuff out. I assume this is the end of it with Brenda, but we still need to take some precautions. I need to call Kayla and Tally. And I'm sure they're going to freak out a little bit too when they see this."

"We need to get on the road no later than 4 to make our dinner reservations on Tybee," Mitch reminded her.

"I had completely forgotten about that," Tally admitted. "Tonight's not really a good night for this, is it?" Going out to dinner and having to look happy to be there was the absolute last thing she wanted to do.

Mitch was crushed and tried not to let it show. But he also wasn't willing to let his plans get ruined twice. Tally saw his face and tried to adjust her attitude.

"I think it's a great night for it," he countered. "Everybody on the island is going to be talking about us tonight so let's get the hell out of Dodge. You need a break and I really want to try this restaurant that Joe has been talking about."

He said it in a way that broached no argument from Tally, so she just nodded and kissed him goodbye.

As soon as he left, she set an alarm on her phone to remind her to get out of the shop early enough to make herself pretty for the date. She needed to do something with her nails, too. She'd been stress-picking her cuticles for two days and her hands looked a mess. She'd rather use the time to nap

– they'd been up most of the night, after all - but she would make the effort for Mitch. More than once, he'd had to live with the last-minute, un-showered version of his girlfriend when she cut things too close, and she didn't want that Tally show up for their date tonight.

Chapter 57

Tally didn't know what the whole agenda for the evening was so she dressed for a variety of possibilities. The short blue and white striped swing dress had a sailor-girl vibe to it, so she paired it with wedged navy espadrilles and a white cardigan sweater. She didn't want to wear heels because she didn't know where they'd be walking.

Against her better judgment, she decided to leave her giant purse behind for the night. Tally grabbed a little navy Kate Spade cross-body that would only hold her phone, lipstick and credit card. It was a date and she wasn't supposed to work. She wouldn't need to build a bride and so she didn't need to lug eyelash glue, tweezers, and a big bottle of Advil with her to Tybee.

Tally was ready and waiting when Mitch got home a little bit after 3. He was impressed and told her so. He'd figured he would have to tear her away from her computer.

"I have all kinds of updates for you on Brenda and the investigation, but let me get myself together first, and then I'll tell you all about it in the car. You can make roadies for us while you wait for me." He planted a kiss on her lips and headed for the bedroom.

Mitch closed the door behind him – suspicious because he never did that – but she didn't think too hard on it. Roadies at 3 in the afternoon were stranger. It would truly be a real day off, she thought, as she grabbed two insulated Yeti cups from a cabinet. She decided to be more creative than usual and pulled a bottle of strawberry daquiri mix from the pantry. Some ice and too much rum later, she was quite satisfied with the results. She slid big straws into the mugs and set them on the counter while she worked on drinking the extra from a glass.

Mitch was ready fast – he looked cute in khaki shorts and a white golf shirt with blue stripes. She wondered if he realized that their outfits were color-coordinated, but she wasn't about to be the one to mention it. His thick hair was still wet and he smelled like Etah's shower gel. That made Tally giggle but she didn't say anything.

He double-checked all the doors that Tally had already locked and led her out to his truck. Sitting on the passenger seat was a small plastic box.

"You got me a corsage?" Tally was amazed at his thoughtfulness.

"I'd like to take the credit for it, but..."

"But what?" she laughed and opened the box. It was a lovely little wrist corsage featuring several tiny rose blooms. It reminded her of the ones the boys from Woodberry Forrest got their dates for Homecoming and Prom when she was at St. Margaret's.

"Bonnie got it for me for you, but I didn't ask her to," he confessed. "She had it next door when I stopped in. She'd invited us to dinner tonight a few days ago and I'd mentioned we had an important date planned. So she picked this up for you. I'm not supposed to give her the credit," he laughed. "But I knew you wouldn't think it was all me."

"I'm happy to give you the credit for it since it was your sweet grandmother who had the idea. It's pretty," she said, holding her left arm out to show it off to him.

They'd left early enough to avoid the traffic, and they sipped on their daquiris while Mitch rotated through the 70s, 80s, and 90s on his satellite radio. When they got to Tybee, they drove around checking out what had changed, and what was the same, from the last time each of them had been there. They'd never been there together before.

Tybee was where people in Savannah went to the beach, and with miles of empty beach on Jekyll, there was no reason to deal with the distant, and relatively-crowded by comparison, beach two hours away. But it was fun to visit another coastal island and see what they had to offer. Tally wished she'd checked in advance to see if Tybee had its own flower shop, but she didn't want to pull out her phone and ruin the vibe of the afternoon with work.

Before sunset, Mitch drove by a beach with a huge pier jetting out into the water in front of it and Tally suggested they stop, but he just smiled at her and kept going. He finally stopped by another, smaller pier called Fisherman's Walk.

"This has an amazing view," he told her as he pulled a small cooler backpack from behind his seat and put it over his shoulder.

He must've had that in the truck before he got home, Tally thought. She hadn't seen him load it when they left. Mitch was full of surprises tonight.

They walked to the end of the pier, nodding as they passed people fishing along the way. When they got to the far end, there was one empty bench and they sat down. The sun was just starting to set in the sky and Mitch was right, the view was phenomenal.

Tally watched as her boyfriend pulled a bottle of Prosecco – they both preferred it to champagne – out of the cooler bag, along with two crystal champagne flutes. They looked like Waterford and Tally figured they were likely another contribution from Bonnie, but she said nothing as she watched Mitch spread out a linen napkin and set the glasses on top of it.

"Will you open this?" he asked her with a sheepish smile, handing her the bottle of Prosecco. Tally laughed and took the bottle. As a wedding planner, she discretely popped corks multiple times a week. The last time Mitch had tried to do it, he'd knocked the lens out of his sunglasses.

"Do you have another napkin?" she asked.

"Sure do." He pulled one out of the cooler and handed it to her.

Tally had already untwisted the wire basket that capped the cork, so she draped the napkin over the top of the bottle and gave the cork a little twist and tug at the same time. It popped but stayed in her hand under the napkin. She handed the bottle and the cork back to Mitch.

"You make it look so easy." He sounded so forlorn when he said it that Tally laughed.

He filled both glasses and set the bottle down on the bench seat. Then he got up for a minute before taking a knee in front of Tally.

Tally froze while her brain processed what was happening. Was Mitch about to propose to her? Right now? Oh my God, was it really happening?

A small box suddenly materialized in his hand – Tally didn't see where it had come from – and then he opened it. Tally gasped.

"Will you marry me, Tally?" Mitch asked, locking eyes with her. "I've loved you our whole lives, and I want to spend the rest of our lives together. Please say yes." It was the most serious he'd ever sounded.

"Yes," she replied in a soft voice. Then, as she realized what had just happened, she wrapped her arms around Mitch's neck and yelled "yes yes yes! I will marry you!" just to make sure he'd gotten the answer. Then she kissed him.

Afterwards, he took the ring from the box and slid it onto the ring finger of her left hand. The ring was exquisite and Tally was stunned by the size of it. There was a large round emerald in the center of the ring, and it was flanked by diamonds. The setting was platinum but the band was gold. Just like Tally had once commented that she preferred.

"It fits!" Tally said with surprise.

"I stole one of your other rings to measure," Mitch admitted.

"Of course you did," Tally giggled. "That's why I love you." She kissed him again. And then again. "You think of everything. The ring is beautiful."

"Bonnie helped me with that, too," he admitted, chuckling. "The emerald is from her engagement ring from my grandfather. It had been his mother's ring first. The center stone in your ring began as my great-grandmother's wedding ring. I thought it was perfect since that's your birthstone. Bonnie wanted you to have it since you've been in our family forever already. She said she didn't offer it to my brothers because she always hoped I would marry you."

"It's perfect," Tally struggled to say more but she was speechless.

They kissed again just as an older couple approached from further down the pier. The man held back a bit and looked embarrassed but his grinning wife charged right up to them.

"We don't mean to interrupt," the kind-looking, gray-haired woman explained. "But we saw what was going on and took a picture of your proposal for you. Would you like to send it to yourselves?" she extended her hand with her phone in it.

"Absolutely. Thank you. That was so thoughtful," Mitch told her, taking her phone and forwarding the picture to himself.

"Thank you so much!" Tally told the couple. She would have hated a staged photo, but a candid one taken by a well-meaning old lady was pretty neat to have. "This is so cool. I'll send it to my aunt tonight."

In the picture, Mitch was on one knee and holding the ring box and Tally was grinning like a lunatic at him.

The man dragged his wife away pretty quickly after that and gave them back their privacy. After some canoodling on the bench, Mitch said it was time to head to the restaurant.

"So, this is why you were so insistent that we not cancel our dinner plans tonight?" Tally asked, as they walked back up the pier, swinging their linked hands between them. "I'm glad you didn't let me back out."

"Tally, I've been trying to propose for a long time. I was going to propose the last time we were supposed to come to Tybee, but I got shot the night before it. But I already had the ring for a while before that. I was just waiting for a good time to ask, when you weren't up to your neck in other people's weddings."

"That would have been a long wait," she conceded.

"Exactly. You're always up to your ass in alligators. And for some reason I got it into my head that I didn't want to propose on Jekyll or St. Simons because we've been to all of those places together a million times – I wanted us to make a whole new memory tonight," Mitch told her as they reached the start of the pier.

"We definitely did that. Are we really engaged? Pinch me. I think I'm dreaming," Tally giggled. She held out her left hand and admired her engagement ring. The sunset made it really sparkle.

Mitch gently pinched her arm and said, "It's real."

He turned her to face him and kissed her. Then he held up her left hand to inspect the pretty ring again.

"So real," Tally agreed, thinking she was glad she'd made time to do her nails.

Chapter 58

"We don't need to go to the arraignment this time?" Tally asked the detectives who were sitting at her dining room table the next afternoon. She still had vivid memories of sitting through Tara's arraignment and the media circus outside the courthouse after Mitch's ex-girlfriend tried to ruin her first big wedding and got locked up.

Johnson & Johnson had left them several messages on Tuesday night, but by mutual agreement, Tally and Mitch had turned off their phones after they called Etah from dinner to tell her about their engagement. Tally woke up first the next morning, and she texted the detectives back and told them that they were welcome to stop by in the afternoon. Both arrived on her doorstep at 12 on the dot. Tally had a platter of chicken salad sandwiches and bowls of potato chips waiting on the table, and both men accepted her offer of a glass of sweet tea.

They greeted the detectives by announcing their engagement, followed by the obligatory showing off of the ring, which elicited hoots and applause from Andy and Ted.

"Okay, so break it down for us," Mitch prompted the detectives. "Assume we know nothing at this point because we've heard so many little snippets from multiple sources – including my father - that may or may not be true, it's hard to put it together."

Andy finished chewing a big bite of sandwich and explained about the arraignment.

"You weren't there when the incident occurred so they don't need anything from you at the arraignment," he began. "Brenda is being held in the critical care unit of a psych hospital while her burns still require constant treatment. She's in Florida, not Georgia, right now.

"The arraignment will be conducted virtually in her hospital room, but she'll be sent back to Georgia when she's ready to be released from the hospital. She was arrested in Georgia, so she doesn't have to be extradited. But that's not your problem to worry about anyway – it's mostly just paperwork and a lot of driving back and forth for us."

"I'm guessing that after her burns are healed, they'll move to keep her in custody on a psych hold?" Mitch asked.

"She's crazy," Tally added.

"Oh yeah. I think that's pretty obvious to anyone who's met her. They're not going to put her in a regular corrections facility right now unless it's in a psych unit," Ted agreed. "If her family pops up and offers to pick up the tab for a fancy private psychiatric hospital, the judge might agree to that. But that doesn't negate the criminal charges against her. Those aren't going away just because she sucked at being an arsonist." He rolled his eyes.

"We interviewed her this morning and it was one of the more bizarre interrogations I've ever conducted," Andy added.

"What did she say? Why did she do this?" Tally asked.

"She's not living in the same real world as the rest of us, Tally," Andy said. "But her lies to you started years ago in Puerto Rico. We still have to confirm a lot of what she's told us, but I think you'll find that almost everything she told you after her first engagement was in her imagination.

I don't know if she's schizophrenic or if there's something else going on – that's for the shrinks to figure out – but she definitely thinks she was on a mission to destroy you for ruining her wedding planning career. She may also blame you for at least one of the failed engagements, but she wasn't making a whole lot of sense so I could have misunderstood.

"The interview was recorded. At some point, you can probably watch it if you're so inclined," he added.

"I'll think about it." She wanted to see it but something in the back of her mind made her think it was a bad idea.

"There were some things that she confessed to during the interview that you hadn't mentioned to us," Ted said.

"Like what?"

"Something about cancelling the grooms' room service order..." he looked at his notes.

"No shit." That hadn't even occurred to her.

"Oh, and she said she copied your outfit for the wedding by reading your blog," Andy explained.

"What the hell?" Mitch asked.

He didn't read Tally's wedding planning blog, but he had a feeling that he was going to need to start doing that in the future. He'd looked at it once but, much as he loved her, couldn't get interested in 10 tips for getting a deal on wedding centerpieces. He looked at Tally.

"I wrote that over a year ago," she said.

"Hang on," Ted tapped on his phone and passed it to Mitch.

"Sometimes, I don't have time to get a shower before a wedding if things went badly at setup," Mitch read aloud. "But I still look professional and arrive on time because I plan out my outfits for all of the events – including shoes and accessories – before each wedding weekend starts so it's all ready and waiting for me.

"No panicking at the last minute because I can't find the right shoes or a bag that matches my outfit that's big enough for all my wedding accoutrement," he continued to read. "I hang it all on the back of my closet doors before the clients arrive on the island."

Tally was speechless. The color had drained from her face. She felt sick.

"She bragged, actually, that she knew what you were going to wear because she peeped through your windows and saw it on your closet door," Ted said.

"She wanted to know if you'd noticed that her shoes matched yours, too," Andy volunteered.

"Oh my God," Tally gasped.

"Please tell me that you're going to charge her with stalking now," Mitch said, a frown on his face.

"Oh, I'm sure. She's already facing hefty charges, some of them federal. Prosecutors gotta sort out who is charging her with what. She had a whole bomb-making kit, and multiple badly-built incendiary devices, in her vehicle. She also had a gun that was stolen from Indiana. So now ATF – that's the Bureau of Alcohol, Tobacco, Firearms and Explosives - is helping with the investigation, too."

"Is that where she's really from?" Tally asked. "I thought she was from Virginia."

"Maybe. We're still trying to confirm everything," Ted said.

"Anyway, from what she told us this morning, she'd planned to firebomb your shop and then burn down your house. She thinks you own this place – not that it matters. Obviously, she had no idea what she was doing, thank goodness. They'll probably find searches for how to build a Molotov cocktail in her browser history," Andy said.

"Does she have a lawyer?" Mitch asked.

"Not yet. Right now, she's claiming she's indigent and is entitled to a public defender so that's what she'll have at the arraignment. But once we figure out who she actually is, the judge will decide if that status is appropriate," the older of the two detectives explained.

"The question is whether there's some family out there who'll show up with a high-priced attorney claiming insanity. We couldn't find anybody when we were trying to track her down, and we're still trying to figure out who she actually is. She hasn't asked to make any phone calls yet."

"That's so weird," Tally said.

"She's insisting Brenda Fogel is her legal name, but she didn't have any legit identification with her and we still can't find her in the system. Her Indiana driver's license was fake and the social security card in her wallet was bogus, too," Ted said.

"Now that's shady," Mitch said. "I wonder if she's wanted. Seems like a lot of effort was made to conceal her identity."

"I can't believe she was going to burn the house down with us in it!" The information was just sinking in and Tally was getting angry.

"Karma must be on your side, Tally," Andy said. "The damage to your office was minimal and she never made it to your house. She told us she wanted to burn down your life, but all she did was set herself on fire."

"That said, we did a brief search of your yard this morning to make sure she hadn't set anything up under or around your house," Ted informed them. "It all looked good to us, but it would be helpful if you guys would do a look-see too. You know your yard better to see if anything is out of place.

Mitch and Tally walked the yard with the detectives and they mutually declared it "all clear." Tally's ADD brain was also busy making a list of things to tell the landscapers about – it had been a while since she'd had time to patrol Aunt Etah's fence line. The yard wasn't huge, but it had a lot of vegetation that was only beautiful if it was trimmed properly a few times a year. She needed to get them to clean out the debris in the sago palms, too. Those were pretty when they were maintained.

"Right, Tally?" Mitch asked, blowing her out of her mental yard list.

"I'm sorry, what? I spaced," she said apologetically.

"You're both exhausted, I'm sure," Andy said. "We'll get out of your hair now. But we'll keep you posted on developments as the investigation wraps up. It'll be interesting to confirm who she is. I don't want to press my luck, but I'd put money on it she's wanted somewhere under another name. It's all been too convoluted for a simple explanation."

"Hopefully, we can get back to real life now," Mitch said, thanking them. He shook his fellow law enforcement officers' hands and Tally gave both of them big hugs.

"Welcome to the Blue Line Family," Andy told Tally.

Chapter 59

Etah hosted their engagement party at her house, and she kicked Tally out for 24 hours beforehand, even going so far as to book a room for her in the historic hotel to get rid of her. That was fine with Tally because several of her friends who were coming to town for the party were also staying there for the weekend so it would be like a big fancy slumber party with her besties.

Her aunt had planned the party with Yaya and Kayla's help, and nobody had told Tally anything about it. There was a cone of silence around the details and every time she walked into a room they were in, everybody shut up.

Etah's rationale was that Tally planned parties and surprises for everybody else, and nobody ever got to throw a party for her. There was no way anybody would throw any surprises into her wedding because that was taboo to a wedding planner. The wedding day should be one time that a bride gets exactly what she wants in the order she wants it, rather than spontaneous karaoke solos from inebriated guests. The engagement party, on the other hand, was a different animal.

Aunt Etah asked her for a guest list and a few wedding-free weekend dates to choose from during the summer, and then she told them to block the calendar for the date she chose and what time to arrive. That was all the information the guests of honor were given. Tally suspected that Mitch was in on some of it and probably knew more about what was going on than he was telling, but she didn't bug him because she wanted to be surprised. Nobody had ever surprised her. She was always the one who did the planning for everybody else's celebrations. Letting go of the reins for her engagement party had been difficult but she wanted to reap the benefits of being the guest of honor, instead of the hostess, for a change. She could drink too much and be irresponsible if she wanted to, and she was looking forward to it.

***

Abby and Todd and Cristie arrived on the island before dinner and they walked down to The Wharf together to watch sunset and get a bite to eat. Afterwards, they walked back from the historic pier, across the lawn to the front entrance of the centuries-old club that had once been a playground for the super wealthy.

Tally stopped on the croquet greensward – that was the official name for the grass croquet field in front of the hotel that was first built for Rockefellers, Goodyears, Pulitzers, and Morgans in the early 1800s – and got a little bit goofy. She retold the story of how her friend Cheryl (who they would meet at the engagement party) had quit her job running weddings at the Jekyll Island Club Hotel when two groups of inebriated groomsmen had come to blows on the green after somebody else accidentally scheduled them for the fancy croquet court at the exact same time. One of the grooms had gone down the aisle with a black eye, and the general manager at the time had blamed Cheryl for the nasty review the groom's mother posted online afterwards. Cheryl had unceremoniously quit, after giving the general manager's cell phone number to all of the brides whose weddings she'd been in the process of coordinating. The company that owned the hotel had replaced that guy soon after for numerous other unrelated reasons. But Cheryl told Tally that she liked to think her walkout during wedding season had contributed to his demise.

Patti and Rita, also classmates from boarding school, drove down from Maryland to Georgia together and arrived after dinner. The girls met up for a late-night cocktail and took it out on the porch. Mitch's brothers were in town for the engagement party the next night so he spent the evening with them and slept over in Brunswick at Pete and Robin's house. As a result, poor Todd, as the only man in the group, had the unpleasant job of reminding the women not to get too loud. Repeatedly.

Between the hysterical laughter, the squeals, and the lifelong friends shouting over each other to correct each other's stories, Todd was certain somebody was going to yell at them to pipe down. But that didn't happen and eventually, he escorted all of the ladies to their rooms and put his wife to bed. The scene reminded him of the meme about somebody's ducks in a row being more like squirrels on crack. He could only imagine all of them at boarding school together. It was lucky that St. Margaret's was still standing.

***

The next morning, everybody slept late and then the girls wandered in the shops on Pier Road until it was time to start getting ready for the party.

Etah had pulled strings and had Mayra set it up so that guests staying at the historic hotel or Jekyll Ocean Club could get roundtrip shuttle service to the event. But Mitch would be picking Tally up to escort her to their engagement party.

Tally and Mitch had pre-planned their outfits, but only one of them wore what they'd agreed on. Mitch had traded the lavender, button-down dress shirt for a coral short-sleeved shirt, and Tally just groaned when she saw him. He matched the coral in her floral Lilly Pulitzer dress perfectly. And her purse and shoes. It was like the harder she tried not to be matchy-matchy, the more obvious it was. She just shook her head and laughed because she didn't want to make him feel bad about choosing to wear what he wanted.

They were the last to arrive at the engagement party at her home, and Tally stopped outside to enjoy the décor. Apparently, the night had an orchid theme. There were pink and purple Dendrobium orchids wound in strings of white lights up and down all of the porch columns and posts. She snapped a couple of pictures and made a mental note to get more after it was darker out.

The party was in full swing but everyone stopped to applaud when Mitch and Tally made their grand entrance. Somebody put drinks in their hands and then they were swooped into the crowd of friends congratulating them. Tally stopped to kiss Etah and made her way out to the porch where the volume was a little lower on the music.

Mitch's family was all outside and they greeted her with hugs and kisses. Mitch's grandmother, parents, and Pete and Robin were crowded around one of the highboy tables that Aunt Etah must have rented.

She admired the fishbowls filled with floating orchid blossoms on the tabletops and strategically placed around the room. They all glowed from the battery powered lights somebody had placed beneath the blooms. It was elegant and pretty and Tally loved it. She couldn't wait to see the pictures.

"Are Tommy and Frank here?" Tally asked, looking around to see where Mitch was in the crowd.

"Oh yes. One guess where they are," Robin said, rolling her eyes.

Tally searched the room and started laughing when she spotted them. She should have just looked for a gaggle of single girlfriends. But she was glad to see everyone was socializing with everybody else. Nothing sucked more than when the women stood in circle chatting all night while the men clumped up at the bar. It reminded her of Friday mixers with boys in high school. And sometimes, it even happened at weddings.

There were passed appetizers – stuffed mushrooms, brie bites, beef tenderloin on toast, grilled shrimp skewers, papaya wrapped in prosciutto, and mini crab cakes, of course – and a big buffet of charcuterie and crudités set up inside. There was a bar, but there were more servers than necessary and Tally and Mitch found their cocktails replaced with fresh ones faster than they could finish them.

Tally was a little drunk an hour later when the toasts began and she mentally kicked herself. As a wedding planner, she knew it was dangerous to overindulge when she would be the center of attention. But then Mitch brought her another one of the signature drinks named for her – a "Tally Ho" – and she drank it fast thinking "why not."

Apparently, Kayla and Yaya came up with the name for the drink, but Tally was a little surprised her aunt had blessed it. She knew Etah must have approved though because the names of the two signature cocktails were printed on bar menus and displayed in frames. She'd instantly recognized that the Tally Ho was actually a Vieques Love Martini, a signature cocktail that Isabelle had invented to make clients feel special. It was just vodka and passion fruit juice. But it looked really cool in a martini glass, and the electric orange color made it a popular party drink. All she could do was shake her head and laugh at the fact it was being served in her home. She lifted her glass to Isabelle, who was talking to Etah across the room, and her former boss cracked up.

Mitch's drink was a "Rookie" and it was some vile-sounding combination of whiskey that was sort of a whiskey sour, but not. It amused Tally to see that most of the girls were drinking the neon Tally Hos and most of the guys had beer or a Rookie.

Yaya made the first toast at Aunt Etah's prompting, and then several other girlfriends offered good wishes on the pending nuptials. Nobody told any stories she would have to kill them for later, and for that, Tally was grateful. There was certainly no shortage of material for them to draw from and she was going to owe them.

Mitch's side went next – each of his brothers made a toast and kept it clean, much to Tally's surprise. But then his dad went last and actually did more roasting of his youngest than anybody else had dared to do.

"As you all know, we're a law enforcement family and Mitch is the youngest. He's also the straightest, most black and white – no gray area – member of our family," Tom began. "But what you may not know is that Mitch's career could easily have taken a turn toward the dark side."

For a second, Tally was horrified thinking that her future father-in-law was actually going to mention the ex-from-hell in his toast. But she should have known better.

"Instead of becoming a state trooper, Mitch could have been a professional stalker. Because he spent the better part of his high school summers staring out the window at his grandmother's house just waiting to see Tally. I can't even remember how many times he came flying down that staircase, slipping and bouncing halfway on his ass, to get outside to catch her and say hi before she went in her own house," Tom guffawed and turned to his mother. "Do you remember that?"

"I do!" Bonnie volunteered from the edge of the crowd. "I was afraid he was going to take out my banister trying not to break his neck." Everybody laughed appreciatively. Mitch blushed and shook his head, but he was grinning.

"But seriously, we have all loved Tally since she was born, and felt like she was a true member of the Durham family. Don't worry – she's not. We double-checked," Tom waited for the laughing to die down. "The fact she's becoming legally ours soon is just a bonus. And the fact she's been Mitch's one-that-got-away for most of his adult life makes this union even sweeter."

Tally thanked Tom, thinking the toast was over – her future father-in-law was holding his glass in the air – but Mitch's mom was not to be left out.

"I've wished you were my daughter since you were a little girl digging holes on the beach with Mitch," Roberta said emotionally. "I'm getting my wish. And I hope you live happily ever after."

There was more cheering and hooting and celebration, with the Durham clan making most of the noise. Then Tom shushed them and gave Etah the floor.

Tally was struck by how old her aunt looked standing amongst the young, vibrant Durham family.

"I never expected to have children," Etah began and the room became instantly silent. "My career wouldn't have allowed for it – I was a wire reporter when women didn't have those sorts of jobs. I chose journalism over having a family and I was pretty content with it because I still had all my time with my great-niece, Tally, for weeks in the summer and for lots of holidays. And her father before Tally. I was very close to my nephew, who also lost his parents young.

"When God chose to call Tally's parents home while she was still a child, I knew it was my responsibility to help her continue to grow and succeed and be as happy as my nephew would have wanted her to be. I could never be her mother, but she gave me all the pleasure that having a daughter could ever give." Etah stopped and took a breath, then wiped her eye to stop a tear before it ran down her cheek.

"When Tally escaped back to Jekyll Island after Hurricane Maria, it was as if God had shut a door and opened a window for her," the elderly woman continued. "I was so proud of her launching her own business so quickly and the amazing success she immediately became. Now she's got a flower shop, too, and God only know what comes next for her career – although several of us" she stopped and dramatically winked at Bonnie "are hoping to see some babies before we die. No pressure though." Everybody laughed.

"I have an announcement to make tonight that will surprise many of you, and I'm not trying to steal Tally's thunder. But it goes hand-in-hand with this occasion," she paused to let her words sink in. The only sound in the room was the boom of waves crashing on the rocks in the ocean in front of the house.

"I'm officially retiring from my more than 60-year career in journalism next month, and yes, we'll have another party to celebrate that, too. I took a look at what I wanted my life to look like going forward and I decided that I want to be here, but I also want to take it easy. This house is not easy. No oceanfront home on a barrier island is easy, as everyone who lives here knows. There's a ton of maintenance and, to be honest, I don't need this much space if Tally and Mitch want to live alone, which I assume they will."

Tally started to protest that they weren't kicking her aunt out of her own house but Etah shushed her. "We want babies, remember?" Tally turned bright red as all the guests laughed.

"But I love this house very much, and I would never want to think of other people living in it. The bones are great. There's room to add on, and it's got the best view on the island, in my opinion," she said in a snarky tone that jokingly reflected the age-old island argument about who had the best view – ocean or river side. It elicited groans from her audience, as was intended.

She turned to Tally and Mitch.

"Mitch, you know I love you, right? But if you don't take care of her and keep yourself safe, and her out of trouble, I'll call Bonnie and rat you out and we'll both make your life hell," Etah warned in a joking tone. but she wasn't kidding.

"So, I decided that the best way to help you take care of her and make my life easier was to buy a condo over at The Moorings and give you two this house as a wedding present. I decided to tell you now so that you'd stop house hunting all over the island. You can't beat my price for this place." She reached into her pocket and pulled out a giant gold decorative key and symbolically handed it to Tally.

"Congratulations on your engagement and I hope you have a very long, happy life together and raise a beautiful family in this home," Etah finished to applause and then both Tally and Mitch gave her hugs and kisses.

"Wow," Mitch said. "Thank you so much. I don't even know what to say. This is such a surprise."

"Oh my God, Etah – you're retiring! Talk about bury the lead – what are you going to do with your time?" she'd never known her aunt to spend more than a few months at a time in one place, and that was only because she was guardian to a minor with school breaks.

"I'm still going to give lectures and such, but on my schedule. And I'm going to learn to play bridge because I've always wanted to. And I'm hoping that my babysitting services will be needed in the not so terribly distant future. I'm not so young anymore, ya know."

Bonnie shoved her way into the conversation with a grin. "You have to share with me, too, you know. Ooooo this is going to be so much fun. If we're all here together on Jekyll Island, it'll be just like when you two were kids again."

"Don't forget about me," Mitch's mom told her mother-in-law.

"They're just going to have to have several children," Bonnie declared.

Tally's jaw dropped but Mitch planted a kiss on her lips to distract her, and then tugged her over to the bar to grab refills.

They walked out onto the deck with their drinks and their guests gave them a minute alone in the moonlight. The moonbeam was bouncing off the ocean, reflecting in a million, mesmerizing ways and Tally leaned back into Mitch when he put his strong arms around her.

"This is so amazing. This whole night. This engagement. Etah's wedding gift," she said.

Mitch began kissing her neck, sending shivers down her back, and Tally turned to face him and kissed him on the lips.

"What a fabulous end to an amazing night," she sighed.

"How about an amazing beginning to the rest of our lives?" Mitch suggested.

"Oh, I like that much better."

Acknowledgements

Special thanks to Susan McLemore, Kayla Blunk, and Kelsi Welch for their patience, suggestions, and endless brainstorming and proofreading. Also, thank you Rita Rich for the marketing and media relations assistance. Full credit for the beautiful cover goes to graphic designer, Patricia Tait.

I would also like to thank all my new readers and cheerleaders who have encouraged me to keep writing. There are so many more real stories to tell, fictionalized to protect the guilty, of course.

About the Author

Sandy Malone is best known for starring in TLC's reality TV show "Wedding Island" and writing hundreds of wedding advice columns that were published in BRIDES, WeddingWire, and HuffPost. She wrote a DIY wedding planning book in 2016 that was traditionally published, and she released her new fiction series - Gem of the Golden Isles - in April 2024. She has also ghostwritten books for well-known reality TV stars (including a Real Housewife). Most recently, she was editor of The Police Tribune.

Sandy got her journalism degree at The Ohio State University and was a reporter and editor for major news publications before she returned to her hometown of Washington, DC, for a career in public relations and government affairs. She began planning destination weddings professionally after her own was nearly a disaster, and ended up planning more than 500 weddings in the Caribbean in 11 years with her retired SWAT-commander husband.

Sandy and her husband, Bill, recently moved to Jekyll Island, Georgia, with their coonhound Sherlock. "In Bloom on Jekyll" is her second fiction novel.

Also by Sandy Malone

Escape to Jekyll Island — Gem of the Golden Isles Series Book 1
Twenty-nine-year-old destination wedding planner Tally Davis lost her
home, her job, and her boyfriend in one fell swoop when Hurricane Maria
hit Vieques Island, Puerto Rico. After she's finally evacuated, she goes
home to Jekyll Island, Georgia, to start over. There's no wedding planning
company on the island, so Tally launches Jekyll Weddings. But not everyone is happy that Tally is home or wants her to succeed. She's unknowingly
kicked a hornet's nest by reconnecting with a childhood friend. Will a
10-year-old grudge ruin her first big wedding on Jekyll Island?

Treasure on Jekyll — Gem of the Golden Isles Series Book 3
Tally Davis is struggling to act like a bride and plan her own wedding to
her childhood crush while her event planning and floral company is going
gangbusters on Jekyll Island, Georgia. She takes her state trooper fiance
back to Vieques Island with her on an errand and opens a Pandora's box
while they're there. Will her past in Puerto Rico ruin her future on another
island, or will Tally live happily ever after with Mitch?

How To Plan Your Own Destination Wedding: Do-It-Yourself Tips From An Experienced Professional, Skyhorse Publishing 2016
Ten years ago, when Sandy was planning her own destination wedding in the Caribbean, she learned everything the hard way. After 11 years in business and more than 500 successfully executed weddings, she wrote a DIY guide that any wedding couple can follow to create a fabulous destination wedding for themselves anywhere.

Check out Sandy's blog and sign up for the newsletter at
www.SandyMalone.com
to find out about upcoming novels and book signings.

Made in the USA
Columbia, SC
12 August 2024

39822640R00183